BET THE FARM

Staci Hart

BET THE FARM

Staci H

Copyright © 2020 Staci Hart
All rights reserved.
stacihartnovels.com

No part of this publication may be reproduced, distributed, or transmitted in any form or by any means, including photocopying, recording, or other electronic or mechanical methods, without the prior written permission of the publisher, except in the case of brief quotations embodied in critical reviews and certain other noncommercial uses permitted by copyright law. This book is a work of fiction. Names, characters, places, and incidents either are products of the author's imagination or are used fictitiously. Any resemblance to actual persons, living or dead, events, or locales is entirely coincidental.

YOU AGAIN

Olivia

A VERY UNLADYLIKE GRUNT GRATED OUT OF ME.

Every muscle engaged as I dragged a ridiculous pink suitcase off the baggage belt of the tiny airport. The curl of my toes kept me braced. My glutes were hard enough to bounce a quarter off of. Shoulders bunched, abs tight, fingers burning.

It was more than I'd worked out in a year.

In a brief and awkward moment, I second-guessed everything I'd packed to come home to California. At the time, I'd been absolutely certain that every article of clothing was necessary. But when I stumbled backward from the force of freeing my luggage, I questioned the inclusion of the rain boots. And the overalls. And all that plaid.

It'd been ten years since I'd moved away from my grandfather's farm and two years since I'd been home. My New York wardrobe wouldn't do—I had to look the part. And "the part" demanded plaid.

The worst part of growing up on a dairy farm was being lactose intolerant.

Growing up, butter and cream, ice cream and cheese, and tanks brimming with milk had been inescapable. As a sweet, innocent child with no clue of the tragic fate my digestive system had in store, I didn't *have* to escape it. I remembered sneaking hunks of cheese from the creamery and eating until I was sick in the hayloft. Or sitting across from my grandfather, warm brownies and teeming glasses of fresh milk before us, the sounds of crickets floating in on the breeze through the open windows of the farmhouse.

These days, it was almond milk and soy cheese, margarine and sorbet. I'd abandoned cream for my coffee, opting to drink it black, which made me feel like a true badass—no easy feat at five feet and change, with hair the color of a penny and enough freckles to find constellations in the array. I was about as badass as a paper towel or a guinea pig or a carrot. Or a guinea pig on a paper towel eating a carrot.

When my suitcase wheels were on the slick tiled floor of baggage claim in the eensy airport, I brushed my hair back from my clammy forehead, scanning the belt for my other suitcase.

It was equally as ridiculous a shade of pink as the one I'd propped myself on to catch my breath—a bubblegum hue fit better for a little girl than a grown woman. A New Yorker, no less. But I couldn't seem to curb my inclination to the color. That sweet, creamy shade of pink that instantly brought cheer—you couldn't tow a suitcase that vivid and hopeful without maintaining the distinct impression that everything would be all right regardless of where you were going.

Even a funeral.

The second hulking pink plastic suitcase rounded the corner of the belt like a shiny-shelled gumball. At the sight of it, I stood and stepped up to the whirring metal track. Remembering my bag behind me, I cast a suspicious glance to the people nearby, noting their distance and attentiveness. But no one paid me or my bag any mind. They probably figured the suitcase was filled with glitter glue and stuffed unicorns.

Not that pink rain boots were much better.

I braced myself as the bag came closer, developing a strategy to attempt to master the physics of it all, hoping I had enough berth to drag the brick factory off the belt. With a fortifying breath and my lips screwed in determination, I reached for the handle and yanked with all my strength, which got me as far as upending the thing.

A pair of very large, square hands slid into my periphery.

"Here, let me help you with—"

"I've got it," I huffed, shifting to put my back to him.

With another heave, I pulled, leaning back in the hopes that my weight would help me, but gravity had other plans. The suitcase thumped back onto the belt, drawing everyone's attention in the vicinity. People shifted out of the way as I walked alongside it, shackled by way of the handle in my fist.

Mr. Square Hands chuckled and stepped around me, reaching for the bag again. "Seriously, you're gonna hurt yourself. Let me—"

"I said, I've *got* it," I shot, ready to stomp his foot or kick him in the shin if he didn't back off.

But then I lifted my gaze.

When Kit, the farm's cook, told me someone would be here to pick me up, I'd expected her, not the hulking expanse of Jake Milovic.

His hands weren't the only square—or large—thing about him. My thirsty eyes drank in the sight of him, cataloging every detail, noting what had and hadn't changed in the years since I'd seen my grandfather's right-hand man. He was a beast of a man, so tall, I only came to the divot in his broad chest. Square pecs, wide and solid as granite under his heather-gray T-shirt, which was almost too small. Small enough that it bordered on pornographic.

It was obscene, really.

His shoulders were square too, sturdy and straight and proud, and between them stood the column of his neck, corded with more muscles. Muscles on top of muscles, a display of brawn few humans were equipped with, though not enough to feel unnatural or gratuitous. My gaze hung on his jaw, which I instantly decided was my most favorite square—sculpted and strong, masculine and shadowed with dark stubble. That jaw framed a ghost of a smile on wide lips.

I'd kissed those lips once upon a time. But the boy who'd owned *those* lips was gone, replaced by a man who looked like he belonged on an ancient battlefield, wielding a mace and dressed in furs. Even the word *man* seemed too bland, too thin to describe him. He was a bear, grizzly and wild, loping through a forest alone.

His eyes sparked with amusement, crisp and flecked with greens and golds and honey browns, like the first turn of the leaves in autumn on the last moments of green grass.

"Jake?" I said stupidly, not realizing I'd stopped until my suitcase dragged me off-balance.

He moved more gracefully than a man of his size should have been capable, somehow catching me with one arm and lifting my suitcase with the other. I found myself tucked into his chest and inhaled greedily, my lids fluttering and senses full. He smelled of pine and hay, of old wood and loamy earth. He smelled like he was made of the woods and the soil and the salty sea air.

He smelled like home.

His hand was so big, it spanned the small of my back, which held me to him while he turned us like we were dancing. For a moment when he released me, I stood mutely, blinking at him.

One of his brows rose with the corner of his lips, just a flicker, just a glimpse. "You okay?"

"Oh, I'm tougher than I look," I blustered, smiling. "Are *you* okay? You didn't pull anything, did you?"

"I think I'm all right," he said, hefting my suitcase with one hand. His bicep turned into a mountain range, with veins snaking like rivers down his forearms and hands. "That one yours too?" He nodded to the suitcase's twin.

"How'd you guess?"

Jake gave me a sidelong glance, that corner of his mouth still just a little higher than the other. "I figured you'd outgrown the whole pink thing."

I shrugged to cover my wounded ego. "It's my signature color."

"I can see that," he said, snagging the other suitcase by the handle without breaking stride.

"That has wheels, you know."

He held one out for inspection. "Sure does," he noted and kept walking toward the exit.

We walked through the sliding doors toward the parking garage of the Humboldt airport, which was smack dab in the middle of Nowhere, California. The crisp spring air drifted over us, carrying his scent in the draft.

God, he'd grown. He'd been big for his age at sixteen when we met, but by my measure, he'd grown nearly a foot taller in ten years—two in shoulder width. One of those shoulders just in the last two years since I'd seen him.

When he'd shown up at the farmhouse looking for work, Pop didn't think twice. It was clear to all of us that Jake had nowhere to go, so Pop took him in, cared for him just like he'd cared for me when my parents died. In turn, Jake had worked his ass off for Pop, earning every bit of his room and board and then some.

Of course, we'd only really known each other that first summer, at the end of which I left for New York to live with my aunt. Jake stayed on the farm indefinitely, and I was glad for his presence there. It excused my guilt for leaving Pop.

Pop.

A sharp pinch in my chest brought my palm to the spot, followed by the familiar sting at the corners of my eyes. Tears were never far these days, the endless well forever surging without warning. I'd been at work when Kit called to tell me he was gone. On my way out of the office, I turned in my resignation at my aunt's marketing firm. Went home and packed a bag. And here I was.

Jake stopped, and I slammed into his back, bouncing off him like a rubber ball. Unfazed, he glanced over his shoulder at me.

"You sure you're okay?"

I waved a hand and made a noise of dissent. "Please. I run into brick walls all the time."

The quietest chuckle left him. He picked up one of the suitcases like it was empty and set it in the bed of his old Chevy.

A low whistle slipped out of me as I inspected his truck. "A '67 K20? Boy, she sure is pretty, Jake." I ran a hand across the shiny cream stripe, crisp against the fire-engine red. "Did you lift it?"

"Just a couple inches," he said, depositing the other bag with a thump. "Didn't figure you for a gearhead."

"I *did* grow up on a farm, you know," I teased, nonplussed. "Pop loved his old Chevy. When I was little, I helped him tune it up, fix it up, replace parts. He thought it important that I know the difference between a ratchet and a socket at a very young age."

"It's useful knowledge. Not that you have a chance to use it in the city."

Something in the way he'd said *city*—like it was week-old garbage—set my lips in a frown. But I followed his lead when he got in the truck, sliding in next to him. The tan leather bench was bouncy, and with a smile, I tested it out. He cut me a look when the squeaking of springs hit his tolerance threshold.

Warmth blossomed on my cheeks. I reached for the seat belt as he turned the key, and the truck rumbled to life around us.

Jake didn't say a word as he backed out of the space, then the lot. But it wasn't that comfortable, companionable sort of silence. It was awkward, weighted with half-conceived thoughts and yawning distance.

I wasn't accustomed to this kind of quiet. I started a dozen conversations in my mind but couldn't find the wherewithal to actually speak. Instead, I played every conversation into a dead end, because I figured that was where it would go. Nowhere.

It wasn't as if he'd ever been any other way, though he'd definitely gotten worse with age. Really, I didn't know why I'd always been cowed by his quiet judgments or lack of conversational skills. He was and forever had been the brooding farmhand, the silent workhorse. Lone wolf and all that. To him, I was the same silly girl with the pink suitcases who'd abandoned the farm all those years ago.

He'd said so himself a few years ago when I came home to help after Pop broke his leg. Pop told me to go back, that all was well. Jake insisted I should stay, that Pop needed me. I argued that Pop would tell me if that were true. And Jake had accused me of abandoning the farm before I ran back to my life in New York.

I'd spent the last few days regretting that choice with every painful heartbeat.

I snuck a quick look at him, tracing the rugged lines of his profile with my gaze. He wasn't wrong. But I was here to make that right, to atone by doing what I should have done years ago—drop absolutely everything to take care of the farm.

I didn't know why I'd thought Jake would behave any differently than he always did. Maybe I'd expected him to be different *because* of how utterly affected I was by him, my memory paling next to the real thing. Or maybe I wanted him to want to talk to me. Maybe I wanted to connect.

Jake was like a grandson to Pop, making him and me the only family Pop had in the end, my final connection to the man who had raised me. But Jake didn't seem to want to talk to me, and that knowledge made me feel desperately alone.

All these years, I'd been firmly on the other coast, working my dream job, using my degree in communications to work in social media at my aunt's marketing firm, telling myself my absence from the farm wasn't felt, that I'd only be in the way, that I had time. But I'd been wrong, and now it was too late.

The tears came again, almost too fierce to stop, halted only by a solid pinch of my thigh and a long, hard look at nothing outside the passenger window. Almost immediately, we were in the countryside, the sky cloudless and sun beating down on the truck, heating the cab like a greenhouse. Sweat prickled at my nape, across my forehead, down the valley of my spine. A fat droplet rolled between my breasts and into my bra, and I reached for the window crank in the same moment he reached for the air conditioning.

I beat him to it, rolling down the window with gusto, reveling in the feel of the cool coastal air against my overheated skin. The current whipped my hair into a copper tornado, curly and wild, and I gathered it up, searching my bag for a hair tie.

A lock of hair broke free, twisting toward the window, and the sight of the brilliant red against the cornflower-blue sky and the rolling grasses that stretched to meet it left me thinking of Pop. Of summer days in his truck with the windows down and Merle Haggard on the tinny old radio. Home became a presence, washing over me with the breeze. This place would forever be occupied by my grandfather. He was here, everywhere—whispering on the wind that soothed my sadness, living in the warmth of the sunshine.

The weight of my loneliness drifted out the window, the burden on my heart easing just a little, just enough. I sighed, leaning back in the seat with my eyes on the horizon, where blue met green.

It took me a moment to realize Jake was watching me, and when I turned to meet his gaze, I was struck.

It was only a second—a fleeting, fluttering second—but I saw the honesty of his own pain, of his loss, etched in the lines of his face, the depth of his eyes. Because it wasn't just me who had lost the most important person in my life.

He had too.

And so I decided right then that it didn't matter if he didn't want to talk to me or that we were virtual strangers. It didn't matter if he didn't want to connect. Because he needed me just as badly as I needed him. We'd never survive the next few days without each other.

We were in this together whether he liked it or not.

"So," I started, deciding dead-end small talk was better than the silence, "how's Kit holding up?"

He didn't answer right away, his eyes on the road and face tightening almost imperceptibly. "As good as you'd figure."

I waited for him to elaborate. Unsurprisingly, he didn't.

"How many trays of biscuits has she stress-baked?"

That earned me a smile, small though it was. "About fifty. You'd think she was feeding an army. But they've just piled up. None of us feel much like eating."

"No," I said quietly. "I wouldn't think so."

His eyes flicked to me, then back to the road. "I think she's planning to take a basket down to the VA later, if you want to go with her."

"I think I might." I paused, considering what the next few days would bring. "I don't know if I'm ready for this. Any of it. All of it."

"None of us are. You won't be alone in that."

That thought was an ember of hope in my chest.

But before I could respond, he doused it. "You sure did bring a lot of suitcases for a weekend."

"That's because I'm staying for a few weeks."

At that, he cut me another look. An accusatory, possessive look. "What for?"

"Because this is my home," I answered with a frown. "Because I want to spend some time with my memories." *Because I'm about to inherit the farm, and I'm not quite sure what that will mean,* I thought, keeping it to myself so as not to upset him.

Suddenly, I got the feeling that he wasn't going to be too happy to work with me, and that was alarming. There was no way I could run the farm without Jake.

He simmered but didn't press. Of course, he didn't acknowledge what I'd said, either. "Kit's got everything ready for you, and Pop's lawyer is meeting us at the house. He's anxious to talk to you about the will."

I swallowed hard. "Now? So soon? Can't it wait until … after?"

Jake's jaw flexed until the muscle at the joint bulged like a marble. "Probably, but he insisted on seeing you the minute you got here."

With a long exhale, I sat back, not realizing I'd straightened up. My gaze landed on the scratched-up lock on the glove box as the knowledge that I was about to deal with business I wasn't ready for sank in. The farm hadn't been doing well, and I had a lot of ideas on how to turn things around, ideas I hoped Jake would help me implement.

But I didn't want the farm right now, not yet. Not until I had a chance to say goodbye.

This time, I couldn't stop the surge of tears. I couldn't ease the twist in my chest or the vise of my throat. I couldn't temper the sting of my nose or the unfurling pain as it filled up my ribs.

Because my grandfather was gone. He was gone, and I was alone again.

I only remembered my parents in wisps and snapshots. In memories I couldn't be sure were real or pieced together from stories and photos. But I remembered every night Pop had tucked me in, every book he read me. Every scrap of homework he struggled through on my account and every night counting fireflies on the porch. It came to me in a fierce rush, and my pain dug up every loss to use as fuel for my tears.

I couldn't see for the shimmering curtain, so I closed my eyes. Held my breath, stifling the hitch of my lungs as best I could. Which wasn't very well.

"It's going to be okay, Livi," Jake said, his voice rough as gravel. "If Frank taught me one thing, it was that there is always hope. In the darkest night, at the lowest low, there is *always* hope."

A sob broke loose, my hand moving to my lips to stop the rest. And without thought, I slid across the bench and into his side, hanging on to his arm like an anchor.

He stiffened in surprise, leaving his hands on the wheel while he sorted out what to do with me. When I didn't let go, when my tears soaked his sleeve, he softened, shifting to pull me to his chest, holding me to him with his massive arm and that square hand on my shoulder. And I cried. I shuddered, face buried in his chest, his shirt fisted in my hand. For that one moment, I was stripped to the studs, exposed and frayed after two days of trying to keep it all contained.

Because no one in this world understood like Jake. That fact was as comforting as it was painful.

When I finally caught my breath, I shifted away, swiping at my cheeks and nose.

"I-I'm sorry," I blubbered, moving back to my side of the bench.

"Don't ever apologize to me for missing him," he said.

And when our gazes met, I decided I wouldn't.

IF YOU DON'T MIND

Olivia

T**HE SECOND JAKE TURNED ONTO THE LONG DIRT DRIVEWAY** of the farm, the vision of home overwhelmed me.

For a breathless moment, I took it in, my cheeks smudged with color and my eyes pricked with tears I'd only just put away. Ancient oaks lined the drive, reaching overhead to thread together, a hundred years of growing just so they could touch branches in a whisper. Rolling hills spread in every direction of the valley beyond, green and lush—every direction but one. In the distance behind me, beyond the sharp cliff face, the Pacific Ocean surged, the salt and brine mingling with the loamy earth, kissing my skin, feathering through my hair.

Beyond the canopy of trees was a slice of the farmhouse, white and crisp, proud and solid.

Two years had changed nothing, and I doubted another twenty would. It was the first view I'd had as a little girl, turning up this drive with my grandfather after my parents died. As we drew closer, the house grew, the trees falling away to reveal the farmhouse in all its glory. The wraparound porch set with rocking chairs and a bench swing that shifted in the breeze. The eaves faced with gingerbread scallops, the porthole window in the attic. The ancient door in need of a new coat of paint. Pop's truck in its spot at the side of the house, like he was waiting inside to see me.

The second Jake's hand touched the shifter to park, Kit shot out of the house with a smile on her face and tears in her eyes as she marched straight to me. I'd barely gotten out of the truck before I was wrapped in a hug that smelled like Christmas and felt like I'd been swallowed by a marshmallow.

She rocked me, holding me to her. "Oh, baby. Oh, honey." Her voice cracked, her arms squeezing tighter. "You're here. You're here, and it's all gonna be okay, I promise. I promise," she rambled, crying into my hair as I cried into her chest.

It took a minute for us to pull ourselves together, but when we did, she leaned back, hands on my arms so she could get a good look at me.

"So grown up. I barely recognize you. If I'd seen you in passing, I'd swear you were your mother."

I tried to smile, but everything hurt. "How are you, Kit?"

"Oh, I'm here and whiskey exists. Was your flight all right?"

"Let's just say, I'm here and whiskey exists."

With a laugh, she said, "There's my girl. Let's drink to that just as soon as you deal with Jeremiah Polluck. That old coot has been pestering me for an hour. You'd think he was blind, as well as he noticed I was busy with a fleet of pies."

Jake snorted, passing me with my suitcases in his hands. "And you'd have to be blind not to see he's sweet on you."

Kit rolled her eyes. "He's sweet on my cooking. And he's not winning any points coming here today just to pounce on poor Livi the second she got home."

My anxiety spiked at the thought of Jeremiah waiting in there with Pop's will. I didn't know what it'd say, but given that I was his last living kin, the answer seemed obvious.

I didn't want to know all the same.

That was the thought on my mind as Kit took me under her arm and walked me into the house, chattering about nothing just to fill the quiet, which I appreciated. We followed Jake's wide back, wound with muscles and tapering down to his narrow waist, then to his substantial rear end, which was at my eye-level for a single glorious moment as we climbed the steps.

Walking through that door was another snapshot in a flip book of snapshots. I was hit with the familiar scent of baked goods and the aroma that only this house contained, an amalgamation of a hundred and twenty years. It was knotty pine and smoky embers. It was pipe tobacco and antique iron. It was smells that weren't smells so much as they were memories, as if the house lived and breathed in this space and had its own stories to tell.

Old man Polluck hopped off his stool—which really meant he sort of slid off, pausing to balance himself—before heading for me with a bit of a bounce in his step.

"Olivia," he said, his face sad and touched with pity, "I am just so sorry, dear. Frank's loss is felt deep and wide. And I'm sorry to bother you when you haven't settled in, but Frank was very clear in his instructions. As his executor, I had to come, you see."

Again I tried to smile, and again I failed. "Thank you, Mr. Polluck."

He waved a hand. "Oh, now—you've been calling me Jeremiah since you were just a little thing with legs twice as long as the rest of you. Don't stop now. You'll make me feel my age." He smoothed his tie over his paunch as if to right himself.

Jake cleared his throat and headed for the stairs with my suitcases. "Want these in your old room?"

"Son," Jeremiah started, "I'll need you here too."

Jake stopped mid-stride, his face bent in confusion. "What do you need me for?"

"Come on and sit down, and I'll tell you."

Kit's eyes bounced between us as we headed into the kitchen. "I'll put some coffee on," she offered, hurrying to keep herself busy so she wouldn't burst.

I couldn't say I blamed her. I'd have given just about anything for a list of things to do.

I took a seat at the table, Jake at my side. Jeremiah shuffled to the other side to face us, his ancient briefcase in hand, then on the tabletop, creaking open. The shuffling of papers preceded the conversation that would change the lives of everyone in this room in some way or another.

"First, these are for you." Jeremiah extended his hands, each holding a letter.

I took mine gingerly, my eyes misting again at my name in Pop's hand on the envelope.

"Do we have to read these now?" Jake asked, his voice tight.

"No, those are for you to read whenever you wish." He took a breath and straightened up as best he could for possessing a crooked back. "A few years ago, Frank updated his will. I don't think any of you would be surprised that all of his money is tied up in the farm. And this asset is your inheritance." His rheumy eyes shifted from me to settle on Jake.

Jake frowned. Blinked. Glanced at me, then back at Jeremiah. "You mean Olivia."

"I mean both of you."

A silent moment, crackling with questions, passed. And with it came my relief. My only shot for success with the farm lay in Jake's hands, which was help I hadn't been sure I could rely on until that very moment when his stakes became the same as mine.

Jeremiah reached into his briefcase, his hands returning to view with identical packets, which he handed to us. "Frank Brent's will states that Brent Dairy Farm is to be equally distributed in its entirety to the two of you, fifty-fifty, with the exception of the farmhouse, which goes to Olivia. What you do with it is solely up to you, but Frank made sure you'd have to come together to decide."

Jake nodded. "That's easy. Olivia isn't staying, so I'll take over for Frank here, and she can just collect a paycheck." He looked at me with his entire stupid, handsome, clueless face. "That'll work, right?"

"*No*, that won't work," I said, my cheeks on fire and my brain ready for a fight. "I'm not leaving."

His face quirked in confusion. "Just to live in the farmhouse? What else are you gonna do here?"

"I'm going to work."

"Remotely for your job in New York?"

"I quit so I could work *here*."

"*Here*?" A haughty burst of laughter hit me like a slap in the face. "You don't know the first thing about running this farm."

"Maybe not the cows and the hay—"

"What else is there?"

"Social media. Newsletters. Our website hasn't been updated in fifteen years."

He stiffened. "We don't need any of that internet stuff."

"That *internet stuff* is the way businesses run now whether you think we need it or not."

The only acknowledgment was a derisive noise before he changed the subject. "What use do you have for a farm? I bet you can't even remember how to milk a cow. Hell, you can't even *drink* a glass of milk."

I looked at him like he had several heads touting feelers. "That doesn't mean I don't want some part in running my family business. I can't believe you expected me to hand it over without a fight. I can't believe you thought I'd leave."

"Why not? You did before."

The heat in my cheeks flared. "Pop told me to go."

"And you knew better than to believe him. That was his pride, but you'd have taken any excuse to leave. And you stayed gone. You *left*, Olivia, and you didn't come back. You weren't being noble—don't pretend otherwise." Before I could argue, he collected himself and tried again. "Listen—nobody expects you to stick around. Leave running the farm to me and go home. You know I'll take care of it, so just go back to New York where you belong."

"No," I said quietly, voice trembling. "We have to decide together, and I'm not going anywhere."

He drew an impatient breath through his nose, his eyes narrow and fiery. "I'm not going to spend my days fighting with you, and that's exactly what it'll be—a fight. I know what I'm doing, so just let me do my job without interference."

"It'll only be a fight if you make it one," I pointed out.

His eyes narrowed when he swallowed an argument. "What'll it take to get you to turn it over to me?"

"How can I answer that when I haven't even had a chance to try my hand at it?"

A pause, the time marked by the ticcing of that muscle at his jaw.

"Well," Jeremiah began, clearing his throat and shuffling things in his briefcase with no purpose, "no one has to decide anything right now. Olivia, your grandpa wanted to make sure you had time to make necessary plans once you decided what to do. So take some time. Get through what's coming. It'll be here waiting." He closed his briefcase with a squeak and a snick of metal latches. "Call me if I can be of any help."

When he stood, so did we. But before I could offer to walk him out, Jake steered him away, the two of them talking like I wasn't even there. And I fumed at their backs with painful disbelief licking at my ribs.

Jake was indignant, shockingly presumptuous. His surprise at my willingness to stay confounded me almost as much as his rejection. I wanted to make excuses for him, and for a moment, I did. Because he wasn't any better off than me when it came to losing Pop. Because his whole world was this farm, and its well-being had been placed on our shoulders—or his alone, if you asked him. And I was about to disrupt that world when he'd been so sure I'd pass it all over simply because it was hard.

That self-righteous asshole thought he had me all pegged. He thought I was in over my head, but he was wrong.

And I was going to prove it to him.

SHUCK IT

Jake

The second I showed Jeremiah out, I stormed toward the old red barn with my chest full of thunder.

Somehow, I hadn't even suspected she'd want anything to do with the farm, and the fact that she *did* didn't sit right. It was an invasion, an intrusion by a foreign general toting pink suitcases. A stranger uneducated in the way of things, with grand designs to meddle with things she didn't understand.

To change the place I'd poured my whole life into.

It wasn't like I hadn't known she was going to inherit the farm. I just assumed she'd come back for the funeral, get her affairs in order, and leave the rest to me as the overseer of the farm. There'd been a chance I could have kept things as they were, run them just as Frank had. But if the last ten minutes were proof, Olivia wasn't going to let that happen.

The only upside was that I owned half the farm too, so if she wasn't going to leave, I could stop her.

A shock of realization blazed through me. Half of everything I loved—everything I'd thought I'd have to hand over to Olivia—was mine.

It didn't feel real, couldn't be possible. I hadn't known my father, but all the imagining I did when I was a boy were nothing compared to the truth of Frank Brent. He was more than a father to me. He was a savior. A mentor. He was the indestructible, unchanging peak of a mountain that had crumbled without warning, leaving my view forever changed.

And he'd loved me the same it seemed, to have left me half of his legacy.

Half of this place was mine. And there wasn't a chance in hell that I'd let Olivia Brent ruin it with her inexperience.

I was absolutely certain there was no way she could tackle the task before her. Olivia, who'd been home a handful of times in ten years. Olivia, who couldn't lift a hay fork if her life hung in the balance. Her exit was as sure a thing as ever existed.

I could see the outcome spread out before me like a game of chess. She'd fumble around the farm. Figure out how complex it was to run. Realize that nobody gave a goddamn about a dairy farm's Twitter account. She'd give bored, give up, turn tail, and run back to the city where she belonged, just like she always did.

Maybe I'd have felt different if she'd stayed when I asked her to. Back then, I was stupid enough to think she could do some good around here, first and foremost by coming back for Frank's sake. If he'd been standing here before me, he'd laugh at the suggestion. He'd play it off, wave a hand, insist she was where she needed to be. But I knew better. I'd spent enough sunsets on the porch with him, seen the look in his eyes when he talked about her. He was lonely, and I was poor company. Having her here would have been a blessing to him, a light of joy in his final years.

But she hadn't stayed. It wasn't important enough for her to give up her New York life. And by proxy, neither was Frank.

This time wouldn't be any different. But I told myself not to worry. She wouldn't last until September before she got bored and left me to do my job uninterrupted. I could survive Olivia for one summer.

I had before, though God knew I'd never forgotten it.

I suspected I wouldn't soon forget this summer, either.

My palm smacked the small side door of the barn so hard, it hit the wall with a crack and rebounded back at me.

Old Mack spun around, wild-eyed and peaked.

"Good God, son," he said, weathered hands shaking as he pulled off his baseball cap to wipe his brow. "What's got in your Jockeys?"

"Sorry," I shot, unable to actually sound sorry. "I didn't mean to scare you."

"Doesn't take much," he said on a chuckle, and it was true.

The Vietnam vet had been homeless for a decade after the war, his PTSD debilitating. He couldn't find—or keep—a job, but Frank brought him in, just like he had all of us. Gave him a job and fresh start. He'd saved Mack.

He'd saved me too.

I whipped off my shirt, tossing it over a stall's fence. Ginger, the mare inside, whinnied at the intrusion.

I ignored her, snagged a hay fork, and went to work.

For a minute, Mack watched me shuck hay, sitting on a bale, catching his breath while I slung straw with more force and speed than was necessary.

"You knew Frank was gonna give her the farm," he finally said.

That shock again, sharp and quick. "That's not the problem. She's not leaving."

"Oh," he said in an unreadable tone. "She fire you?"

"Nope. Because Frank left *me* the farm too. Fifty-fifty."

Silence behind me as I drove the fork into the pile.

"Well, I'll be damned," he breathed. "Congratulations, son." A pause. "So how come you're so pissed?"

"Because she wants to work the farm when she doesn't know

what she's doing," I fired, dumping the load onto the little trailer hooked up to the ATV.

"I see." He didn't at all sound surprised.

"She's got all these big ideas about social media and who knows what else. She wants to change things—I know she does. I can smell the city all over her. She mighta fed chickens and milked cows when she was a kid, but she didn't know this farm. She doesn't know the day-to-day. She doesn't know how much we've worked for. What *Frank* worked for. It'll be a cold day in hell when I let her sink what he built."

"Change ain't never easy, Jake. And there's gonna be a lot of change around here now Frank's gone."

That familiar heaviness sank in my ribs.

Frank. There was only one directive—run this place exactly as he'd done. I'd known him well enough to know what he'd do in any given situation, and the best way to honor him was to act as he would. Anything short of that would be blasphemy. Sure, we were in the red, but there were plenty of conventional ways to turn that around. And if I ever got a handle on running the entire farm alone, I'd get right on that.

It didn't matter that I was afraid of failing him—there was no choice to be made. I'd stepped into his place whether I knew what I was doing or not. I *had* to preserve him. It was the best way I knew to make him proud.

Another pause, leaving me to mark the feel of the smooth handle in my fists, buffeted by calluses I'd had since forever. The burn of my shoulders was a comfort, a punishing ache to remind me that I was here. That this was my place.

"I wish I could say I was surprised she wants to step in," Mack said. "But she's Frank's kin, after all. Giving up isn't in the Brent genetic makeup."

I stopped, turning to him with my brows strung tight. "You figured she'd want to stay?"

He rolled one sloped shoulder. "Oh, I dunno. But I didn't

figure she'd give it all up, either. I wasn't convinced she'd just pick up and leave. Frank was just as much a father to her as he was to you."

That thought hit me in the softest of places. "You let me go on thinking it was a sure thing, her turning it over to us."

"Well, you seemed real sure of yourself, Jake. None of us coulda told you any different. Kit figured there was a chance you were right and didn't want to upset the apple cart for no reason."

"Kit too?" I snapped. "And all this time, I thought you were on my side."

"Oh, quit it. There's no side to pick here."

"Doesn't matter," I said, taking back to my task with a little more determination. "She's gonna fold like a lawn chair, just watch and see. If she really knows what's best, she'll let it go. Her meddling is only gonna make things harder around here, not easier."

"Guess we'll see," he said like he knew something I didn't. "I'm getting out to the barns to check on the milking crew. Want me to keep the news buttoned up?"

"They're gonna find out anyway. Better from you than me." I dumped the hay, irritated that the trailer was full.

"Don't be too hard on her, Jake. She wants what's best for the farm, just like all of us."

"Except she doesn't know what's best for the farm." Annoyed by my own petulance, I added, "I'll give her a fair shake. I promise."

With a dubious look, he nodded once and turned, leaving me with my thoughts.

Which were largely consumed by Olivia.

I turned for the stalls, hoping if I mucked them, I might muck her too.

When I'd seen her at the airport, that red hair flaming, I'd barely recognized her. I hadn't seen her in near two years, and the truth was, I avoided her as best I could when she came home. It hadn't always been like this—once upon a time, I reveled in her homecomings, hoping for ... I didn't know for what. Another kiss maybe. Something more. She always said she'd come back straight after college, but after that trip home when she dismissed the truth so easily, I never looked at her the same.

I'd told her right then that Frank needed her, but she left anyway. And when she graduated and got a fancy job, we all knew.

Olivia wasn't coming back to the farm. Not if she could help it.

And here she was now that it was imperative, just like I'd figured.

When she'd reached for that pink suitcase on the belt, there was no denying it was her.

She was small like I remembered, a delicate thing. A wisp of fragile bones and wild hair. Her skin so fair, ten minutes in the pasture would boil her like a lobster. She seemed porcelain, breakable. And the farm was no place for breakable things.

Maybe she had more mettle than I figured, but I hoped that possibility was nil. Because if there was one thing I'd protect to my last breath, it was this farm. Every cow and calf, every acre and blade of grass.

And I'd be certain to make good on that vow whether Olivia liked it or not.

KNOW-HOW

Olivia

I STOMPED UP THE STAIRS WITH ENOUGH FURY, EVEN KIT knew better than to follow.

I'd known I wasn't ready to hear what Jeremiah had to say, but whatever I'd imagined, this was a trillion times worse. Not for the knowledge that I'd split the farm with Jake.

But that Jake hated me so desperately.

I flew into my old room blindly, closing the door behind me with a slam.

It had remained unchanged, and when I passed the threshold, I was teleported back in time. I was sixteen again and had gotten the news that I was going to live with Annette, my mother's sister, in New York. The tears were the same. The rip in my chest was identical. And there was nothing to do but take a minute to wallow.

I'd been handed a bucket of lemons, and I wanted to squeeze them all into Jake's eye.

I sank onto the bed, curling into myself, but along with the squeak of the old mattress came a crinkle of paper.

The letter in my back pocket beckoned, momentarily forgotten. Holding it in my hands was surreal, the weight of the words inside as tangible as the paper itself. These words were the last he'd ever speak to me, and that knowledge left me as reluctant to open it as I was desperate to devour the words inside.

Wasn't that how it always went? The moments you needed your lost one the most was when they were gone.

And I needed Pop.

With shaky hands, I tore open the envelope, begging the slip of paper for guidance.

Livi,

Seems like a million years ago that you and me rumbled up to the house after losing everyone we ever loved. You were just a pocket-sized little thing, and I remember lifting you out of the truck, thinking of how precious you were to me. I remember realizing just how badly you needed me and the answering understanding that I needed you too. Because we were alone. But we could be alone together.

So I made myself—and you—a promise. I'd never leave you alone again.

Lately, I've been thinking a lot about that promise. It comes to me on the wind sometimes, on cricket songs, in the sound of my rocking chair on the porch. It comes to me in moments when I feel every mile between us, and there you are, as alive in my mind as if you were standing in front of me. Someday, I'll be gone, and what will become of you?

I can't leave you alone. Not again. So I'm leaving you with Jake.

I hope you don't hate me for splitting up what's yours by right. But I suspect that the two of you will need each other, even if just for the farm's sake. I also suspect that Jake will not take kindly to your interference any more than you can stop yourself from interfering. But promise me you'll listen to him. Never have I known a man so devoted to the farm or to me. I know that between the two of you, you'll make something of our farm that none of us could have imagined. Truth be told, that thought makes writing this letter that much easier.

I love you, Livi. I'd wish for you to be strong, but you already are—you don't know any other way. You persist with joy in your heart, and you'll keep going despite my absence. But I'll wish for you to take care of yourself and the farm. Take care of Jake in the way I hope he takes care of you. And try not to miss me all that much. Because I'll always be here, with you.

All my love,
Pop

It took me much longer to read the letter than it should have, for both the unceasing curtain of tears and the hungry wish to hear his voice.

I can't leave you alone.

I remembered that day, the day I'd come to the farm in Pop's truck, teddy bear in my arms and my little pink polka-dot suitcase stuffed with my belongings. I remembered the way he'd smelled, the song on the radio—"Blue Eyes Crying In The Rain" by Willie Nelson. The squeak of the seat as we bumbled up the drive. I remembered Kit, who was unchanged in my eyes. I remembered the loneliness I'd felt up until the moment Pop picked me up from the airport and swept me into his arms.

I can't leave you alone.

So he'd left me with Jake.

It was a comfort and a curse to have him as my partner—he knew what he was doing and how to run the farm, that much was true. But I had a pretty good feeling that companionship was out of the question.

He'd left me with Jake. But Jake didn't want to be left with me.

I swiped at my tears, reading the letter again, then once more. The farm had been left in our charge, and his final wish was that we take care of it.

So I'd make sure we did. I owed him that.

I owed him more than that.

This was my chance to prove myself, to right my wrong in leaving. Jake had accused me of avoiding coming home, and in so many ways, I had. I thought I had time when I didn't. I hadn't been ready to come back, but that shouldn't have mattered.

All I had now was my purpose.

Determination filled me up like sunlight in a bottle—light and bright and warm. It was purpose I'd found.

And that seemed to make all the difference in the world.

I popped off the bed like a jack-in-the-box, ready to unpack and settle in. But then I remembered Jake hadn't brought my bags up, and I'd flown right past them in my fury. So with my chin up and my back straight, I trotted down the stairs, hoping Kit could help me up. But she was nowhere to be found, and I wasn't willing to leave the safety of the house—I didn't know where Jake was, and the last thing I wanted him to know was that I needed help. So I stood there in front of those suitcases and gave myself a pep talk before grabbing one, hoisting it with all my strength, and propping it on my leg to ease a little weight as I struggled toward my room.

Up the stairs I went, huffing and puffing and trying not to scuff the walls. By the time I reached the top, my fingers burned and slackened. Another three stairs, and I might have gone tumbling down to the landing, which would have been an unmitigated disaster. I couldn't exactly save the farm with two broken legs.

There was no way I'd be able to get the second one upstairs, so I prayed when I opened it that it was the one with the things I needed. And when I unzipped that glorious suitcase, my prayers were answered.

I unpacked my clothes and toiletries and my blessed rain boots. They'd been a silly purchase, honestly. The likelihood of me using them in New York were slim to none—I might have been laughed out of Manhattan if someone had spotted me on the subway in pink rainboots. The only place I'd ever wear them was here. But I saw them in a shop window in April a few years ago and stopped dead. I'd had to have them, even if just to stand up under the coat hooks for looks.

But their time had finally come.

The old dresser drawers groaned and hung, its handmade pieces uneven and warped from years of use.

It was a far cry from the slick IKEA drawers that lasted a grand total of one year before coming apart at the seams.

Reverse culture shock was what it was. Once upon a time, this had been my whole world. But now I had New York to compare it to.

I found I preferred it here. When I was sixteen, Pop and my aunt Annette decided that New York would provide more opportunity than Maravillo, population: tiny. I didn't want to go at the time, but when I got to Manhattan, I fell in love like most people did. For the first time since my mom died, I had a surrogate mother in Annette, someone to guide me into womanhood.

I loved the city still, but here? Well, here was home. Here there was quiet. Space. It was slower, easier in so many ways. More real estate than I'd seen in one place in some time, enough to be a little disorienting, like swimming in open water.

Don't get me wrong—I'd loved living with Annette too. I loved my job, and I loved my life. Over the years, I'd convinced myself that New York was home, but the second I'd set foot on the ground in front of the big house, I knew that wasn't true. This was my home, and it always would be, no matter how many years I spent away or how many miles stood between us. The decision to quit my job and move here had been simple and easy. For that, at least, I was grateful.

Jake would love to see me leave, and I'd hate to give him the satisfaction.

"Tell me I can't milk a cow," I muttered as I pulled on jeans and buttoned up a blue plaid shirt. "Oh, I'll milk a cow," I said to my boots, shoving in one foot, then the other. "I'm gonna milk her so good, she's gonna need a smoke when it's over."

I stood, checking my reflection. I looked like a proper farm girl, except for my hair, which was as unruly as ever. So I slipped my fingers into my locks, humming tunelessly as they wound a French braid to keep the tresses contained while I did exactly what Jake said I couldn't.

Nothing motivated me quite like being underestimated.

Down the stairs I bounded and out the front door. Golden sunlight cut through the branches of the oaks shading the drive and house, dappling the ground along with the breeze. That breeze was one I'd missed—the crisp California air, touched with a nip, even in the thick of summer.

I wound around the porch and toward the old barn. The meadow rolled on past the fence and up a hill dotted with heifers and calves out to graze. We'd provided local dairy since the late 1800s, our stock growing over the years to over a thousand heads of cattle. The big barns stretched off in the distance, all built to allow plenty of space for our herds with long and regular access to pastures.

We were part of the foundation of the town before the Pattons came along. They were cattle ranchers, known for rustling, thought themselves above the law. Legend went, they'd stolen Brent cattle and drove them to Wyoming, and when they came back, the Brents were waiting for them. In the scuffle, one of the Brent boys was shot by a Patton, and the elder Brent had the elder Patton arrested and hanged. With the law watching them, the Patton heirs decided ranching wouldn't be lucrative enough. So they went into dairy, and they went in big, their number one goal seeming to be to put our farm under.

It was a miracle our farm had survived. But the feud never ended, passed down generation to generation, ad infinitum. My grandfather and the late Billy Patton had been at it since birth.

James Patton and my father had nearly beaten each other to death over my mother.

I didn't know where Chase Patton landed.

When I was nine years old and didn't have a single friend, Chase was the one who sat next to me at lunch. He played with me at recess and told me he liked my red hair when the other kids teased me for it. He was my first friend in a time when I needed a friend. Until his father found out. And then he came to school, pushed me off a swing in front of his other friends, and sneered down at me as I lay crying in the dirt that I was a dirty, fire-crotch Brent.

I didn't even know what it meant, only that it hurt brutally.

Pop did. James sported a black eye for a week as a result.

But I always believed Chase was only doing what he'd been told, not what he wanted. Quietly, he'd shown me kindness. Silently, he'd protected me more than once from ridicule from the girls and worse from a few of the guys.

And I couldn't ever understand how the old feud still had teeth.

The old barn had been opened up to let the sunshine in, and I passed the threshold filled with sentimentality. The smell of hay and ancient wood, of livestock and barley. The horses nickered in their stalls when I passed, the wide floor covered in hay, and in the back corner with a mouthful of cud was Alice.

My smile spread when I saw the heart-shaped spot on her flank that set her apart from the rest of the herd.

The summer before I'd moved away, I'd helped birth Alice, which proved a harrowing affair. Her mother nearly died, and we thought Alice might go with her. But by some miracle, they both lived, and after my constant attention and the attachment that came along with it, Alice and I became best friends. She found me when I visited her herd, followed me around while I marked heifers for the vet. She'd nestle and nudge me with her snout until I paid her attention. When she started following me to the gate, I brought her up to the house with me to give her a good old-fashioned brushing. And when she wouldn't go back to the pastures, nudging me back to the old barn instead, I asked Pop if she could stay near the house. He indulged me as he so often did, and forever after, that was where she preferred to be—in the old barn with the horses and hay.

She always pastured with the rest of the cattle, but then she'd come to the gate and moo her request for passage, which was always granted, sometimes simply because she'd stand there bleating until someone let her in.

I approached her with the fondness of an old friend. Her rear was to me, but she caught sight of me almost instantly, her three-hundred-degree periphery serving her well. She stopped chewing. Chuffed. Turned to me with her ears flicking in my direction, her big, sweet eyes full of recognition.

I could have cried at the sight of her.

"Heya, Alice," I said with a trembling voice, reaching out to scratch the wide space between her eyes.

Those eyes closed, and she leaned into my hand.

"I missed you too. Are you mad at me for staying away so long?"

She mooed, and I laughed, glancing around to get a good look at her udders.

"Did you have another baby?" I petted her shoulder. "Lucky for both of us. I've got somebody to prove wrong."

"And who might that be?"

I jumped about a yard at the sound of Jake's voice, whirling around like I was being held up. "Jesus," I breathed, pressing a hand to my thundering heart. "What are you doing in here?"

And shirtless.

Indecent was what it was. His body was chiseled and solid as stone and absolutely *indecent*. His broad chest was streaked with dirt and flecks of hay, the same tiny flecks that caught in the valleys between his abdominal muscles and that V his hips made.

I'd never actually seen one of those Vs in person, and something in me squeezed at the sight of it.

He caught me looking and smirked just a little, just enough to flame my cheeks and snap my gaze to his.

"Nice boots," he said, snagging his shirt off Ginger's stall wall.

God, even watching him put it *on* was hot. The graceful stretch and tug, the mussing of his dark hair, the fanning and flexing of biceps and fluttering muscles of his forearms as he pulled the hem into place.

I turned to Alice, not wanting to look at him anymore. Well, I *wanted* to look at him—I'd have liked to spend a good long while drawing a map of those muscles with the interest of an anatomy student. Because truly, I couldn't understand where they'd all come from. I hadn't even known most of them existed.

"Don't make fun of my boots," I snapped, petting Alice, who broke from me to head to the wall where the bucket was nailed.

She mooed and nudged it off the nail with her nose, unfazed when it hit the ground with a clang.

I chuckled. "That bad, huh? I'm here to help."

"Lucky, since you have something 'to prove.'"

I scowled at the bucket, pulling the stool into the room. The second I sat, Alice parked herself right in front of me.

"All right, girl," I said so only she could hear. "You ready to dismantle some misogyny?"

With another chuff and a stomp of her foot, I figured she agreed.

For a moment, I assessed the terrain. Surely, this was like riding a bike. I'd milked a million cows but not for at least five years, and as I looked at her udders—and as Jake watched me with a critical gaze—I second-guessed myself. Opposite nipples, I knew that. I needed to strip them first.

With the objective remembered, I moved the bucket out of the way and clutched a nipple in each hand, taking a breath before the moment of truth.

I squeezed, dragging down in the motion that felt both familiar and foreign. Something was off, my grip maybe—I could tell by the feel of the motion, confirmed when nothing came out.

Undeterred, I tried again. Again, it was wrong, and Alice mooed her discontent.

"Grip it up higher, closer to the bag," he said from my side where he leaned against a post with his arms folded.

"Don't tell me what to do."

"Fine, but when Alice kicks you off that stool and knocks the wind out of you, don't come crying to me."

"I wouldn't dare," I said, hating myself for doing what he'd said. Another stroke told me I was still wrong.

I let out a noisy breath through my nose and tried again, adjusting the pressure and pinch, but I got nothing out of her.

With a huff, I let her go, digging through my brain for an answer as Jake watched from his perch, smug as all hell. When I thought I might have some direction, I grabbed her teats again only to get smacked in the face by her tail.

I spat out the coarse tail hair and wiped my lips with the back of my hand while Jake laughed. It wasn't a small laugh, but a big, happy sound I hadn't suspected lived in him. I was too annoyed to appreciate it.

"Bump the bag like a calf would," he said when he caught his breath. "It'll let her milk down."

"I know how to do it," I bit out.

"Coulda fooled me."

Ignoring him, I nudged her udder with my hand.

"Good. Now grab her up high, fill your hand with her teat, and—"

"I know how to do it!"

He held up his hands in surrender. "Fine. Then let's see it."

But once again, I did what he'd said, and as I pulled, I knew it was right—I was rewarded with the first stream of milk.

I crowed, stripping each udder a few times to clear them out.

Cheerfully, and perhaps with too much confidence, I clutched the bucket between my legs like I used to do and milked the damn cow like a champion milkmaid.

"Told you I could milk a cow," I said over the tinny sound of milk hitting the metal bucket.

"Sure. You're a regular pro. How long you think you woulda sat here before Alice got impatient and tossed you?"

"I would have figured it out," I defended.

"Guess we'll never know."

"If you hadn't interfered, we would."

"I was just trying to help," he said.

"Were not. You were making fun of me."

"I didn't think you'd wear those boots if you didn't want people to make fun of you."

"I don't really give a damn what you think of them."

"They look brand new. Have you ever even worn them?"

"What does it matter?" I hedged, my eyes on Alice's udders, imagining my fists were around his neck instead of a cow's nipples.

"Only in that you look about as green as you are."

"You forget I grew up here."

"That doesn't mean you know what's what. You couldn't even milk old Alice without my help."

"I don't think that's indicative of my business acumen."

He snorted a laugh. "Acumen, huh? So tell me, how do you think you're gonna run an entire dairy farm?"

"I'm not. *We* are."

This time, the noise he made wasn't a laugh at all. "So I'll do everything while you what, come in here and talk to Alice like she's your diary?"

"There's plenty to be done, things that have been neglected and ignored for years. I'm here to turn the business around. You can keep doing whatever it is you do."

"Whatever it is I do?" he shot. "By that statement alone, your argument's invalid. You're in over your head, farmgirl."

"Farmgirl, huh?"

"City girl, showing up in her city getup, pretending she's a farmgirl. One tumble into the pigsty, and you'll be running for Saks where I bet you bought those stupid boots."

"*Your* boots are stupid," I shot back. "My boots are pretty and pink and they make me happy, which is more than I can say for you. Now if you'll excuse me, I have a cow to milk."

"What for? You can't drink it."

I stopped, turning my fury on him like a siren. "What the hell do you care? If you came in here just to bully me, you're even worse than I realized."

"I was here first."

"Technically, I was here first," I volleyed. "This farm was born of my blood, so don't go on trying to convince me that I don't matter. I matter, Jake. And I own half this farm, same as you."

"Tell me how to get you to turn it over," he said sternly, echoing his demand from earlier, a demand I didn't suspect he'd relinquish. "You can run your financial half, if you feel you have to. But it'll be easier for everyone if you do it from New York."

"Easier for everyone or easier for you?"

His jaw clenched.

"You know, the worst part of all this is that you won't even give me a chance. You won't even let me *try*."

Jake pushed off the post and spoke too quietly to be as intense as he was. "All right then, big shot—I'll tell you what. I'll make you a deal. If you can turn things around in one season, I'll give you one percent of my share, and the whole thing can be yours. And if you don't, you give *me* one percent and go home."

"I *am* home."

The look on his face said *bullshit*, but rather than speak, he extended his hand for a shake.

And I took that big, dumb hammer of a hand and squeezed it as hard as I could when I gave it a pump.

"I'm not going anywhere," I promised again.

His eyes were dark, brows drawn, his lips touched with a ghost of a smile. "We'll see about that," he said.

Before I could sling my bucket at him, he turned to go.

By God, if I wasn't happy to see the back of him. And for more than one reason.

"It's you and me against the world, Alice."

And with a moo of agreement and a nudge for me to finish the job, I was left hoping I'd come out on top.

SURVIVAL INSTINCT

Jake

I COULDN'T GET MY TIE STRAIGHT.

With a huff and a tug and a slip of silk, it was undone again, and so I made to try once more.

I could count on one hand the times I'd worn a tie, and every single time, I'd had Frank to help me fix it when it was crooked or the tail was too long. But today, on the day of his funeral, it was only me and the mirror.

My face was fresh-shaven, my hair combed neatly, fingernails scrubbed clean. The tailored shirt I'd pulled out of the depths of my closet was nearly too small, the fabric taut around my chest and biceps, but nobody'd see it anyway. Kit had let out my coat to fit, at least. It'd do.

If I had my way, I'd burn the whole outfit the second this day was over.

A hard swallow did little to open my throat, and the urge to bolt overcame me. I didn't want to do this. I didn't want to say goodbye. I didn't want to pretend like it was all going to be okay, and I didn't want to comfort the people of the town, the friends and loved ones who would be here today.

All I wanted was to sit in the kitchen with the people who loved him best and remember him. For a moment, I daydreamed about that impossible scene where Kit baked and I sat at the island, picking at the results. Olivia would be there too, and I found I didn't hate the idea. Because if there was one person in the world who knew and loved Frank as well as me, it was her.

I imagined her crying and knew I wouldn't know what to do. Her emotions were big and loud and subject to change without notice. Mine were quiet and simmering and stewed until they boiled over. I didn't know how to deal with her big loudness any better than she seemed to know how to deal with me. She wanted to talk. I wanted to listen. And in that, I figured we'd do well enough. So long as she didn't expect me to talk back.

That pain I'd carried around since Frank died was deep and dull and constant. It was a feeling I knew well, one that I'd had since I was sixteen and motherless, trucking across the country, working odd jobs on farms. I kept quiet and kept my head down. Used my size and strength to keep a roof over my head and my belly full. And when I'd knocked on the old farmhouse door, I'd found a home when I thought I'd never know family again.

Homeless and alone at sixteen, that summer marked the beginning of a new life. Frank brought me into the family in ways I'd never expected or imagined. All I'd wanted was maybe a cot in the barn and a few weeks' work, but he gave me a home. He gave me hope when I'd convinced myself no such thing existed.

So I did whatever he'd asked, without question. I kept my head down, as I was like to do. But I watched Olivia. We'd both lost our families, both been saved by Frank. Given a home, shown kindness and love. And I spent so long marveling at her unsinkable optimism when there wasn't an ounce of optimism in me. There was rarely a moment when she wasn't smiling, never a time when she didn't find joy where I could find none.

When she found me up in the hayloft that night long ago, staring out the open gable window at the moon, we talked about the losses we shared. Well, she talked. I listened, my heart aching with understanding I couldn't find the words to express. She'd been younger than I was when my mother died, but when she spoke of her parents' death, I found myself jealous that she hadn't seen them go—she was at school when the accident happened, their coffins closed. For years, she said, she expected them to just walk in the door, told herself they were just away and would be back at any time.

And I told her how I'd held my mother's hand and watched her take her last breath, leaving me alone in the world.

Maybe it was the recognition on her face. Maybe it was the honesty of the tears in her eyes. Maybe I'd never met anyone who understood me until her.

But I kissed her. And that kiss made me wish I'd kissed her the second I met her instead of the night before she left.

She'd never truly returned. And her loss was felt by Frank every single day.

It was me who had found him the day he passed. I heard the crash and rumble as he fell, taking a shelf down with him. A moment was all it took. One flicker and thump of his heart, and the man I'd known faded away in my arms well before the ambulance arrived. But I pumped his chest all the same with Kit at my side, praying to a God I didn't believe in to save him.

It wasn't the first time He'd let me down. Watching my mother wither away, neglected in a county hospital bed, I'd prayed. I bargained and begged. But in the end, she was taken from me too. There was no insurance for an immigrant, even if she'd come here seeking refuge from war. There was no compensation for my father dying in a valley in Croatia, and there was no place for me anywhere. There was no quarter for any of us.

So when Mama held my hand with tears in her sunken eyes and begged me to survive, I promised her I would. But it wouldn't be in the foster system. I didn't even know what would happen to me if I let them take me, but the fear of deportation to a country I'd never known was enough to set me out on my own. I was young and strong and knew there had to be work for me, if I looked for it.

So I headed west, certain there was a place at the end of the road where I'd find what I was looking for, even if I didn't know what that was.

Farm after farm, harvesting corn, breeding livestock, learning everything I could to expand my résumé, to make myself useful, indispensable. But I never stayed for long, never set down roots. Mostly, people were kind. Plenty of times, they weren't. But in the end, when I made it to the West Coast, I found the gold at the end of the rainbow.

I'd found Frank. And Frank had given me everything.

I did not want to step foot out of my house, nestled on the edge of the big house property. I did not want to walk into this day, a day I knew would be unending and exhausting in ways I couldn't even fathom. I didn't want to say goodbye to Frank, not with an audience, not ever.

But I had no choice. There was no way to avoid it, and the people of this town needed someone to accept their condolences.

My only comfort was that I wouldn't be alone.

Olivia and I had stayed out of each other's way the last couple of days, resulting in some kind of unspoken truce. I was still as unhappy about the whole situation as she was. But today, we needed each other. Today, nothing mattered but Frank. So we'd stand side by side and accept everyone's grief, piling it on top of our own. We would sit shoulder to shoulder in a pew and do our best not to break in front of the whole town. We'd get through today and put the rest off until tomorrow.

I swore under my breath, undoing my tie again. It was hopeless. I was hopeless.

An idea struck—Kit. Kit knew everything about everything. She had to know how to tie a stupid tie. With the slip of silk in my fist, I headed out, snagging my coat on the way.

The morning was cool, the sun only up enough to shoot shafts of sunlight through the dewy leaves of the trees. Even the grass glittered, struck with that burst of light that made the whole world look like it was weeping.

The path wound around the other cottages, one for Kit and one for Mack and one for Miguel, our vet. I smelled Kit's biscuits well before I reached the back door and hoped I'd find the faces I knew. Hoped we'd have a moment to ourselves before this day began.

But once again, luck was not on my side.

The kitchen was empty except for one person, a face I barely knew anymore, one I was accustomed to seeing screwed up with irritation. But in that moment when I walked in, Olivia's face was soft, her eyes glittering and shoulders slumped. For the first time since I'd picked her up at the airport, she looked like the city girl I knew her to be. A tailored black dress with sleeves capping small shoulders. Her neck, long and pale, exposed by the twist of her hair, smooth and red. Her lips, lush and bowed and turned down.

She was unarmed, and the sight disarmed me too. Everything about her was delicate and vulnerable—from the curve of her chin to her long, threaded fingers—the spitfire doused, leaving her nothing but vapors. And when she met my gaze, we shared that sentiment, the thread of connection deep and tangible between us.

But she looked away and took the moment with her.

"Kit just ran back to put on her dress," Olivia said, swiping at her cheeks, her back stiffening. When she looked up again, then at the tie hanging in my fist, she frowned. "Did you need help?"

I scoffed. "No."

"Then why's your tie in your hand and not around your neck?"

"You said Kit's at her house?"

"Getting dressed," she added, slipping off her stool. "Don't be a baby, Jake," she said without heat. "Let me help you."

I let out a noisy, resigned breath as she clicked her way toward me in heels higher than I'd ever seen. They were black and shiny against the snow of her skin, her legs long and her stride sure. This was her element more than the stupid pink boots. And in this element, I was as lost as she was in mine.

She took the tie from my hand when she came to a stop in front of me. "You look nice," she said, her eyes on her hands as she flipped my collar and slid that tie around my neck in a whisper.

"So do you," I offered, meaning it.

For a moment, she said nothing, just watched her hands as I watched her. Her nose, small and pert. Her lashes, long and feathery. Her cheeks, dotted with freckles. She smelled like flowers—not the old lady kind. The kind that made you sigh in the summertime and wish you lived in a meadow.

I swallowed, disturbing her work with my Adam's apple.

"Get any sleep?" she asked.

"Not a wink. You?"

"None. I watched the sun come up wishing it would go back down." Her voice trembled. "I don't think I want to do this at all."

"Neither do I. Only thing that makes it a little easier is knowing you'll be there with me."

Her face turned up to mine, her brows creased. "Me? I thought all you wanted was for me to give up and go home."

"Oh, I do." A smile flickered on my lips but faded away. "But not today."

Her eyes filled with tears, chin wobbling. She sniffled. "Thank you."

"What for?"

"I thought we'd be at odds like we have been."

"I'm not a monster, Livi. I know I might act like one, but I'm not."

The smallest smile touched her lips. "I don't know. Bridge troll comes to mind."

I huffed a laugh. "At least let me be something with style. Like a werewolf or something."

With a chuckle, she smoothed my tie. "There. All set."

"Thank you. Only person who ever knew how to do it was Frank."

"Well," she started, tamping down her tears for the sake of me, "I think he'd be quite proud of you."

"Oh, I dunno. When it comes to you, I'm not so sure."

"Don't worry. There's still time."

When she smiled up at me, I was overwhelmed by the urge to draw her into my chest. To fold her up in my arms, to take away her tears. To shelter that delicate thing from what might harm her.

I almost did. Right then and there, for no reason at all, I almost did.

But before I could, the back door opened and Kit flew in looking like a mad scientist—hair in disarray, dress buttoned crooked, dashes of mascara under her eyes.

Olivia and I broke apart like an eggshell. She frowned, taking Kit in as she rushed to the oven to pull out a tray of biscuits.

"How can I help?" Olivia asked as she approached Kit like she was a wild animal.

"Oh, I'm all right, just in a rush. Didn't want to burn the biscuits."

"Whatever would we eat?" Olivia teased, gesturing to the two dozen biscuits already stacked on the counter.

"Hush," Kit said, setting the baking sheet on the stove. "Come here and help me move these to the rack, Livi."

"How about I help you fix your dress?"

Kit blinked, then looked down and laughed. "Why do I get the feeling the whole day's gonna be like this?"

Olivia smiled sadly and stepped around Kit, smoothing her hair into a bun. "Bobby pin," she commanded, holding out her free palm, the other holding the bun in place. When Kit patted her apron, Olivia added, "I know you've got some in there."

"If I didn't shed them like scales, I'd argue," she joked, depositing a couple of bobby pins into Olivia's hand.

I watched as they talked, as Olivia soothed and anchored Kit, lest she fly away. And once again, I was glad to have her by my side. I could see Frank's kindness in her, that light that never went out glowing under her skin. She was unsinkable, facing her loss with a smile and her pink suitcase in tow, eyes on the future and sun on her face.

And in that moment, I didn't even care that she might be the end of the farm as I knew it. Because if ever I needed that joy, it was today.

HOTHOUSE

Olivia

THE DAY WAS ENDURED WITH A CURIOUS LACK OF OXYGEN. My lungs seemed to have shrunk, and no matter what I did, they stayed pinned in my ribs with only enough room for sips of air. Jake and I stood in the receiving line and shook the hands of hundreds of people, and all the while, my voice was small and far away, someone else's voice, one made thinner for lack of that all-important oxygen. We sat in the front of the pulpit with so many people at our backs, there was barely room left to stand. And songs were sung. Scriptures read. A speech by me, halted and squeaking with a paper in hand, damp from my palms and tears. A speech by Jake, endured with my hand over my lips and my shoulders shuddering in the circle of Kit's arms.

And all the while, I couldn't breathe. Least of all when everyone was gone, headed up to the big house for the wake, leaving Jake and me to say goodbye well and truly.

Frank Brent lay in a bed of satin, hands folded over the breast of his best suit. His silver hair was combed, his skin pallid but for an unnatural rouging of his cheeks. It wasn't garish. But it wasn't him.

He didn't look asleep like they said the dead sometimes did. He looked empty. Even in sleep, his brow was animated. His lips broad with the smile that always seemed to be waiting. But when his heart stopped, the light in him went out.

He was gone. And saying goodbye shredded what was left of me.

There wasn't enough air, not when I told him how I loved him. Not when I held his cold hand, resisting the urge to jerk it back for the knowledge it would be the last time I ever touched him. I smoothed his hair. I told him I was sorry. And Jake stood stoically at my side until I turned away, unable to catch my breath for the hitching sobs, unable to keep my eyes open. Then Jake wasn't at my side. He was everywhere, all around me, crushing me to his chest and holding me in his arms. There were no words, only the quiet sobs I tried to contain but couldn't. He held me for a long time, rocking back and forth, his big hand on my back, thumb circling gently.

There would be no catching my breath, but I found enough composure to leave his space. Our eyes shifted to the coffin, and I moved to his side, taking his hand.

"It's your turn to say goodbye, Jake."

He didn't move, didn't take his eyes off Pop. "I already did," he said with his voice rough and whispery. And before he swept me out of the church, he laid his hand on the shiny dark wood and said a thousand words with the gesture.

The ride back to the house was quiet, the windows down and the breeze whipping my hair out of its confines, but I didn't care. I sat in the middle of the bench next to Jake, felt the warmth of him across the thin space between us. And I watched the world sweep by without seeing anything at all.

But as the wind spun around us, I found for the first time all day, I could finally breathe.

As we rolled up the driveway, I worked on my hair. The yard was packed with cars in such a haphazard manner, I didn't know how anyone would leave unless they all left together. I was marveling over this when Jake slapped the dashboard, scaring the ever-loving shit out of me.

My face swiveled to find him tight with fury, his lips the thinnest line and brows sharp. "Goddammit. Goddamn them all. Today of all days."

"Who? Goddamn who?"

"The Pattons."

A crackling anxiety flitted over me, through me. "Why would the Pattons be here? I thought they and Pop hated each other."

"They do. Did," he corrected darkly. "I saw them at the funeral and thought that was enough gall. But to come here? To the farm they've tried to destroy for more than a hundred years? I could turn Chase Patton's face inside out for this. I could turn his face inside out for a lot of things, but especially this."

"What do you think they want?"

"To make a show of it all. To posture. To pretend they care for the sake of the town. To be a couple of entitled dicks. I don't know, and I don't care. I just want them off the property. *Now*."

He pulled around to the old barn and parked in its shadow. But before we left this last quiet, safe place, I stayed him with a hand on his arm.

"You can't make them leave, Jake."

"Like hell I can't. And why shouldn't I? Give me one good reason not to chuck the Patton pricks out the front door and down the steps."

"Today isn't about them—it's about Pop. The whole town is here, Jake. Everyone's watching."

His jaw clenched, but he didn't argue. He didn't say anything.

"If we're going to turn this place around, we have to play nice, especially with the Pattons. They could make our lives hell if they really wanted to. So let's not give them a reason."

Again, he was silent, that muscle at his jaw bouncing and ticcing with the grind of his teeth as he considered.

"All right, fine. But they'd better not put a toe out of line, or there won't be diplomacy. Only force."

"Then I guess it'll be my job to make sure they keep all their toes in their shoes where they belong."

He almost smiled—I saw the glimmer of it. But it disappeared in place of concern. "You ready for this?"

"Absolutely not. You?"

"Never. But in a few hours, it'll be behind us. That's something to celebrate."

"Amen to that."

"And if I break a Patton limb, we'll celebrate that too."

I laughed as he opened the door and stepped out, offering his hand to help me out on his side. And as I took it, I wondered over this man, the gentle—albeit grumbly—man who held me while I cried and helped me out of the truck like a proper gentleman. I barely recognized him, much preferring this version of him to the smug fellow who would love nothing more than to see me crash and burn before putting the entire country between us again.

People had gathered in clusters outside and on the porch, so we snuck around back to avoid the first wave. We headed inside in silence, sharing a look before he opened the door and ushered me inside.

The house was full to bursting and warm from the crowd. The only space not occupied by people was occupied by furniture, and when we entered, every face in the place turned to us.

There was a collective sigh and a flurry of hellos and brushes of arms and *we're so sorry*s and *he'll be missed*. And Jake and I wound through the throng, stopping when we could, hugging when it was required, shaking hands when they were offered.

Eventually, we exited the crowd into the kitchen, which hadn't filled with people simply because no one could get in Kit's path without paying for it with a burn or a potential shanking. Kit tended to run with knives.

"Oh, there you are," she said, wiping her brow with the back of her hand and leaving a streak of flour in its wake. "Everybody's been asking about you. Here. Take these out to the table, Jake." She shoved a platter of delicate pastries at him.

"Can I help?" I asked.

"No, honey. I've got my hands full and prefer it that way. If I stop, I'll ..." Her chin wobbled. "Well, I just can't stop, that's all."

"Then don't," I said with a small smile, turning to leave her to it.

Jake was held up at the table by a little old lady I didn't recognize. Beyond her hovered a host of others with sad, hungry eyes, waiting for their chance with him. I couldn't remember the names of most of them, though I recognized their faces. Plenty I didn't know at all. And looking around, standing in the warmth of the kitchen, there was suddenly no air again. Too many people in too small a space.

Somehow, among a crush of people, I was alone. Jake was the center of this universe, the living connection to Pop, blood or not, and I was just a girl on the edge of the crowd, looking in on something I wasn't truly a part of.

The urge to escape overwhelmed me. I hurried for the back door and reached it unobstructed, slipping out onto the porch that circled the house, seeking solitude. For a moment, I found it. Closed my eyes and leaned up against the side of the house, relishing in the feel of the cool air on my overheated skin.

"Long day, huh?"

I bolted off the wall, my eyes flying open to find Chase Patton leaning against the railing.

He'd always been a tall drink of water, his smile easy and his body long and lean. Blond hair artfully mussed, eyes crisp and blue as a summer day. He was handsome, and he knew it. As the only son of the man who owned the town, he got anything and everything he wanted. I wondered briefly if anyone had ever told him no and decided they hadn't.

Of course, I hadn't seen him since before I moved away. I

knew him—everybody did. But I'd seen a side of him he hid from others, first and foremost, his father.

We watched each other as he brought his cigarette to his lips to take a long, lingering drag, and when he exhaled, he breathed slithering smoke like a dragon.

My heart thundered, my cheeks flushed despite myself. "Oh, I'm sorry. I didn't realize anyone was out here. I'll leave you to it." I started to turn, hoping I could avoid an actual conversation with him, but he snagged my hand.

"Please, don't. Don't go back into that hothouse on account of me."

I withdrew my hand from his and folded my arms.

"Smoke?" he asked, cigarette hanging from his lips as he reached into his back pocket.

"No, thank you."

He settled the pack back where it'd been and took another drag. "It was a beautiful service. Frank's gonna be missed around here, no doubt about that."

I almost laughed—he certainly wouldn't be missed by the Pattons. "Thank you."

"When my grandfather died, it was the longest day of my life. He was the epicenter of this town, and the hoopla was almost unbearable. All any of us wanted was to be alone, but we found ourselves in the middle of everyone else's grief. It's brutal. But tomorrow will be a different kind of hard. Because that's when it really hits you."

I swallowed my tears, nodding. "Thank you for coming to pay your respects."

He smirked even as he took a pull. "All you've done is thank me since you came out here."

At that, I did laugh, relaxing just enough. I leaned against the house again, facing him. "Can I ask you something?"

"Anything."

"Why did you come? The Pattons and the Brents are the

Hatfields and McCoys of this town. You can imagine it's a surprise to see you here, at the house."

He nodded thoughtfully. "Would you kick us out if I said it was politics?"

"You? No. Your dad? No promises."

"The honest truth is that I've been holding out hope he'd have the courage to mend fences. I can't say I subscribe to a hundred-twenty-five-year-old feud—no good has ever come of it. I'll keep holding out for a change of heart, especially now that Frank is gone," he said with a nod toward the house. "There's no reason to keep it going—not one that makes sense. But I couldn't let him come alone. So here we are."

I glanced in through the window to see James Patton talking with all the gusto of a politician, and the sight turned my stomach. I tried to tell myself perhaps the song and dance was just how a man like him dealt with regret. By pretending it didn't exist.

"I heard you inherited the farm. Congratulations."

"Thank you."

"You're welcome, infinity," he teased.

I chuckled, looking down at the slats of the porch.

"So what are you going to do with it?"

"Well, if you know that I inherited, you know Jake inherited half."

"I do."

"And you also know we have to decide everything together."

"Naturally. Of course, I didn't figure you'd stick around. I thought you'd be back to New York."

I frowned. "You and everybody, it seems."

"It makes sense, that's all. Don't take it personal," he said, somehow sounding reassuring. "You know Dad's been trying to acquire your farm forever. Maybe one day, it'll be up to you and me. We can put the feud to bed by joining forces. I'm sure you know we could do a lot for your farm. How we could use our reach and money and expand."

"I'm sure you could, but I think we'll be just fine on our own. We've lasted this long."

He smiled sidelong at me so amiably, not a single warning bell rang. "You have. And I'm sure you'll outlive us all. But it's a nice thought, isn't it?"

I was just about to thank him again for a laugh and excuse myself, but before either of us could speak, the back door flew open, and Jake blew out.

He stormed. He brewed and crackled. He rumbled and thundered with whorls and eddies of darkness.

His eyes were locked on Chase.

But Chase watched him approach, unfazed. He took a final lazy drag of his cigarette and flicked it into the yard. "Heya, Jake. Condolences."

"Fuck you, Patton."

Chase put up his hands in surrender and straightened up with the fluid grace of a cat. "Come on now. You don't want to do this today, do you?"

"Today feels like the best day to do it. If I had my way, you'd already be in your car on your way to your daddy's house with a broken nose."

"And since you didn't have your way, who did?"

Neither of us answered, but I swore I heard a battle cry rattling in Jake's chest.

"I see," he said with that cavalier smile on his face. "Well, I think I'll say my goodbyes." He turned to me. "It was nice seeing you again, Olivia. Hope next time it's under better circumstances."

I didn't know how to respond, and he didn't seem to need me to. He and Jake eyed each other like wolves as Chase passed and mercifully left our presence.

I exhaled, sagging against the wall. "God, thank you for—"

"What the fuck did he want, Olivia?"

My brows drew together in confusion. "Excuse me?"

"What did he want with you?"

"Nothing. He just happened to be here when I snuck out for some air."

"He wants you to sell, doesn't he? He wants you to sell to his greedy daddy."

"He talked about working together, but—"

"What did you say?" He loomed over me, everything about him accusing. "What did you tell him?"

"Nothing! If I wouldn't sell to you, why the hell do you think I'd sell to *Patton*?"

"Chase Patton gets what he wants. This farm. You too, if I know anything about him—and I know too much. He gets whatever he wants, and he'll take it before you've even had a chance to refuse."

"I cannot believe you," I said, my hands shaking from fury. "I cannot believe you'd accuse me of—"

"You know better than to get in bed with the devil, Olivia. Don't give me any more reason to fight you for this farm."

I stood, dumbfounded, as he gave me his back and headed for the door.

With a slam, he was gone.

And I was alone once again.

FARMGIRL

Olivia

I DESERVE A GOLD STAR.

The shower stream pinged my skin like hot little knives, but I didn't touch the faucet. Instead, I sighed, closed my eyes, and tipped my head up.

Really, I should have made one of those adult chore charts. Do laundry? Get a star. Make your bed? Shiny little sticker. Shower? That should be worth two. Fill it up, and you get a pair of designer shoes. Not that they'd do me any good out here, but think of how pretty my closet would be.

I'd spent the last three days in bed. Chase Patton had been right about one thing—the day after the funeral had been worse. Even the rest of the wake was unbearable, the sting of Jake's dressing-down fresh and raw. We avoided each other like a couple of south magnets, the force too great to fight. It was easy to stay away given the density of the ring of people around him. By the look he'd worn, you'd think he was trying to take a nap on a porcupine, but he stood there and listened as everyone offered their condolences. Occasionally, one of them sought me out, offered a few words, and headed away again. But few of them knew me, not after all this time. Some of them had a look in their eyes, a quiet hurt, directed at me.

I wondered how many people thought along the lines of Jake—with accusation that I'd abandoned Pop and the farm—and decided it was more than I was comfortable with.

It wasn't long before I snuck out the back and wandered into the little patch of woods behind the houses, heels hooked on my fingers and spring grass between my toes. I found the old rope swing and sat there swaying, staring at the spot beneath my feet that had once been bald from use, now as thick as the rest. And I thought.

I thought about nothing and I thought about everything, caught in that state of static, wondering how I could feel so much and still be empty. Flickering memories fluttered in my mind, peppered with questions about my future and the future of the farm. But the threads were impossible to grasp. I stood at a nexus with innumerable paths stretching out before me. I could go one of so many directions, but I didn't have a single hesitation about which way I wanted to go.

What I didn't know was how far I'd make it. Not very, if Jake had anything to do with it.

With another sigh, I ran my hands over my crown, the water sluicing down the tail of my hair and to the old claw-foot tub with a slap. For three days, I'd been unable to think about anything except Pop and what we were going to do without him. But today when I woke, I knew it was time.

Can't gain any ground if you're flat on your back, Livi, Pop would have said.

So with a resigned sort of peace, I'd hauled myself up and taken my first shower since the funeral.

It was well *past* time for that one.

While I washed my hair and over-conditioned it on behalf of my curls, my mind wandered to the farm and the quandary I faced. It'd been in mild decline when I moved to New York, but at some point in the last few years, the drop-off had been dangerously steep. I didn't know why yet, and I wouldn't until I met with Ed, the accountant. Fluctuations in the price of milk maybe, thinning livestock, upkeep of the farm. Farmers were rarely rich folk, and farms did not run cheap. Even the slightest economic shift could have a serious impact on us.

What I *did* know was that we needed money. And to get money, we needed more business.

That I could do.

Once I was clean, I dried off, scrunching my hair in an old T-shirt—again on behalf of my curls. A blob of curl cream was the extent of my styling, a bonus of farm life. No blowouts, no eyeliner. There was no point in spending an hour straightening the mess that was my hair if it was going to get hay or mud or who knew what else in it. And the heifers didn't care if I had mascara on, so why should I?

A few minutes later, I trotted down the stairs in a pair of jeans and a white V-neck in search of my boots. But on a cursory scan of my dump zones for such things, I found nothing.

"Kit?" I called, hinging at the waist to look under the coffee table. "Have you seen my boots?"

"Those pristine pink things?" she asked. "Out on the porch."

I gave her a look. "They're gonna get spiders in them."

She waved a hand. "You'll live. I cleaned the mud off them."

"How come? They're just going to get all mucked up again."

"Well, I know that, but they're so shiny and new, and I wanted them to stay that way," she rambled, her cheeks flushing and a dish towel twisted in her hands. "Plus, you know how I am. I can't stop doing things or ..."

"I know." We shared a long look. "I want to hug you, but I'm afraid we'll both cry."

At that, she laughed, tears already shining in her eyes. "Then you'd better get out of here quick."

So with a smile and a stinging nose, I headed off in the direction of the porch.

My boots sat proudly right next to the front door. They were so cheerful against the white siding and the whitewashed planks of the wraparound porch that I had to take a picture. Phone in hand, I walked down the steps to get the boots closer to eyeline, kneeling on one of the lower steps to line up the shot. An idea struck.

The flower garden.

With a spreading smile, I flitted toward Grandma's garden, which now was just an overgrown patch of anything and everything with a path cut through it. Every season, Pop would go out there with a variety of seeds he'd mixed up and spread them across the patch inside the white picket fence. Another sprinkling—this time of manure—and in a few weeks, with a bit of rain, the garden would teem, spilling out of its confines in abundance.

He always used her favorite flowers, and this time of year was when the peonies bloomed, which was exactly where I headed. The little open shack next to the garden housed a few tools, so I grabbed the gloves, glancing inside dubiously, imagining a mama spider next to an egg sac in their depths. But in the end, I shoved both hands in without getting bitten, picked up the shears, and trucked into the flower bed.

It was an explosion of color and scent and texture so intense, one didn't know where to look. Wild roses wound through sunflowers and dahlias and foxgloves. Honeysuckle climbed along the fence, occasionally reaching into the bed to mingle with the other more delicate stems. There was no rhyme or reason to it, just beautiful chaos. Pretty to look at but not easy to find what you were looking for, should you be looking for something specific.

Peonies in every color of pink caught my eye, the fuchsia plants first. Their blooms sagged, too heavy for the long stems to keep upright. The one unchanging feature of the garden was Grandma's peony bushes in creamy peach, soft pinks, rosy petals, and into the deeper shades until they hit this crazy hot-pink.

I leaned in and lifted a bloom, bringing it to my nose for a deep breath of heady perfume. And with an outrageous smile on my face, I began to cut stems until I had a gradient of my favorite color cradled in my arms. A couple of white foxgloves and a handful of Russian sage later, and I had enough for two bouquets.

Perfect.

It wasn't until I reached the porch again that I realized I was all cut up. Fine slashes on my arms from thorny roses, a deeper gash on the side of my index finger, and my bare feet scuffed up and raw on the bottom. Shrugging it off, I plopped down on the patio in front of my boots with my haul and arranged them in the necks, thinking of my grandmother.

She'd died before my parents, the stroke swift and fatal. I was six, so my memory of her was foggy and vague, but I knew her from stories Pop and Kit had told, from the remnants of her left all over the farm.

My hands paused. The old store—*her* old store—sat hidden behind a thatch of trees near the barn. Pop had locked it up when she died, and as a little girl, I used to sneak up to the porch and look inside. It was a time capsule, dull with dust, her wares spread over tables and displayed proudly on the walls and in the windows. I finally drummed up the courage to ask Pop to let me in, expecting a hard no and a potential talking-to. But he agreed, walking me silently up to the front door. Once unlocked, I wandered inside with my mouth hanging open, my hungry eyes eating up everything they saw. But when I turned to ask Pop a question, he was still on the porch side of the threshold, watching me with an unreadable expression on his face. At the time, I was too young to understand it was a mixture of pain and fear and deep, unanswered loss that kept him out. But then he smiled, told me not to break anything, and hoofed it to the barn.

I didn't ask him again—I just snuck the spare key Kit "didn't tell" me about and wriggled my way inside to sit among her things. Maybe it was the mystery of the place or that it felt like a secret, but for years, I couldn't stay away. Sometimes, I'd read a book in the rocking chair. Others, I'd play with the old register. I was too little to think about cleaning the place up, but it didn't seem to matter that the shop was a mess. Some of the candy was even still good.

But then I got a little older, and the place got a little sadder, and after a few years, the magic was gone.

Now? The magic was back. And the first of what I hoped would be many brilliant ideas struck me.

But first—

Once the bouquets were perfect, I scooted back, holding my camera low to take a series of pictures in every orientation. That giddy feeling slipped over me, that manic joy you experienced when something not even that funny happened and the giggles wouldn't quit. The feeling grew until it was too big for my skin as I opened an editing app and filtered it to be crisp and bright.

And then I opened Instagram.

In the throes of my three-day fog, I'd thought a lot about starting an account for the farm, but I'd gotten stuck on a username—everything good was taken, and nothing was catchy enough to grab someone's attention. But as I opened the app that morning, I knew what I wanted to do.

When it was available, I squealed, slapping my feet on the porch planks.

@TheAdventuresOfFarmgirl

And I uploaded my first post, using every hashtag I could think of, including #farmgirl and #BrentFarm. I even tagged and hashtagged the well-known brand of the rain boots in the hopes I'd get more visibility.

The second it posted, I popped off the porch and scooped up the flowers, flying into the kitchen as I called for Kit.

Her head appeared in the doorway of the pantry before she stepped into the room. "What in the world's the matter? Don't tell me there really was a spider in your boot—"

"Nope! Where's the key to Grandma's shop?"

Kit wasn't moving, but she somehow stilled. "On the hook, where it always is." She nodded in that direction. "What's this all about?"

I deposited the flowers in her arms and snatched the key. "I know how I'm going to save the farm."

Her mouth gaped like a bass, but before she caught a thought, I was out the door and stomping my feet into my boots. I zoomed down the stairs and toward the little house with ideas zinging around in my skull. The easiest way to get people were attractions, and we had attractions galore. The shop. The farm. We could do tours and hayrides. Pumpkin patches and holiday festivals. Petting zoo. The creamery made goods for local stores, but we could add our fare to the shop. Maybe expand our distribution and start delivering milk, use the website to make it convenient and accessible, use social media to—

"What are you doing?"

Jake's voice scared the bejesus out of me, and I jumped, whirling around.

"God, Jake. You sure have light feet for an ogre."

He frowned and folded his arms. "What are you doing?" he asked again, this time with authority.

So I frowned right back. "None of your business."

"Everything that happens on this farm is my business. What do you want with Janet's shop?"

For a second, I assessed him, considering what to tell him and how many words to use to do it. But there was no keeping it from him.

"Well," I started, an unbidden smile stretching on my face, "I was thinking about how to increase our revenue. Did you know most farms do tours and have a shop?"

"Of course I know that," he snapped. "But that's not us."

"Grandma would disagree." I gestured to the house. "Before she died, we had both."

"How are we gonna make money if we have to hire a bunch of people to run tours and work at the shop?"

"I was thinking we could see if anyone here wants to help out with it. Who better to tour than our people? And we could limit it to the weekends, keep it simple at first."

"You're going to put us in the ground, Olivia."

Something about the way he'd said my name sounded like a curse.

"We're not maximizing our earning potential. We could do a pumpkin patch. Festivals. The Fourth of July is coming up, and we could—"

"No."

I blinked. "No?"

"No."

I blinked some more. "No to what part?"

"All of it. We're not whoring the farm out for money."

I jerked back like I'd been slapped. "Excuse me?"

"You want to exploit this place, taint it with strangers just to earn a buck. I don't know a better definition of the word." He pointed at the barn. "I didn't think much of you to start, but I thought more of you than *this*."

Cheeks flushed and nose burning, I could barely tamp down my fury. "I don't know who you think you are—"

"I think I'm the only person who knows how to run this place, and I think *you* are full of more shit than the manure yards."

"Well, *Jake*," I spat, "I think you're a miserable asshole who's so scared of change, you'd rather see the farm fail than admit defeat. And you'll bully everyone around you until you get your way. But guess what? You don't scare me, and I won't be told what I can and can't do around *my* farm."

He kicked his head back and laughed so heartily, a bird flew out of a nearby tree. "Your farm. That's rich. Call it whatever you want for the next three months. Because after that?" When he met my eyes, his smile went cold. "You're gone."

My muscles ached to launch myself at him and push him with every bit of strength I had. I clenched my fists at my sides, the ridges of the key cutting into my palm.

"We made a deal," I said quietly, my voice trembling from restraint. "I can't save the farm if you won't let me. If you're going to make this fair, you're going to let me do whatever I want."

He glared down at me, those stupid, angry muscles bouncing at his jaws. They were huge, bigger than a normal person's, probably from excessive use.

"Every other farm *whores* their farms out because it's good business. You won't have to do anything—I'll take full control and responsibility for it. Otherwise, I'm considering you in breach of our agreement, and the deal will be off the table."

For a second, he just kept staring at me with his eyes hot coals in their sockets. It went on so long, I wondered if he'd answer at all.

"Terms," he finally ground out. "You won't ask me for any help—this little endeavor is yours to fail, and I won't dirty my hands with it. Whatever you spend becomes your debt to the farm and will be repaid in full. And when you lose, you won't argue when I say I told you so."

"Fair enough." I tried to explode his head with my eyeballs. It didn't work.

Hot, hostile energy sizzled between us, our thoughts almost loud enough to hear, almost sharp enough to cut.

"It's not going to work."

"Not with that attitude," I said with mock cheer before whirling away from him.

I didn't check to see if he was watching, just unlocked the door with shaking hands and ringing ears before slipping inside.

The shop was quiet and still, the dust thicker and the smell mustier. But everything else was the same.

My pulse slowed as I wandered toward the back, occasionally pausing to brush the dust off things. And when I reached the shiplap wall, I turned around and surveyed my domain.

He was going to be so mad when I won, and I was going to be *so smug* when he lost.

And fueled by that fire, there was nothing left to do but get to work.

HOGWASH

Jake

A STRING OF EXPLETIVES BLEW THROUGH MY BRAIN LIKE A rope in a tornado.

The second she closed the door to the shop, I turned on my heel and marched away. Three days without seeing hide nor hair of Olivia hadn't been enough distance, if my fury was any proof. I'd thought I'd mostly gotten my anger put away, but one look, and *poof*—there went the lid on that particular box.

For a moment, I'd thought there was a chance we could work together. And then I caught her smiling at Chase like he was a goddamn angel, talking about *our* farm with a man intent on seeing it fail.

After that, nothing could convince me anything Olivia said was a good idea. Every little infraction piled onto the next. Her intrusion. Our shared responsibility, one I hadn't ever planned on having in the first place, but one I couldn't stomach sharing with her and her cockamamie ideas that resulted in her changing the sum of my world. The sight of her with Chase Fucking Patton and the knowledge he'd do anything to get ahold of our farm for his crooked daddy. Even use Olivia, and in any capacity he could.

Any capacity.

And now she was going to rifle around in Janet's shop, knowing full well Frank wouldn't step foot in that place. I could feel his discomfort from beyond the veil, and it made me feel sick. My stomach was a rusty bucket of rocks, clanking and grinding with every step I took.

I didn't think anyone in the world had ever made me so goddamn mad as Olivia Brent.

"Well, what's gotten into you?" Kit asked.

My gaze snapped to her, unaware of her presence in the barn. Her face was screwed up in a mixture of curiosity, surprise, and maybe a little judgment. In her hand was a bucket half the size of a trash can, full of kitchen waste, and she stood at one of the pig troughs in the barn with the slop poised to pour. I barely heard her over the squeal of a handful of hungry pigs.

"*Her.*" I jabbed a finger in the direction of the shop.

Kit gave me an accusing look. "You're always grumpy, but this is a whole new level of hot under the collar. Only other times you've been this mad is over a Patton."

"Yeah, well, screw them and her both."

That earned me a full-blown look of reprimand. "Jakob Milovic, you watch your mouth. Olivia is just trying to help, and I for one don't think opening the store is a bad idea."

"Do *you* run the farm?" I shot.

Immediately, I regretted it.

The flush in Kit's cheeks rose, her mouth pinching with the flex of her chin. The shine in her eyes gutted me—the rocks in my belly thunked to the ground.

"No, I don't suppose I do. But neither do you."

Ashamed, I sighed and raked a hand through my hair, affording me the opportunity to look at the ground where I couldn't see what I'd done. So I could take a second to loosen the clamp on my throat.

In the dirt under my boots, I discovered a truth I hadn't acknowledged.

This wasn't about the store. It was barely even about Olivia.

The only father I'd ever known was gone, and I wasn't ready to let him go. I wasn't ready to fill his shoes, my feet too small and unpracticed to do anything but flop around uselessly. I'd spent three days avoiding that truth, working from dawn until I dropped so I wouldn't have to think anything or feel anything except my anger at Olivia.

That was so much easier than facing the truth.

"I'm sorry." Two words, rough with emotion. "It's just … nothing is … I don't know how to …" I shook my head, fighting emotion. "Frank's gone, Kit. What the hell are we supposed to do now?"

Before I knew it, I was somehow wrapped in Kit's arms, which was a feat of physics, given her height and mine. But she managed, rocking me and shushing me and crying, from the sound of it. The pigs had gotten louder when she set her bucket on the ground, just out of their reach. One of the sows was working hard to wedge her head between the stall slats, which would be a disaster. I'd have to bust the fence to get her undone.

"You'd better feed those pigs before Susie tears the pen apart," I teased, rubbing Kit's back.

She laughed around her tears, dabbing at her eyes with her apron. "Wouldn't want any more work for you, given your hands are so full with a pint-sized redhead, would we?" Kit picked up the bucket. "Hush, Susan. Don't be dramatic."

The second the scraps hit the trough, the only sound was their sloppy eating.

"Come on, Jake—I think you need something to eat too," she said, slipping her arm into mine.

I took Kit's bucket and let her lead me away.

"Alright," she started once we were out of the barn. "You've been bottling yourself up long enough. Go on and unload it."

I glanced down at her, unsure if anybody was ready for that.

But she gave me a look. "Go on, chicken."

So I took a deep breath, and for the length of the walk, I did.

It was much of the same, centered around Olivia's ideas and punctuated frequently by the words *stupid* and *no*. I heard the petulance in my voice as I neared the end of my exchange with Olivia and hated it, hated how petty I sounded. But not as much as I hated the prick of realization that I maybe wasn't entirely in the right.

By the time we reached the house, I'd gotten it out, even if it wasn't gone—the film of it clung to the space it'd occupied. Sullenly, I let her guide me inside, taking the bucket back before depositing me in a chair at the kitchen island.

For the length of time it took her to put the bin under the sink and wash her hands, she was silent. But when she moved for the fridge, she said, "She's right, you know."

My nostrils flared.

Kit didn't wait for me to answer, which was good. I'd rather have jumped off the roof of the barn than admit either of them were right.

"Every successful farm in the tristate area has a shop and does tours, and you know it. Only reason Frank didn't was because it reminded him Janet was gone. Easier to ignore her absence if he didn't deal with her part of the business. Why let somebody else run the shop? That was *hers*. Letting somebody else in would have erased her, he thought. I didn't have the heart to tell him it was just another way to hide. But I don't have any problem telling *you*. And if there was one person he'd let open it up, it's Livi. I think you know that too."

She didn't put me on the spot by making eye contact, instead keeping herself moving first with a container of fresh lunchmeat and brioche buns she'd probably baked at three in the morning.

"We need to up our income, and Olivia has all the tools to do it. But you've gotta let her. Nothing's going to change if we don't, and none of us know how to do it, except Livi. We are one trip around the sun from the farm falling into a deficit we can't recover from. And then we won't have a choice. We'll have to sell, and who do you think the highest bidder will be?" she asked the bun in her hand as she slathered it with mustard.

The thought of selling to those crooks sent a roaring burst of fire through my chest. "That won't happen."

"As it stands, we can't make enough to make up for the last few years. You can't promise we won't have to sell, especially if you do nothing but bury your head in the sand like Frank did."

"There are other ways. More livestock. Higher production. Raising our wholesale prices."

"That won't be enough—the cost of livestock alone will take years to recoup. Frank held everything still, pretending like it'd work itself out as the world changed around him. Maybe he was too scared of the risk or skeptical of any solution's success. He wasn't willing to adapt. And if you aren't either, you'll be the one carrying the burden of the farm's failure regardless of whether it was your doing or not." She set the knife down with a clang, her face tight with emotion when she finally met my eyes. "You won't survive that, Jake. So if you won't listen to Olivia for yourself, do it for me. Do it for the farm. Get out of her way and let her try. Frank risked this farm's survival for you. Don't you dare let that be in vain."

The twist in my chest was so tight, I thought it might choke my pulse to a stop.

Because that was where she had me. She'd just spoken the truth more plainly than I wanted to hear.

The farm had been in decline when I found it, but it hadn't gone into this margin of debt until Frank took out a mortgage on the farm to fund my immigration. My mother had come here from Croatia under asylum, and when she died, my immigration status had to be reviewed and renewed. I didn't know, not until I settled into the farm and ICE came to call on an anonymous tip that wasn't anonymous at all. Deny it all they wanted—I knew exactly who'd made that call.

The Pattons had me detained, a fact Chase waved around like a battle flag. And it'd taken Frank mortgaging the farm and a near two-hundred-thousand-dollar debt to keep me here.

This farm's downfall was more my fault than anyone. It was my debt.

I couldn't walk away from that. I couldn't let the farm fail.

Even if it meant getting out of Olivia's way.

Heavy resignation settled on my shoulders, sloping them. "All right," I conceded quietly. "But if she's the reason we lose the farm—"

"I know you don't trust anybody, but do your best to trust me when I say she won't be."

And with a nod, I promised the only thing I could.

"I'll try."

KNOCK YOUR SOCKS OFF

Olivia

I STARED AT THE PRINTOUTS ON THE DESK BETWEEN ME AND Ed, the farm's accountant, and pretended like I knew what I was looking at.

"So," Ed continued, "you can see that the bulk of the farm's debt is due to the two mortgages Frank took out on the farm—one a decade ago, the second two years ago. The first put us in the hole, and the second made it worse."

I flipped the top paper over and skimmed the second one for information I understood without finding anything. "But what caused the decline in the first place?"

"Market prices, upkeep, expansion. That sort of thing."

Something in his leathery voice sounded like avoidance. I glanced at him in search of a clue and found enough in the craggy lines of his face to confirm.

"So the first mortgage was for …"

He fiddled with the stack like he was looking for something, avoiding my eyes. "Well, ah, equipment mostly. Modernizing. Cattle. You know, farm stuff."

"Right. Farm stuff." I gave him a look.

"How about I get you access to the books? You can see what all Frank spent it on, if you'd like. And I'm always here to answer questions, if need be."

"That would help." I flipped back a few more pages. "It's a lot of money to spend modernizing without a return."

"Sure, but while Frank modernized the equipment, he didn't modernize elsewhere, as you've mentioned. I don't know much about the new way of marketing, but I can see it's not what we're doing." He leaned in a little. "Don't tell Jake, but I think you've got the right idea. My grandkids taught my wife how to use Instagram, and she's been showing me your pictures there. I have a hunch you're what we've been missing around here. Wish you'd come along a few years ago," he said on an amiable chuckle.

A seemingly harmless thing to say, an offhand musing. It cut me open right there in his office. He couldn't know my guilt, wouldn't have realized just how desperately I wished I'd stayed when Jake asked me to.

I smiled through the pain. "Your secret's safe with me. Here's to hoping I can help."

"Not a doubt in my mind, Livi. Have any other questions for me?"

What aren't you telling me? "No, I think that'll do for now. Just send me those records, if you would, and I'll take you up on that offer to help me make sense of them."

"Deal," he said as he stood to see me out.

We said our goodbyes, and I wandered away from our offices—built in one of the old converted barns—toward the farmhouse with the papers he'd given me under my arm.

Papers that showed us several hundred thousand dollars in debt.

It made sense—equipment alone was a massive expense, and with the market constantly falling, dairy farmers all over the country were losing their farms. We weren't alone. It was so hard to turn a profit, we operated hand to mouth. A couple hundred thousand seemed like nothing in comparison to the value of the farm itself, but with our profit in a constant freefall, there was no way to get caught up. We just kept falling further behind, hemorrhaging money every quarter.

And it was my job to stop the bleeding.

On that thought, I popped into the house, depositing the papers in Pop's messy office before grabbing my things to head out to the pastures for a little photo shoot with the calves.

The day was warm and humid enough after last night's rain to draw a trickle of sweat as soon as I was out of the shade. The sun kissed my bare shoulders and cheeks, and I wondered how long it'd been since I'd had so much vitamin D. I probably should have worn a hat and some heftier sunscreen than the SPF fifteen I put on daily as a rule. But I had an aesthetic in mind, and it didn't involve hats. Plus, I wouldn't be out long enough to burn. Hopefully.

I trucked across the farm in my pink rain boots and overall shorts, with a white tank underneath and a bubblegum bandana tied around my crazy bun. I passed the newborn yards where each calf was separated from the others. Without knowing the reasoning, people sometimes thought it was cruel or that the separation and confinement was to sell the calves for veal. But the truth was that calves were as germy as babies, and just like babies, they put everything in their mouths and had brand-new immune systems. So for a couple of months, they lived in small pens, socializing with their neighbors through the grid fence. This way, if a calf got sick, it was easy to contain and sterilize. If we kept them together, we'd lose calves en masse when even one got sick.

In an open space between the calves and the barns, larger pens held small groups of older calves where we socialized them, learned their personalities, got them used to each other before they ended up in the teenager herd, which caused as much trouble as the human variety. But I was headed for the pens where the calves were still smallish and less likely to prank me.

"Hey, girls," I cooed as I approached a pen and worked on attaching my tripod to the metal fence.

The three calves hurried over and fitted their noses through the fence squares.

"I'd be flattered if I didn't know you were just looking for food."

The albino calf licked her nose, her lashes batting.

"Don't worry. You'll get all the treats once we get the money shot."

I checked the screen to make sure I had a good view of the pen and scenery. The oak trees rose in the distance behind us, the land between us and them green and lush. The craggy, mountainous hills that created our valley cut into the sky, the view comforting, familiar, as beautiful as it ever was.

I had no real plan other than to muck the stall and brush the calves. It was usually done in the afternoon with a separate shift for the refilling of hay, feed, and water, and I timed it so I wouldn't interrupt anyone's work.

Or so I'd thought.

I wasn't far into my task—boots planted in the mud and shovel in my hands—when I heard an ATV in the distance. I looked up, shielding my eyes from the sun, squinting at the figure on the four-wheeler, just in case my eyes deceived me.

They hadn't.

Jake motored straight for me, towing a trailer of hay and feed.

Shirtless.

He was tanned and strapping, his posture more relaxed than I'd seen since coming home. There was something elemental about him, as if he were made from the earth itself, and in its presence, he was at ease, at home. This was his domain, and his authority was absolute, particularly when held up next to my knock-kneed manure shoveling.

I knew the exact moment he saw me.

He turned to stone.

Every soft line straightened, sharpened. I could feel the heat of his eyes on me from a hundred yards away, and my pulse doubled in preparation for a fight.

When he stopped at the far end of the pens and got to work without acknowledging me, he left me more confused than relieved. But not by much.

I put my back to him before filling up a blue wheelbarrow the old-fashioned way, and I tried to pretend like he wasn't there.

The task was impossible.

I could feel his presence as if he were standing next to me. Every sound he made held my attention, my mind obsessing over what he was doing. A whisper of hay. Metal grazing metal. The pebbly sound of feed in a shovel, then the plinking against the plastic bucket for consumption.

When it got to be too much, I plodded to another section of the pen with my boots slopping in the mud. The calves followed me expectantly, so I propped my shovel against the fence and gave them a little love, watching Jake out of the corner of my eye.

He'd made it closer to me, just a couple of pens down, his muscles bunching and easing. The sun reflecting off the sheen of his skin was blinding. Or maybe that was just the effect that sort of stature demanded. Utter and complete blindness.

I'd stopped petting the albino calf, and she nudged me. Then one of her buddies gave me a push from behind, knocking me into the albino. A squeal, and I tried to move out of the way before the third shoved me in the chest.

I would have made it out of the crush too, if my boot hadn't been stuck in the gloppy mud.

I went down like a windmill, one socked foot in the air and arms wheeling. The calf had still grazed me, and the force, combined with my graceless fall, slammed me into the ground.

My ribs quaked, my lungs empty from the shock and locked by the pain. Stunned, I watched the calves tromp around me, knowing I needed to curl up or crawl away or call for help. Only I couldn't move or speak, too busy trying to pry open my lungs and hear past the ringing in my ears.

A sharp whistle cut through the chaos, and the calves trotted to the other side of the pen. The sun hammered me into the mud.

Breathe, I can't breathe, I can't—

Shade cast over me, and I cracked my eyes to see a silhouette of Jake against the crisp blue sky.

He gathered me to sit, bracing my body against his and inspecting me as best he could. "Are you hurt?"

I shook my head. "Can't ... breathe ..."

"You can, just look at me."

When I met his eyes, I would have told him that was the dumbest thing he'd ever suggested, provided I could speak. Because it was impossible to breathe with his face inches from mine. His eyes were narrowed in concern, the green of his irises crisp and vibrant, even in the shade. Maybe it was the lack of oxygen. I was probably hallucinating. No one could be this perfect, every feature symmetric and aligned. He had to have a flaw besides his shitty attitude. Hairy ears, maybe.

When he turned his head to check my limbs, I noted his stupid ears were perfect too.

Jerk.

"Slow breaths. That's it." With his free hand, he checked my ribs.

I wriggled in his arms, coughing instead of laughing. "Stop it," I rasped. "Laughing hurts."

I caught a flicker of a smile as he sat me up all the way and let me go. "You could have been hurt, you know. Where's your shoe?" he asked with his brow quirked.

"Over there."

The errant boot stood in the mud like a soldier who'd been abandoned at its post.

"You got knocked out of your boots?"

I shrugged and hauled myself up to stand. "I'm disappointed. I've always wanted my socks knocked off, so this feels like a real fail."

"What are you even doing in here?"

"Filming," I said as I inspected myself, my hands covered in mud and worse.

He set the boot next to my socked foot, which I hadn't had the courage to fully plant in the mud. "You should have asked me."

I shot him a dirty look. "I don't need your permission."

"Not for that—you're doing it wrong."

"I'm *shoveling* wrong?"

"First, your shovel's too long for your height. And with that handle, you're working harder than you have to. Plus, you've got the wrong head—a flat head would be easier."

"Jesus." I stomped my foot into my boot. "Are you enjoying yourself?"

"I'm not getting onto you. I'm trying to help."

"Don't ever go into teaching. There are much easier ways to make kids cry."

He folded his big arms over his chest. That chest I'd been ogling was streaked with mud, as were his jeans and hands and forearms. He had a little mud on his face that I should have told him about but didn't.

"So you did all this and nearly got yourself trampled for a stupid video?"

I folded my arms right back at him. "These stupid videos are going to bring people to the farm, so don't knock it. No one's asking you to make a fool out of yourself on film. What do you care what I do?"

"If you weren't being irresponsible, I wouldn't care."

I snorted a laugh. "The shop isn't irresponsible, and you'd rather eat glass than leave me to it."

"The money it's costing *is* irresponsible."

"Well, Mr. Fixit, what's *your* big idea to turn the farm around? Because I haven't heard any suggestions, just more of the same."

A shadow fell across his face. "I've been in charge for a week. How the hell should I know? I barely know whether or not I'm doing this right, never mind how to change things."

I paused, cowed. "Isn't this what you've always done?"

With a huff, he dragged a hand through his hair, groaning when he remembered it was muddy. "Some of it, sure. I shadowed Frank enough to know what I'm dealing with, but only in the loosest terms. I … I haven't done it, not without help. Not without his guidance. So forgive me for not finding the time to put together a business proposal for a job I didn't even know I'd have."

My gaze dropped to my shoes, my eyes pricking with tears. Pop would have known what to do. We were adrift without him.

And if we didn't help each other, we'd both drown.

"Can I make a suggestion?"

"If it has anything to do with the fucking internet, I swear to God—"

"What about local deliveries?"

He scowled.

I eyed him. "Are you mad because of the idea or because it's me who suggested it?"

"You don't want me to answer. Tell me your big idea."

"Well," I started, perking up, "we're selling milk to local stores, and the surplus is sold for distribution. What if we distributed less wholesale in favor of a local milk delivery service? We could make so much more selling it for retail prices rather than the market value of wholesale milk. And it wouldn't be hard. We're already bottling and packaging for the stores. We wouldn't even need a special transport for now, just a cooler solution for the back of a truck. I could set it up on the website so people could order from us online. We can put up fliers, and I can advertise on the *you-know-where*."

He was still scowling, but it was a different kind of scowl. This one I had a feeling was a direct result of me being right.

"Get something together that we can take to Ed and the team. If it's viable financially, it might work."

I tried not to smile too big. "Is that a yes?"

"It's a *we'll see*." He watched me for a beat. "How come you can't come up with *more* ideas that don't cost an arm and a leg?"

"I'll look through my diary and see if I can dig something up," I joked.

A quiet chuckle through his nose. "You should probably go shower—you smell like shit."

"You're no better. You're the one with actual shit all over your big, naked mantitties."

Full-blown laughter barked out of him.

"I mean, you're wearing *jeans* but no shirt? It's like turning on the heater with the windows down."

"*You* try shucking hay in shorts and tell me how it feels."

"Maybe I will," I said smartly, heading for the shovel to finish cleaning up.

"And maybe next time, think about sunscreen. That's gonna hurt in a couple hours."

"But I've only been out here a—" I glanced at my shoulder and huffed. "Son of a bitch."

Jake laughed, petting the albino's head as he passed her to vault over the fence with such ease, I wondered if he really was some sort of wild beast.

"Do me a favor and stay out of trouble," he called over his shoulder.

"I can't promise that," I shouted after him, enjoying the view until he picked up his hay fork again.

Once I put my tools away and given the girls the treats I promised, I unhooked my phone from the tripod and leaned on the fence to scan the video frames. There were some cute shots of me and the calves, some great ones of me shoveling manure, then the sequence of me getting head-butted by a calf and knocked flat on my back.

But that was nothing compared to the shots with Jake in them.

I'd seen a few pictures of Jake around the house, and in every single posed picture, he was wearing one of those fake, toothy smiles. Like somebody'd told him to say cheese while they stuck him in the ass with penicillin.

When he wasn't paying attention, he was perhaps the most handsome man I'd ever known.

As I rolled through the frames, the sight of him getting into the mud to pull me into his lap did something melty and hot to my insides. The worry on his face made me wonder if maybe he *did* care about my well-being. But my favorite shot was the two of us faced off with our arms crossed and mud all over us.

I thought of a handful of captions in a millisecond, weighing the value of putting shirtless Jake on the internet he loathed versus what he'd do to me if I did.

"Hey," I said in his direction. "I'm going to use these pictures on our social."

He gave me a look. "Wasn't that the whole point?"

"And you're okay with it?"

"Do I have a choice?"

"Not really."

"Then thanks for asking," he deadpanned.

"Look at us, being a team and all."

"Don't get your hopes up, farmgirl."

"Too late!" I cheered, letting myself out of the gate to skip toward the house for a shower.

But nothing could wash the smile off my face.

NO GOATS

Olivia

A WEEK LATER, I STOOD IN THE STORE ADMIRING WHAT I'D accomplished in such a short amount of time. Two weeks had to be some sort of a record, not only for the strides I'd made in getting the farm ready to welcome to the public, but for Jake's lack of interference.

Begrudgingly, he'd let me do what I would. So far, I'd cleaned out the shop and washed all the floors and windows. Ordered goods both local and otherwise, decked out the shop with a trio of glass-front product fridges, and started the process of organizing the displays. A tree-trimming company had come last week and cleared out the underbrush, paring down the tree branches to give a gorgeous view of the house from the gravel parking lot I'd had poured. A local woodworker had provided us with furniture and decor, not only to use, but to sell in a consignment deal that saved us a considerable amount of money.

Jake had banned me from getting goats for the petting zoo—too much trouble, annoying, ate more than their share—but that was milk and cheese I could actually consume. What was the expression? *Ask for forgiveness, not permission.* As inconsiderate as the proverb was, I didn't know that there was any other way to handle Jake.

I'd learned quickly that just because Jake didn't try to throw down with me every time we crossed paths didn't mean he was happy about what I had planned. Sometimes, I'd catch him watching me with that annoyed, skeptical look on his face, and nothing could stop him from frequent and sassy notations on whatever I was doing.

I'd also learned the he didn't like being called sassy.

Obviously, it became his new nickname.

My little speaker sat on the ancient register counter, blasting Fleetwood Mac. I sang too loud with Stevie as she reminded me about when thunder happens (when it's raining), when players love you (when they're playing), et cetera., but my hands were busy arranging pots of ivy in the pockets of a cream-colored macrame hanging planter. A girl in the next town over had made them, and I was almost certain that with this display, it'd become a bestseller. It was so inviting, in fact, that I positioned the creaky white ladder I'd just climbed down at an angle, set some of my gardening tools on the steps, and stepped back to take a picture for Instagram.

The lighting was perfect—sunshine brushed everything it touched with an inviting, ethereal glow. Humming behind a smile, I threw on my filter and posted the picture with a reminder of our opening next week.

My farmgirl account had taken off, thanks to some strategic brand tagging and hashtags, the rain boot company in particular. They'd shared several of my pictures and tagged me back, and between them and the local vendors I'd taken on, I had almost twenty thousand followers.

But my most popular posts were my adventures. Or more often *mis*adventures. The selfie I had taken, smiling in my sun hat in front of the barn, had over a thousand likes, and while cute, it had more to do with the blistering sunburn I'd acquired and the caption: *SPF 1000 couldn't save me. Somebody send for @bananaboat!*

Baby cows were also a crowd favorite. With eyelashes like that, likes were a sure thing.

I was in the middle of checking my notifications—the time lapse of me setting up the store went over well, particularly the segment in which I lay on my back in the middle of the store like a starfish and the part where I took a brief dance break.

The tap on my shoulder scared me straight, and I yelped, whirling around to find Presley Hale smirking at me with a wooden crate full of wares on her hip. Her three-year-old daughter, Priscilla, was very, very busy doing ballerina twirls to "Gypsy."

I turned down the volume on my phone, smiling. "I forgot you were coming by today," I admitted.

But she laughed, unfazed as she set the crate on one of the tables. "I've been here every day for a week, so I'm putting that on you. Store looks almost ready to open."

"It's the rug. Really pulls the room together." I leaned down to the toddler's level. "Hi, Cilla."

"Hiyee," she answered, still spinning.

I mouthed *Candy?* at Presley, and she nodded.

"Guess what I got in today?"

She ignored me.

"*Lollipops.*"

She stopped on a dime, her eyes wide. "Wollipocks?"

"Yup." I bent at the waist. "And I got the good ones."

Her face lit up, and I extended my hand, which was instantly filled with Priscilla's small, slightly sticky one.

"The store's looking good," Presley said, looking around as we walked to the counter where I'd hidden a massive apothecary jar full of Tootsie Pops. "I'm so glad you're selling Julie's macrame. Who knew it could be actual art? All I think of when you say macrame are those scratchy brown '70s things our grandmas used to make."

I chuckled, unwrapping the strawberry lollipop while she bounced impatiently. "Thanks for the hook-up. Have you seen her hammock? She almost had to dump me out of it. I might never have left."

"I have been drooling over that hammock since she posted it on social a few weeks ago."

"Me too. I commissioned a couple of the hammock chairs from her to hang in one of the trees out front too."

She sighed happily. "Genius. You're a genius."

"Nah, I just like pretty things. Like this little bean." I picked up Priscilla and set her on the counter. She didn't even know I existed, too busy with her lollipop and the display on the wall behind me to register I was talking about her. "I've been wondering about her name. Priscilla and Presley?"

"Oh, well—I have a thing for Elvis."

My brows nudged each other. "A … thing?"

"My Nonnie loved him—like *love*, loved—and had this big curio cabinet in the dining room full of memorabilia. And given my name, I convinced myself he was my grandpa. Mom always rolled her eyes and stated the math again, which conclusively proves that my grandfather is actually my grandfather. But as a little girl, no logic could sway me. I listened to Nonnie's stories and decided Elvis was my grandfather, and that was why I was named Presley. For a few years, I listened to Elvis exclusively, and I had every one of his movies on old VHS tapes. Do you know how hard it was to find posters of Elvis in the early 2000s?"

I hadn't stopped laughing since she started talking.

She smiled. "The bad thing about people knowing you have a 'thing' is that all anyone ever buys you is that thing. I have enough Elvis shit to fill a studio apartment."

Priscilla pointed at her mother. "Bad word, Mama."

"Mama can say bad words because Mama knows how to use them."

She opened her fat little hand, palm up. "Monies."

Presley rolled her eyes, reaching into her pocket for a quarter, which she deposited into Priscilla's hand. With a smug look on her face, the little girl closed her fist.

"My mother started a swear jar," Presley said. "I've spent a small fortune on quarter rolls."

"And how's that going?" I asked, still laughing.

"Cilla's college should be paid for by Christmas."

I wiped a tiny tear out of the corner of my eye. "That is the best story I've heard in weeks, and I've heard some whoppers."

"Any of those from Jake?" she asked with a shrewd smile.

Just like that, nothing was funny. "You act like he talks to me. Other than the opportunities he takes to be an ass."

"Oh, come on. He's not that bad."

I folded my arms and popped a hip. "Just today, when I ran into him in the creamery, he spent a solid eight minutes teasing me about not being able to eat cheese. Cheese! He was all, *Are you sure you're lactose intolerant, or have you just been milking it for years?* Like I haven't heard that before."

One of her brows rose. "You've heard *that* joke before?"

"Maybe not that one, but there have been plenty. Where do lactose intolerant farts come from? *Your dairy-air.* What did the cheddar say to the ghost? *I'm lac-ghost intolerant.* I've already run out of comebacks for Jake. I only had three to start."

"Well, what are they?"

"*Dairy is an inferior culture. Sorry, I can't handle cheesy jokes.* And *It's just a curdle I have to overcome.*"

"I somehow can't imagine Jake using puns."

"Well, he does, and they're stupid," I said indignantly. "He's the worst. Did you know he almost never wears a shirt? Why does he need to be shirtless all the time? I was nearly trampled to death last week because his naked chest distracted me to the point of hazard. Someone should call OSHA."

"Maybe he's just trying to keep his shirt clean."

I made an airy, defiant noise.

"But no more fighting?"

"More bickering than fighting. He told me I couldn't get goats!"

She pouted. "But goats are so cute."

"*So* cute. So I got some anyway. They came this afternoon," I said with a smirk.

She shook her head at me with an appraising look on her face. "See? Genius."

"We needed them for the petting zoo, and I want to sell goat milk and cheese, so he's just gonna have to deal with it."

"I'm sure he'll take that really well. I bet he even thanks you."

"You joke, but he will. When I prove him wrong, he's going to be a groveling baby."

"Jake? Jake Milovic? We're talking about the same guy, right?"

I rolled my eyes. "Well, he'll at least tell me I was right."

"The best you can expect is an admission that you weren't wrong," she said on a laugh, moving her crate to the counter. "So I brought over everything you asked for, and I packed a sampler so you can decide what you want for your next order."

"Perfect. I've got a five-gallon milk can for you. I just need Mack to bring it around."

"And with it, I will make you all the goodies. Lotions, creams, soaps, the works, specially branded for you."

"You know, of all my partnerships, this one is my favorite."

"I won't tell old Regina. If she hears I've beaten out her scarves, none of us will hear the end of it. Come here, pumpkin," she said to Priscilla, picking the little girl up. Presley leaned back, eyeing her shiny hands. "Did you thank Miss Olivia?"

Priscilla smacked her mouth a couple of times before saying, "Tanks, Wivia."

"Hey," Presley started, her voice taking a new tone, "a bunch of us are going to Buffalo Joe's tonight. Mom is watching Cilla. You should come."

I was ready to refuse but realized I had no real argument. I knew just about everyone from school, but that felt like a trillion years ago. I also realized I hadn't been off the farm for fun since I'd gotten here.

So with a smile, I said, "Sounds fun."

Presley bounced, and Cilla giggled from her hip. Her little hand flailed, and just like that, the lollipop was stuck in Presley's dark hair.

"*Son of a bitch,*" she hissed, reaching for the offending candy.

"Mama, gimme monies." She opened her palm where a sweaty quarter already sat.

"It's highway robbery," Presley said as I made my way around to help.

I was nearly finished when the door opened, and in stalked Jake with a milk jug hanging from that hammer he called a hand.

"Tell me I didn't just hear a fucking goat out there, Olivia."

"Bad word!" Priscilla called like she'd just gotten a bingo.

Jake's cheeks flushed, but his face was still furious. "Sorry, Cilla. Hey, Presley." He turned up the heat once he met my eyes again. "I thought I said no goats."

"And I thought I said it's a good business plan." I pulled the lollipop from the last of Presley's hair, but before I could take it to the trash, Priscilla snatched it and stuck it in her mouth.

Presley sighed.

"Goddammit, Olivia—I didn't agree to this."

"Monieeeeeees," Priscilla said, leaning his direction with enough force and speed that Presley had to catch her before she fell.

"You know, we'd better go. I'll text you later, Olivia."

I offered a weak smile but said nothing as she set Priscilla down, hefted the milk jug, and waddled out. Jake didn't notice a thing. He was too busy trying to send me to hell with his glare.

"It's my money, isn't it?" I challenged.

"Technically, it's the farm's, and the farm doesn't have a sack full of hundred-dollar bills to spare."

"You said you'd stay out of my way."

He took a step closer. "And I have. But you're pushing it. First with that stupid picture of me you put on your social without my permission—"

"You said I could—"

"Post about the *farm*, not me."

"That was the most popular post I've ever had, thanks to your refusal to wear clothes."

He pointed at me. "Pushing it, Olivia. And I said *no goats*."

"What's your problem with them?"

"You gonna clip their hooves? How about mend all the fences when they bust out, because they're a pack of brainless Houdinis. How about deworming? And you've gotta breed. You ever smelled a goat buck? Tell me, smartass—have you ever seen goats mate?"

I shook my head.

"Let's just say, there's a reason the devil has goat horns, and you're gonna have a front row seat to the horror show. If you knew anything about anything, you'd never have started all this."

Another step, his arms folding across his expansive chest, which was covered. And thank God. I couldn't think when he was shirtless.

Part of me thought he knew it too.

"Lemme tell you something, Olivia. It's gonna be *me* who deals with the fucking goats, not you. And I told you no."

"Fine. I hereby take all responsibility for the goats. All hoof-clipping, fence-mending, and deworming will be done by me."

He stared me down for a second, and whatever he was thinking tugged at one corner of his lips for that whisper of a smile. He stuck his hand out for a shake.

I took it, aware of every nerve touching his skin. The rough of his calluses. The warmth in his palms. The odd sensation of my hand being almost completely enveloped by his.

I squeezed and pumped our hands once.

"Just promise me one thing," he said, still holding my hand.

"What?"

"Let me know when you're clipping their hooves so I can make popcorn."

He still had that almost-smile on his face when he let go of my hand. I made an impatient sound.

He laughed.

God, it was a nice sound, a deep, rolling baritone. I wondered what happy meant to him and how he could get more of it. Because laughing Jake was better than asshole Jake any day of the week, even if it was at my expense.

When he was through, he shook his head, his eyes twinkling. "Good luck with your goats. They're as stubborn as you are."

"*Me* stubborn?" It was my turn to laugh. "You'd argue that Alice's spots were white on black instead of black on white, and she can't even argue back. Never mind when somebody actually disagrees with you. I don't come out to the milking station and tell you how to run your equipment, do I?"

"You could, but since you don't know what you're doing, you wouldn't have much of an argument to make, would you?"

"Nope, but you came in here just yesterday and flipped through the journals and declared, *Nobody wants paper without lines on it,* and that it was *for looks, not function.* In fact, you've been in here every day to pick on me for something."

"Picking on you?" He still had that amused look on his face. "What are we, eight?"

"You tell me. You're the one always needling me."

"Oh, so buying the goats had nothing to do with pissing me off?"

"Believe it or not, I really do want the farm to make money, and the goats will help. Pissing you off was a bonus."

He humphed, scanning the store. Looking for something to mess with me about, no doubt. When his eyes narrowed, I braced myself for whatever he threw at me.

"Did you hang those shelves?"

"I did," I said, straightening up. "I used a drill and everything."

Another humph as he walked up to them and tested their bearing. When it wiggled, then slipped out a little, he gave me a look. "Go get me the drill."

"I can fix it," I insisted. "Just tell me what I did wrong."

"These walls are sturdy, but these shelves are too big not to anchor them in a stud."

I stared at him. "You lost me at anchor."

"Exactly. So go get me the drill, and I'll show you how to do it so you don't kill somebody and get us all sued."

As I headed for the toolbox, I wondered over him. He really *had* been in here every day, plus he'd followed me around while I trained the tour crew, using the script and talking points I'd drawn up. I'd thought it was just to intimidate me—it worked—but as I watched him move around the store looking for things to fix, I asked myself if there was more to it. If maybe he *did* want me to succeed. Or maybe he didn't give a shit if I succeeded so long as the farm did too.

But the reason didn't matter. Goats or no goats, he was on my side.

And that was something to celebrate.

PROBABLY KNITTING

Olivia

I STOOD IN FRONT OF MY CLOSET THAT NIGHT WITH MY HANDS on my hips, staring at the clothes like they were a calculus problem.

The issue was that I'd brought clothes for two occasions—milking cows and a funeral—and I could only guess what townies wore to a bar. But I figured it was safe to assume heels weren't required. What I really needed was a sundress, and I made it a point to ask Presley where a girl shopped around here.

This is not a real problem, Olivia.

With a sigh, I pulled a tank top that was more fashion than function and tugged it on, half-tucking it into my jeans.

"Easy enough," I said to no one, walking to the bathroom to get a last look at myself.

My hair was big and poofy, and I wondered how I'd gone all day without anybody telling me so. After a little product and some fancy fingerwork, I inspected my reflection. My cheeks were pink from all the sun I'd gotten, my skin 'tan', which meant a darker shade of pale. I leaned in, inspecting the bridge of my nose.

Pretty sure my freckles had multiplied.

I sighed, putting on a little mascara. I pulled my phone out of my back pocket, held it above me at an angle, and took a selfie that I texted to Presley.

Formal enough?

My phone buzzed immediately. *Are you wearing mascara? If so, you're overdressed.*

I smiled at my screen. My phone buzzed again.

Already here. How far out are you?

Ten! Be right there.

Should I get you a PBR, or do you prefer Miller Lite?

I paused. *I can't tell if you're kidding or not.*

I'm definitely kidding, but fair warning: they've only got two types of wine. Red and white.

Guess I'm drinking whiskey then.

Now we're talking.

My phone was back in my pocket when I reached the stairs, trotting down them like a baby deer. The house was empty and quiet, and I found myself grateful I had somewhere to go. And a Jakeless escape at that. If there was one thing I doubted Jake did, it was hang out at the bar, and if there was one thing I needed, it was a Jake-free night.

It was strange, the feeling I had as I pulled on my canvas sneakers and grabbed the keys to Pop's truck. Like I was still a teenager with a brand-new license, feeling very adult and very responsible. Only now there was no one's permission to garner, no one to kiss me on the cheek and tell me to be safe. In this house, I didn't feel like an adult.

I was a passenger, unable to grasp that the house was mine. That the farm was mine.

Or half mine, as it were.

Once the house was locked up and I climbed into Pop's truck, I glanced at Jake's house, one of several at the back of the property. Golden light spilled from the windows, filtered through curtains I wished I could see past. Because whatever did Jake do in his free time? I couldn't imagine him doing anything but working.

The thought made me sad.

The truck roared to life when I turned the key, and I thought I caught a flicker of motion at one of the windows. I wondered if he had any hobbies. Maybe he read books. Perhaps he was a secret baker, and I laughed at the thought of Jake in an apron with flour on his nose. I bet he knitted, and another burst of laughter filled the cab of the truck. Knitting needles would look like chopsticks in his big hands.

It made me wonder what chopsticks would look like.

I amused myself with imaginings of Jake knitting a sweater in a rocking chair by a fire. As I rolled down the drive, I gave him a cat too, a big, fat tomcat that was too proud and pompous to give a shit about anybody but himself. I figured the two of them would get along nicely. Just a couple of assholes, scratching at anyone who got too close.

Jake hated change, maybe even more than Pop had. I'd convinced him deliveries were a good idea, and I'd already set up the website and a plan for the creamery. It was very nearly all profit, our overhead the hourly cost of deliveries, and my hope was that it'd put some money back in the coffers after everything I'd spent over the last few weeks. My heart lurched at the thought of the running clock, the summer days already ticking by at an alarming rate.

I had to speed things up. Hopefully with an idea for the Fourth of July that just might make up for everything, if I played my cards right.

The road into Maravillo was deserted, winding through thick woods only to bend close enough to the coast to hear the distant crash of waves and see the cliff's edge. But the closer I got to town, the more cars I saw. And then I reached Main Street and the four-way stop that marked the center of town.

Buffalo Joe's was the only place open after eight and one of two places to eat in town—the other being Debbie's Diner, where Presley had worked since high school. Though we'd become instant friends since working together, she and I hadn't been friends back then, which was interesting, given there were only sixty people in our class. But she was a cheerleader and I played the clarinet. Even in a school that small, our groups didn't mingle. I had one good friend, Carol Ann, who was the other clarinet player. And that was all I needed. But then I moved, and Carol Ann moved away for college. She already had a couple of babies and was living in Milwaukee with her husband. Our lives had split, and though we followed each other on social, we hadn't spoken in a few years.

But boy, did I wish she were here now.

I pulled into a spot in front of Joe's and killed the engine, thinking again about how strange it was to be a grown-up in a place I'd only otherwise been a kid. Those old cliques and social constructs still existed under the surface of everything—I felt like a freshman after the juniors asked me to hang out. I realized this in truth when I walked through the door and saw about a third of my old high school right there in Joe's.

Everyone mingled, everyone talked. In a town this small, it was easy to snub people when you thought you were getting out. But nobody ended up leaving, and as such, they were stuck with each other. So it seemed the lines had dissolved, leaving nothing but a trace. But you could still see it, if you looked hard enough.

Presley waved me over to where she stood at the bar, parked between two stools while she waited on Joe to get her a drink. Eyes followed me as I made my way over to her. I did my best to hold myself up straight and pretend I didn't notice.

"Whatcha drinkin'?" she asked when I approached.

"Maker's and Coke," I answered, wanting to keep it simple—I was a lightning rod for gossip without ordering a French 75 at Buffalo Joe's.

Joe—whose giant stature and very virile body hair really did remind me of a buffalo—nodded and went about making it for me.

Presley turned to me, leaning on the bar with a smile on her face. "I'm glad you came. Wanna sit up here for a little bit?"

"Please," I said, taking a seat when she did. I glanced over my shoulder at half the old high school cheerleading squad. Their gazes snapped away from me. "Looks like the gang is all here."

She sighed. "Nothing around here ever changes. Same old fools as always, except instead of sitting around a bonfire in a field with a keg of Natural Light that John Planter's big brother bought, we're sitting in Joe's, drinking Budweiser like the sophisticated adults we are." When Joe set our drinks down, she thanked him and picked hers up for a toast. "To the same old, same old."

"Hear, hear," I answered, touching my glass to hers. We took our obligatory sips. "So how long did it take you to scrub the sticky off Cilla?"

"About an hour. Thanks for that, by the way."

"I aim to please."

"How'd it end up with Jake?"

I bobbled my head. "Fine, I think. He let it go under the condition that I take care of the goats all by myself."

She made a stinky, sour face. "Have you ever taken care of goats? If not, I'm siding with Jake."

"YouTube," was all I had to say.

"The instruction manual of go-getters. I'm more concerned with how much you'll hate it."

"It's that bad?"

She nodded with an air of condolence. "But they're cute as shit, so that helps." Before either of us spoke, her eyes flicked to the door before sweeping the ceiling. "Ugh, Chase Patton just walked in."

"Is that a bad thing?"

"Maravillo's golden boy lives on admiration and applause, and he's made an art form out of selling himself. Whatever it takes to win."

"Win what?"

"*Everything.*"

"He wants our farm," I said quietly, unsure how far away he was and unwilling to look.

"Then you're double screwed. Dammit, he's walking over." She slapped on a winning smile. "Chase, hi. How are you?"

"Good as ever," he said, leaning in to kiss her on the cheek before turning to me. "Well, look at this—Olivia Brent has made it off the farm."

He didn't say it in a snobbish way—he seemed to be genuinely glad to see me.

"Blame Presley. She's very convincing."

"Guilty," she said, raising her hand shoulder height.

"Well, I'm glad you're here. Maybe we'll get a chance to talk without Milovic sulking around."

I opted for the fake smile Presley had donned to cover my discomfort.

"Come on," Presley said, sliding off her barstool. "Let's go grab a seat."

"Grab one for me too," Chase added, smiling down at me.

I didn't know how he did that—made me feel all squirmy and warm and uncomfortable with just a look. There was another guy who did that to me but for entirely different reasons.

The thought that those reasons weren't actually that different flashed through my mind, and I let it zip away without acknowledging it again.

"Sure," Presley said, taking my arm to drag me away.

Chase watched us the whole way, along with everyone else in the bar.

A cluster of people sat around a big table they'd made out of smaller ones, and at our approach, greetings rang out. Chairs scooted, and a couple of guys who used to be on the baseball team pulled up seats for us.

Chase was on his own, I guessed.

"You all remember Olivia Brent."

They nodded and said their hellos with cheer. The group was composed of half cheerleaders, half misfits. Chantel, Courtney, Kendall, and Kaylee—the cheerleaders—and Amanda, Megan, Celeste, and Shannon, who had been goth girls. Now it seemed they'd all mingled. The guys peppered between them—husbands, by the look of it—were baseball players and burnouts. Stewart had almost burned the school down playing with a lighter and some hairspray when he was high. Now he looked like an accountant. Jared and James—twin baseball players—had once been the hottest guys in town, shortstop and first baseman for the high school team. Now they were forty pounds overweight and already balding.

They were a living testament to a simple fact of life—*nothing turns out like you think it will.*

Chantel, who had never spoken to me in school, smiled sweetly at me, her hand resting on her very pregnant belly and the other hooked in Stewart's arm. "It feels like we haven't seen you in a thousand years. I'm so sorry to hear about your grandfather."

"Thank you," I said, clutching my drink.

"How's it going at the farm?" she asked. "I heard you and Jake had to split it. That can't be easy—I don't think I've ever seen him smile."

"It's a rarity and generally at someone else's expense."

She rubbed her belly. "I don't know how you stay so skinny with all that ice cream around. They'd have to cart me around in a flatbed if I lived on a dairy farm."

"And all that cheese," Amanda mused. Heads nodded in agreement. "I'd make meals out of wheels of cheddar. You'd have to fight me off."

"Seriously," Chantel started, "if you tell me you don't work out, I might pitch myself off the roof over the unfairness of it all."

"Please don't swan dive on account of me. I don't have magical metabolism—I'm lactose intolerant."

They blinked at me. A laugh shot out of Stewart.

"You're kidding. You inherited a dairy farm, but you can't drink milk?"

"I mean, I *could*, but it wouldn't be pretty."

"Not even with Lactaid?" Shannon asked with a sad look on her face.

I shrugged. "Such is my curse."

"That's awful," Chantel said with a wavering voice.

Stewart looked at her like she was a bomb about to go off. "You're not about to cry over Olivia's digestive system, are you?"

"No," she shot, brushing the corner of her eye with her index finger. When Stewart started laughing, she nailed him in the arm. "It's your fault I'm like this. You did this to me." She gestured to her belly before hesitantly accepting a kiss on the temple.

Kaylee smiled and said., "My little boy, Braden, caught wind of a petting zoo, and I think his smile was bright enough to power the town, he was so excited. I mean, the Pattons have one, but the animals look depressed. You're going to give them a run for their money."

"Somebody should," Stewart said into his pint glass before taking a sip.

"It is true. I even have goats with bunch of babies in the mix. I got them onesies, which everybody told me was crazy. Obviously I'm a terrible listener."

They chuckled, but their attention shifted when Chase pulled up a chair next to me.

The guys all got up and clapped his hand or shoulder, and the girls all said their hellos—some with disdain, some with a celebrity sort of longing, a few with friendly enough apathy. But everyone seemed to have a reaction.

Chase Patton demanded attention without having to say a word.

"What are we talking about?" he asked.

"They were just asking Olivia about opening the farm to the public," Presley said proudly and pointedly with her eyes on mine.

"I think I heard something about that," he said, hanging his arm on the back of my chair. Everybody at the table noticed.

I did my best not to squirm, partly because I was under scrutiny, partly because he was supposed to be the enemy, and partly because I didn't necessarily want him to be.

"You're opening up the old shop, right?" he asked.

"She is, and she's putting my soap in the front window," Presley said. "Aren't you, Livi?"

I chuckled. "Guess so."

"It really is something, guys. You've got to come see what she's done with the place," Presley added.

"Oh, it's nothing, really." I hated that I blushed and hoped my barely-tan helped cover it.

"We've seen bits," Kendall said. "We all follow you on Instagram."

Everyone nodded their agreement, even Chase.

I gave him a questioning, smiling look. "Well, thank you."

Courtney laughed. "Oh my God, the video where you mucked out the stalls and fell in shit had me and Dave laughing. Didn't it, honey?"

Dave nodded. "I thought Court was going to hyperventilate."

"I've mucked one stall in my life, and it went exactly like that," Courtney said.

"And the hashtag," Amanda said, whacking Courtney on the arm. And at the same time, they hollered "*Muck it!*"

Everyone laughed, but not that teasing, cruel sort of laugh—an authentic laugh of relation and camaraderie.

Now I blushed in earnest, my skin steaming hot and my smile immovable. "If I can't laugh at myself, what else do I have?"

"Oh my gosh," Chantel said, slapping Stewart on the chest with her gaze on me. "That picture with Jake in the calf pen? I knew he was fit, but that was just ridiculous."

Stewart wasn't amused. "I keep catching her looking at it on her phone, zoomed in four hundred percent."

"He just has so many abs. There are like twelve of them," she said.

"How'd you get him to let you post it?" Amanda asked.

"By not asking."

The table chuckled.

"I bet that went over big," Jared correctly guessed.

"He barely knows how to work the internet, so really, he's all bark."

"Well, from the bottom of our hearts, *thank you*," Chantel said, pressing her hand to her chest.

Stewart made a derisive noise and took a swig of his beer.

"Oh!" Kendall said, snapping to attention. "Speaking of having to laugh at myself, the other night, the baby was in the bath …"

Chase leaned in as she continued. "You've made quite the impression, Miss Brent."

"I tend to do that. Question is whether the impression is good or bad."

"Oh, I think it's good. The girls have been stalking you on social for weeks."

"I mean, it's not like we've never met."

"Sure," he said with a shrug. "But I'd like to think we're not who we were back then."

The statement had layers of meaning. I almost thought I heard an apology somewhere in there.

"No, I guess we aren't. I hope you're not planning to push me off a swing again—it's been a long time since I've had a skinned knee, and the thought intimidates me a little," I joked.

But he didn't smile. "I think about that more than I should."

I sat back, pretending to assess him. "You mean Chase Patton is a human being with a heart and everything?"

"Hard to believe, I know." For a second, he just watched me. "My dad would love nothing more than to keep the feud going, even if it meant manipulating a fourth grader into doing something cruel."

"It's fine," I assured him, unsure what else to say.

"It's not, but I appreciate you saying so." Another pause. "Let me take you on a date."

"Chase—"

"I think I owe you for what a shit I was to you. Let me start with dinner."

"So the whole town can whisper about us being seen together?" I asked lightly. "So I can take a hammer to the fragile peace Jake and I have going? Chase, you know this can't happen. Right? A Patton and a Brent, even being seen like this"—I motioned to us—"makes me feel like I've broken something."

He nodded. "You've got too much to lose."

"Exactly."

"Then I have a proposal. How about you and me come up with a way to end the feud once and for all?"

It was impossible not to laugh. "Should we sacrifice a goat?"

"Sounds messy. I was thinking more along the lines of working together."

My smile slid off my face and into my lap. "The goat would be more effective."

"I'm serious," he said on a chuckle. "Maybe we could come up with a joint product or something. A special ice cream flavor called Peace Treaty—vanilla cream mixed with candy treats, like Nerds—or Handshake ... make it chocolate malted maybe."

"Sounds like a milkshake made out of hands."

"That's disgusting, and we should work together."

A genuine laugh slipped out of me. "Being seen in public with you is too much for my place in the farm, but working together would be easy peasy? I think they'd rather see me sharing a banana split with you than sign on with the Pattons. No, scratch that. They'd string me up for both."

He sighed. "Think about it. There has to be a way, and when we figure it out, we're sharing that banana split in front of the whole town."

"All that just to get me to go on a date with you? I knew you liked to win, but I think I underestimated the lengths you'd go to," I teased.

Chase leaned in a little closer, flashing that billboard smile of his. "That'll be the last time you make that mistake."

His thumb stroked the back of my shoulder, and I sat back in my seat, tuning back into the conversation just as Kendall wrapped up her story about her little boy pooping in the tub and her calling to Jared, *Honey, get the slotted spoon!*

I listened and laughed and luxuriated in the normality of a night out, but all the while, my mind chewed on Chase and his hand that never left the back of my chair. He had to have some sort of angle, didn't he? Not that it mattered—working together wasn't an option, and dinner was even less likely. If I ended up in bed with Patton, four generations of Brents would roll over in their graves. My ghost would be ostracized. I'd be left to haunt the barn and the goats. And Jake, if I could manage it.

I would haunt the *hell* out of Jake.

I thought of him again, sitting in his house alone. If he'd just let me be his friend, everything would be better, easier. Maybe he could even teach me how to knit.

But only if he did it shirtless.

KEVIN

Jake

ARE YOU STILL WATCHING?

I scowled at Netflix, pointing the remote at the TV to answer, *Yes, asshole.*

It was after midnight as another episode of *Parks and Rec* started. I couldn't remember the last time I'd intentionally been up this late. My mouth stretched into a yawn at the thought, and I blinked at the television screen, only half-listening as Leslie Knope told us about the upcoming *Most Li'l Sebastian Harvest Festival Ever.*

The rest of me was listening for Olivia's return.

My brain had been chewing since I'd heard the truck fire up. Unaccustomed to hearing the sound after dark, I'd checked to see what was what and watched her drive off, leaving me wondering where the hell she'd gone. Given that Presley had been here today made it safe to assume they'd gone somewhere together—Joe's probably. But I didn't know who all she'd met running around town, looking for fare to sell in the store. Maybe she'd bumped into Chase. Maybe he'd asked her out. Maybe they were on a date. Wouldn't surprise me if a degenerate like Chase didn't pick a girl up at her door, and with Olivia being a city girl, she probably wouldn't think twice.

If she'd gone out with Chase Fucking Patton, the throwdown we'd have about it would be a barn burner.

Bad enough she'd put a picture of me on social, even if it was a good one. When Kit had shown me how many people had liked and commented on it, I'd mostly been embarrassed, which made me madder than her posting it in the first place. Even the fucking goats weren't the worst thing, only that she'd gone around me. It made me feel better to know I'd get to watch her try to wrangle a trip of goats, and they'd be a good addition to her stupid petting zoo whether I liked it or not.

But nothing would forgive her and Chase together in any context.

I'd been squirrely since she'd left hours ago. The roads were pitch black this time of night with a new moon, no streetlights to speak of, and plenty of deer and raccoons were making tracks from one patch of forest to another. She wasn't prepared to drive on a night like tonight. One rogue animal, and she could end up swan diving off a cliff in Pop's truck.

I clicked back through my mind to figure out the last time Pop had the brakes serviced and couldn't remember.

Shifting in my seat, my face managed to both tighten and frown. I checked the clock. 12:02.

"This is ridiculous," I said to myself in a huff, turning off the TV.

The room was thrown into darkness. I stood, knowing my way around well enough to navigate blindfolded, chastising myself.

"You're not her fucking mother," I grumbled, unbuttoning my shirt on my way to the bathroom. I flicked on the light, flinched from the shock of light, reached for my toothbrush. Scowled at myself as I scrubbed my teeth.

What do you care where she is? She's probably drinking beer and playing Patsy Cline on the jukebox. Bet Chase is there. Bet he asked her to dance, that crooked, conniving son of a bitch.

I spat into the sink and went back to scrubbing.

He thinks he's so fucking slick. He thinks nobody sees him. But I do. And Olivia will never know what hit her, not if I don't warn her—

A thump in the distance, and I stopped brushing, my ears straining for noise. A pair of female voices, and I rinsed out my mouth, zooming back through the house to the front windows.

Across the yard in the dark, I caught sight of Presley's truck and Olivia leaning in the window. A jingle of laughter. Olivia stepped back—something was in her arms, but I couldn't tell what—and Presley turned the truck around, offering a wave before heading back down the drive.

Olivia looked down at whatever was in her arms, and I thought I heard her talking as she wobbled toward the barn.

"What in the hell …"

My brows nocked together, my eyes narrowed and locked on her as I wandered barefoot out of my front door to follow.

She shifted her burden to one arm to grasp the cast iron handle to the big side door. It took all her weight to slide it open, her body angled about forty-five degrees to the ground with the effort. She disappeared into the slice of darkness.

The closer I got, the better I could hear her talking to something like she was its mama. Goats bleated. A pig snorted at the intrusion. Ginger nickered softly. And Olivia went on talking.

"… and you're gonna live here now with me. You were all alone, but you won't be anymore, will you? No, see? We'll have each other, won't that be nice?" A baby goat bayed. "Stop that, Brenda! Don't—*ahhh!*"

Chaos erupted, and I broke out in a run, throwing the barn door all the way open and scanning for her.

Olivia Brent froze on the spot, her eyes big as ping-pong balls and her mouth opening in a little O of surprise. One leg was thrown over the fence to the goat pen, the other propped on a beam. One hand rested on the top of the fence, and in her other arm squirmed two squinting puppies. A goat on the inside of the pen tugged at the edge of her tank until she jolted back with a squeal.

I was across the barn before she teetered and lost her hold on the fence, scooping her up by the waist. The goat and I had a brief moment of tug-of-war before the sound of tearing fabric signaled her freedom.

Gingerly, I turned us, paying close mind to the tangle of her legs and the fence. Puppies wriggled against my chest, which was partially bare, but what I felt most was Olivia's breath tickling the hollow of my throat. She smelled like whiskey and springtime and trouble, and when I set her on her feet, I stayed close to her without thinking, wanting to breathe her in for a second longer.

Her little face turned up to mine, her eyes black in the moonless night. "I ... what are you doing? Why are you up so late?" The words ran together a little, but she maintained her composure for as drunk as I suspected she was.

"How about a, *Thanks, Jake—I woulda broken my neck in the goat pen if you hadn't saved me.*"

Laughing, she shoved me in the chest. "You're the worst, do you know that?" When she looked down my chest, she rolled her eyes, groaning. "God, don't you *ever* have your shirt on?"

"For your information, I was brushing my teeth when you came home making all that noise."

"Mmm," she hummed in pleasure. "That's why you smell all minty."

I ignored the note, unsure what to make of it and certain I didn't want to find out. "What are *you* doing out here at midnight? And what are *those*?"

"*Oh!*" she said, seeming to remember the wriggly blonde puppies in her arms. "Oh my God, Jake. Listen to this—Presley was driving me home from Joe's because I might have maybe had a little too much to drink, and we were just outside of town when we came up on this cardboard box on the side of the road that somebody wrote PUPPIES on. Can you believe somebody would do that? This world is so fucked up."

I started to laugh at her untethered use of the word *fuck* but cleared my throat. "Okay, but what are they doing *here*?"

"Well, they were so cute, and Presley wanted one and was gonna take the rest to town to—" A hiccup. " 'Scuse me. To town tomorrow to see if anyone wanted them or she'd drive them to the animal shelter. And I was sitting there with that box in my lap and was looking at those little babies with no mama to take care of them, and I ... well, I ..." Her voice wavered, and tears welled in her eyes so high, they touched her pupils. "They're all alone. And so am I. And so are you. So I brought us puppies. This one's yours."

She shoved a puppy into my chest.

"No, wait. *This* one's yours."

She shoved the other puppy into my chest, clutching the first one to hers.

I looked down at the furry, squiggly thing, taking it with no small amount of reluctance. "I don't want a dog."

"Well, that's too bad, isn't it?" she said to the puppy in her arms in a schmoopy voice. "Jake, aren't they just so sweet? I could just eat him up."

"That one's a girl."

She glanced for confirmation. "Well, I guess I'll have to pick a new name. Kevin isn't exactly neutral, is it?" When she looked up, her nose was a little red, but her eyes were clear. Until she got a good look at me and her face melted into that doe-eyed expression girls got when they looked at a baby.

"Awww, Jake! You're holding a puppy." She giggled, but her eyes were shiny again like she was going to cry. "And your shirt's all unbuttoned. And you don't have shoes on! *I can't handle it.*" She brightened up with an idea. "Let me take a picture of you." She was already fumbling for her phone.

"Pass." I dumped the puppy back in her arms with its sibling. "I don't want a dog, and I don't want to be all over your stupid social media."

She made a dramatic grump face and said in a doofy mocking male voice, "*I don't wanna be on the interwebs with the TikTokers and InstantGrammars.* You are such a fuddy-duddy. And you can't say no to the puppy."

The puppy was back in my arms. "Trust me, I can."

I tried to give it back, but she pushed it in my direction, her face twisting in a sad sort of frustration.

"Listen, you asshole—you need this puppy, and she needs you. You won't let me be your friend, so please, take the dog. She doesn't have anybody else to take care of her, and you don't have anyone to take care of *you*. We don't have Pop anymore, Jake. And I don't have you and you don't have me because you're such a stupid jerk and you never have a shirt on when you know it makes me all …" She crossed her eyes and circled her ear with her pointer finger. "So take the goddamn dog! And I'll take mine. And then we won't be alone anymore."

A slice of white-hot pain cut through me at the despair in her words. At the knowledge on their heels. At the look on her sad, angry face and those shiny tears still in her eyes. How she'd gone through so many forms of tears in such a short period of time astounded me. But that was Olivia. She felt everything. And she always tried to find a way to be happy despite her circumstance. Which, at the moment, was pretty shitty.

And all I'd done was make it worse, simply because I was scared of losing anything else that meant something to me. I'd lost enough.

She was right. We were alone. And we needed a friend, canine and human both.

I looked down at the puppy, and it looked up at me, its little pink tongue darting out and its needle nails shredding the outside of my hand. I glanced toward its tail.

BET THE FARM

"One problem."

"What now?"

"This one's a boy."

With a relieved laugh, she rolled her eyes. "I swear, I know my way around genitalia."

We shared a look. The color in her cheeks flared enough to see even in the near dark.

Her chin lifted. "I stand by that statement in any context."

I held the puppy out for inspection. "Kevin's a dumb name—only accountants are named Kevin. He looks more like a Rhett."

"Ugh, you country people. Why can't Kevin be an accountant? Just let him live his life already."

"A farm dog needs a good old-fashioned name. Like Buck. Hank maybe. Nash? Ryder? What do we think of Ryder, buddy?"

"So he needs to be a cowboy?"

"Anything's better than an accountant."

She stepped next to me to assess the puppy with me. "What about Bowie? You can pretend it's after the knife, and I can pretend like it's of the Major Tom variety."

A quiet laugh puffed out of me. "Bowie, huh? I don't hate that."

"That might be the best any of us can hope for, Jake."

I tucked it back into my chest. "What are you gonna name yours?"

"She's so furry and cute and blonde …" She paused. "Maybe Dolly. Think I can teach her to howl 'Jolene'?"

"I dunno. I think she might look more like a Jolene than a Dolly."

Olivia looked up at me, then at the puppy. "You know, I think you might be right."

"I've been waiting to hear you say that for weeks."

She snorted a laugh. "Asshole."

The goats yelled at us in a chorus from the fence, their heads sticking out between fence rungs. I jerked my chin at them.

"What were you doing in the goat pen?"

Her face lit up like I'd screwed in a lightbulb. "Well, I was so excited about the puppies, I knew I'd never sleep, but your lights were off or I woulda come over and given him to you. So I thought I should take them to see the goat babies, and then all the babies could be friends. But then Brenda got all excited and kept trying to head-butt them to death and I got scared and then you walked in."

"Brenda wasn't trying to murder your puppies."

"*Our* puppies," she corrected.

"Fine, *our* puppies. But that's how kids play. You've never seen them do it?"

"Well, we've only had them for like twelve hours, so no."

"Come here. Watch them."

We walked over to the pen, and I reached into the bucket hanging high on the post for a handful of feed. Four seconds later when they finished it, the adults went back to sleep, and the kids started playing. It was admittedly alarming to watch—they took turns making leaping dives for each other's heads, cracking their buddies square between the eyes. One was so good, he landed at least two hits midair.

I glanced over at Olivia—her fingers were over her lips in abject horror.

"Don't be scared. They're the most hardheaded animals on the planet."

"Well, I'm surprised you all don't get along better."

"Never said we didn't get along. Just said I didn't want the pain in the ass."

She cast me an amused, sidelong look. "If only we all could run away from things that were pains in the asses." Her brows quirked. "Pain in the asses? Pains in the ass?"

"I get your meaning." Jolene squeaked from Olivia's arms. "They're little. I think we're gonna have to bottle feed them."

She whirled toward me with her face all lit up. "Oh my

God—please tell me you'll feed it in a rocking chair with no shirt on for my calendar."

"What calendar?"

"The one I just thought of. *Twelve Months of Mantitty, Featuring Jake Milovic*," she said, motioning like she was reading a marquee.

"Not on your life."

"Oh, come on. Be a good sport."

"Whenever have I been a good sport?"

"What would I have to do?" I opened my mouth to say *give me the farm*, but she stopped me with the point of a finger. "Not that. What else would I have to give you?"

"You can't afford me, Olivia."

She laughed and used that pointing finger to poke me in the chest. I hadn't realized how close we were until she touched me.

"That's what you think, buster. Come on, I know you can think of something humiliating for me to do."

"Oh, I can think of plenty, but there's no chance in hell I'm posing for a calendar."

With a shrewd look, she said, "Fine. Then I'll have to take some when you're not looking. So if you could please shirtlessly feed Bowie tomorrow night at six thirty in the rocking chair out front, I will absolutely, positively *not* be hiding in the bushes to take pictures of you for illegal distribution to raise money for the farm."

An unbidden laugh slipped out of me, and she softened at the sound. Her eyes traced the lines of my face with an unfamiliar emotion behind them. It was a sort of fondness, an admiration.

"I love it when you laugh. You never laugh. Or smile. Has anyone ever told you you have nice teeth?"

"Wouldn't you know—that's the first thing anyone says about me," I teased.

With a laugh of her own, she tried to bump me with her hip, but because she was drunk, she just sort of fell right into me. For the second time in ten minutes, Olivia's body was flush against mine.

But this time, it wasn't just the sweet scent of her that I noticed. It was the length of her dark lashes, the endless depth of her eyes. It was that smart little nose and the valley that connected it to her lips. Those lips were full and wide with a bow so deep and sharp, it looked like it'd been carved there by a sculptor. I could have counted the smattering of freckles on her cheeks or the creases in those plump, rosy lips, which parted just a little. Just enough for me to capture one if I tried.

Except she busted out laughing.

Confused, I blinked down at her.

Her eyes pinched shut, her chin kicked up, a riot of giggling rolling through the air. "Jake, oh my God. Were you about to kiss me?" A snort ripped out of her, and a peal of laughter spilled out behind it.

"That's it," I said, trying to tamp down a smile, unable to be sour with her laughing so prettily. I turned for the barn door and snagged her arm. "You're going to bed."

"Why? Wanna come with me?" Another snort, followed by a halt as she hinged over, laughing. A gasp of air, and she stood again, waving her hand like a windshield wiper. "I'm sorry, it's just so funny. You. Kissing me."

"What's so funny about that?" I asked with a teasing tone to cover the rejection as I guided her out of the barn, closing the door behind me.

"Only that you'd want to kiss *me*. You hate me."

"I dunno if I'd call it hate."

"Just the general pains in the asses. Pains in the ass? I can't figure out which one is right."

"I mean, you did get me a puppy."

"Aww, I did! I mean, I saved the puppy from rabid raccoons or a mob of angry squirrels or—God forbid—a bear. I didn't exactly *get* him for you."

"Well, it still counts," I said as we approached the steps of the big house. "And ... well, thank you."

We came to a stop, and she took two steps up, turning around to face me. "You're welcome, Jake. I'm glad you didn't make me give him back because I would have been *so sad*."

A chuckle. "Can't have that."

"I'll remember you said that for next time." With a smile, she turned, ascending the last of the steps.

"Then let's hope I mind my manners."

"It'd be a first for all of us," she joked, stepping through the threshold. "Night, Jake."

"Night, Livi."

And the door snicked closed.

Heading toward my house, I let out a heavy breath and looked down at Bowie. "A puppy. What the hell am I going to do with a puppy?"

He licked my hand in answer, and I thought I might know just what to do with him after all. I needed somebody to love just as much as Olivia said I did.

A hot flush crept up my neck. She hadn't been wrong—three more seconds, and I would have kissed her. I made a vow to never be so stupid again. Not with the farm in the balance and all our futures on the line.

I needed someone to love.

But God help us all if I even considered that somebody being her.

MOTHER HEIFER

Jake

Only a couple cars were left in the gravel lot by the time I finished my rounds on opening day, a day I'd spent trying not to think about how many strangers were on the property.

Olivia had been busy.

From what I'd gathered, our first day had gone off without a hitch. Our staff who ran tours were wide-eyed and brimming with excitement from the fun they'd had. The calves were well fed, thanks to the petting zoo, and the animals in the barn seemed just as wound up as the staff was about the new faces they'd seen. Mack had told me the shop had been so busy, there was barely room to walk. They'd sold out of our creamery fare four times.

To no one's surprise, I was skeptical.

I should have been as giddy as the goats and staff. Instead, anxiety and dread twisted in my chest like a hot towel, steaming and scalding to the touch. Because what if it didn't work? What if she failed? What would it do to the farm, to our finances? What if this was a fluke?

And what would happen when got bored and she left me here to pick up the pieces alone?

As I made my way toward the shop to pick up Bowie, I dunked that towel in ice water and listened to the sizzle. Truth was, we *had* been busy, and busy was good—I'd noted the people, doing quick math to figure about how much we'd made on tours alone at ten bucks a head, twenty per tour, eight tours for the day. The markup on the creamery goods alone would have made a hefty sum when calculated four times over.

In that, I found enough hope to ease my mind, even if it was only by a degree.

Golden sunset light cut through the trees as I rounded the barn and caught sight of Janet's shop. Olivia had painted the door that Pepto Bismol shade she favored, and hanging from a porch post was a logo she'd made. *Farmgirl*, it read in an arch over an illustrated pair of pink rain boots stuffed with flowers.

Olivia meant well, and based on today, I could see how what she was doing would help. But at the end of the day, the responsibility of the farm's debts fell on me, as they should.

They were *my* debts, after all.

As I climbed the whitewashed steps to the shop, I glanced in the big front windows painted with doodly, quirky scrolling and script spelling out the shop's name and social media info along with the phrase, *Easily distracted by cows*. I rolled my eyes and pulled open the door to the sound of the little bell overhead.

It was true. She was distracted by cows and goats and flowers and puppies, and I'd used up a metric ton of energy pretending like I didn't find it as goddamn adorable as it was annoying.

The shop was lit up by the slanting sun, the space bright and cheerful by design. She'd arranged everything on farmhouse tables and shelves in little vignettes, the front table the biggest and best. It was iron baskets stuffed with hay and fake eggs. Flannel and distressed tins. T-shirts featuring the farm and Farmgirl as well as some with funny sayings like *Mother Heifer* and the word

Bad over a picture of a donkey. It smelled like apple pie, and I noted a few of Presley's candles burning in an almost direct trail to a wall of soaps and lotions and candles.

In true Olivia fashion, she'd created a little nook off the side of the register where she'd painted black Holstein spots and the phrase from one of her T-shirts—*Mother Heifer*. The farm's new logo, Instagram handle, and hashtags sat close enough to the phrase to be in the photo but at a size that it didn't intrude. Even though the store was technically closed, a couple of women were taking pictures of each other in front of the wall with full-blown grins on their faces.

And there behind the register counter was Olivia, smiling at a customer with a handled brown paper shopping bag featuring the farm's new logo in her hand.

Oftentimes, I found myself caught in moments such as this, a strange stretching of time where I saw every detail of her all at once. The light illuminating her wild copper hair from behind, blazing it like a halo. The darkness of her velvety brown eyes in contrast to the pale of her skin. The shape of her smile, the little half-circles at the corners. The curves that composed the line of her neck and shoulders, in full display by favor of the cut of her sundress.

That dress held my attention the longest, the gauzy white fabric made of light, the sunshine shading the blurred shadow of her body beneath. Nothing about it was suggestive—in fact, the dress itself held almost no form—but I couldn't help noting the shape of her, as if I'd caught a whisper of a secret I wasn't supposed to know.

"Hey, Jake," Presley said from my elbow in a knowing tone that I didn't like, simply for its suggestion that she'd heard what I'd been thinking.

I covered my surprise at her presence with, "You know you're not getting paid for today, right?"

At that, she laughed. "Do you have any idea how much of my

own stuff I peddled? Trust me—no payment is necessary. How'd it go out there today?"

"Sounds like it went well, but I dunno how much of it is everybody being excited about it and how much was actual profit."

"There's more to life than money," she noted as we waited for Olivia to finish up.

I gave her a look. "Don't act like you don't know that any given farm is one bad season away from dire straits. We don't do this for the money, but without money, we can't do it."

"There's still more to it than—"

Before she could finish, three puppies and Priscilla charged out of the back corner and toward us, barking. Priscilla was the loudest.

Laughing, I crouched to greet the trio, who proceeded to climb over each other in an effort to lick my face. Before Priscilla reached me, Presley snatched her up.

"Ah, ah, ah—I don't think Jake wants licks from you too."

Priscilla donned a mighty frown, but within a second, it was gone—she seemed to remember someone else was within licking distance and went to town on her mother's face.

"Blah!" Presley angled back enough that it broke contact.

Unhappy, Priscilla barked at her.

Presley offered me a sarcastic smile. "We've been playing puppy all day."

"Sounds fun." I scooped up the wriggly puppies and headed to the corner where their beds were. But every time I got one in, the other one ran off.

Four tries in, I sighed and gave up.

When I stood and turned, the customer was gone, and Olivia and Presley were shoulder to shoulder, watching me and whispering. Priscilla panted from her perch on Presley's hip.

"What are you two whispering about?" I asked.

"Well," Olivia started, "Presley agrees that we should make a calendar. Pretty sure we'd be millionaires."

I gave her a look.

"Okay, at least thousandaires." She smirked. "How'd it go out there?"

"Good, I guess. How'd you do in here?"

Her face lit up like New Year's Eve. "Oh, Jake—we kept running out of milk and ice cream, and we had to put away the cheese plate because as soon as we put food out, it was gone. We nearly sold out of Presley's goodies."

"I put out everything I had in the car. I thought I was just being optimistic." She smiled over at Olivia. "I don't think a single person skipped the store after the tour."

"They saw your spread in the window and couldn't resist," Olivia said. "I'm going to have to put in a new merchandise order—a rush order, if tomorrow goes like this. And I think I'm going to need a couple more fridges so we don't run poor Mack to death."

"He's got an ATV at his disposal. I think he'll live," I teased. "Any idea what our profit was today?"

"I've been dying to look," she said with a grin, turning to the tablet she'd set up as a register to click through a couple of screens.

But then she stopped. Her smile fell. Her eyes went wide.

My heart lurched in fear.

Slowly, her face turned to mine. "I rang up almost seven thousand dollars today."

Presley's jaw hung open as she stared over Olivia's shoulder. "You have got to be fucking kidding me," she breathed.

"No bad words, Mama." Priscilla held out her hand, but Presley was too stunned to even acknowledge her.

"I ... you what?" I asked stupidly. There was no way.

"Look." She swiveled the screen around, and I stepped up to look.

And there it was. Two hundred seven transactions, a few which spent several hundred dollars.

"How ..." I breathed, running the math.

"We booked a hundred and sixty heads for tours, and a bunch of people from town came just to show their support. Almost everybody left with something from the fridge at least, but plenty of them bought other things. I've been teasing products all week on social, and people were asking for specifics."

"We even sold the hammock, and that thing was a hundred and fifty bucks," Presley added.

"And what's your markup?" I asked.

"Fifty percent," Olivia answered quietly. "Two hundred for our dairy. And this doesn't include the ten dollars per head for the tours."

I scrubbed a hand over my mouth. "Another sixteen hundred for tours? In one day?"

Smiling, Olivia nodded.

"Jesus Christ," I muttered.

"Do you have any idea what this means?" Olivia asked. "Even if we don't do this much every weekend, we're going to make well over ten thousand a week between the shop and tours. And when we start doing festivals? All the vendors will have to pay a table fee, and we're going to call crowds from a tri-county area."

I frowned. "Festivals?"

"Like Fourth of July. I've been calling around looking for carnival rides and food trucks, and I think I've found a fireworks guy who can—"

My blood pressure spiked. "We're not doing carnival rides and fireworks on the farm."

She frowned. "Why not?"

"Because it'll scare the animals for one, but mostly because we can't afford it."

"But if we keep earning money, can't we—"

"Do you have any idea how much this farm costs to run? Twelve hundred cows cost six thousand *per day* to feed. You add that to the debts we already had, and you're scratching the surface with what you've made here."

"But that's what I'm saying—if we've earned this much in one day with the store, what could we do if we opened the farm up even more?"

My neck was hot with indignation, a prickle of sweat licking my hairline. She didn't understand. She couldn't understand. And she couldn't let anything breathe. She just couldn't leave well enough alone. She couldn't focus on one thing at a time, preferring to pile a new project, a new goal, a new change on top of everything else she'd turned inside out.

"It's never going to be enough for you, is it?" My words were hard, sharp. "Not dusting off Janet's shop. Not erasing the old logo in favor of your stupid goddamn rain boots—"

"Monies—"

Presley clapped her hand over Priscilla's mouth.

"Not the fucking goats and not even a damn good first day. You haven't even locked the door and you're already talking about more. More, more, more."

Olivia's face pinched and flushed. "You are the most miserable, ornery asshole I've ever known. I'm making us money. I'm thinking outside the box. What I'm *not* is an enemy."

"Haven't you invaded? Aren't we at war? All you've done since you stepped foot on this property is blow things up."

"And all you've done is fight back when we could be working together."

A dry laugh shot out of me. "That's what the Romans promised before they enslaved every country they overtook. So yeah, I'll fight to the bitter end. Who else is going to defend the farm? Because you won't. You have no honor, no respect for this place, for what it stands for."

Her body trembled, as did her voice when she whispered, "How *dare* you."

"Oh, don't play the victim," I shot. "I am so sick and tired of you acting like I'm the crazy one when I'm the only one trying to keep this place running. All you've done is run up a bill when we're already crippled from our debts. We're not adding another harebrained idea that's gonna double what you've already spent. I'm putting my foot down."

She razed me to the ground with a glare. "How about you put the other foot down in front of the first and repeat until you're out of my store."

I snorted but turned for the door, vibrating with fury. "Keep on spending, and I'll see you on the next flight out of here."

"Nothing you do will scare me off—*nothing*."

My palm slapped the door as I pushed it open, laughing cruelly, hating myself more with every step I took.

Why? Why do you do it? Why'd you say it? Why'd you hurt her when you could have walked away, you son of a bitch? I asked myself as I stormed away.

But I knew the answer. She'd never get it out of me, and I'd never say it aloud, but I knew.

Olivia Brent held the power to take away everything that meant something to me. And I was too terrified of that possibility to do anything but fight her off.

Even if she might be right.

PRETTY IN PINK

Olivia

I POPPED OPEN THE CAN OF PINK PAINT WITH A SCREWDRIVER and smiled at its contents.

I hadn't seen Jake since he'd stormed out of the store two days ago, which was a feat in itself. Kit had told me that rather than bring Bowie to me like he'd done every day for weeks, Jake rode around with him all day as he made his rounds. There was no way to know his motivation for avoiding me—he was either cooling off or plotting a coup. Maybe he couldn't stand to look at me. Or maybe he knew if I saw him, I'd yell at him.

He'd be right.

There were no words to describe how he'd made me feel, not exactly. There was no single phrase for the wash of emotions that hit me when he shoved the shop door open and walked out to the tune of his laughter. The few silent tears I shed were laden with frustration and audacity and a deep, aching pain. My heart thudded with loneliness and rejection, my pulse racing with a hostile discord I couldn't remember feeling before.

It was impossible not to care, not with the fate of the farm hanging between us. There was nowhere to go, no chance at getting away from each other, not when I could see his front porch from my kitchen. I was trapped here with a man who saw me as a threat, who hurt me in one of the deepest ways he could.

He'd said I had no honor and no respect for this place. Speaking those words was an unforgivable sin, a magnificent lie. All I could do was hope he didn't mean it.

If he did, there was no chance this would work.

I'd had it with the bickering—it was time to settle things once and for all. His time to stew was nearly up, and as soon as his work day was done, I'd march my way over there and force him to hash it out with me. No running away, no insults. Just a real-life, grown-up conversation that wouldn't end until we shook hands.

This morning, I'd awoken with a sense of possibility, all the good sitting in front of me like a basket of kittens. The shop and tours yesterday had gone off with barely a hitch. We'd made a fat stack of cash over the weekend, which I'd designated funds for Fourth of July, the expenses amended to strike fireworks and carnival rides from the list. I hadn't even thought of the animals before Jake said something.

Just one more thing I needed him for.

If I could only get him to realize he needs me too.

You'd think I'd recognize a brick wall, but I was just as stubborn as he was. He'd see what I was showing him eventually.

All I had to do was not give up.

Humming along to the music playing from my earbuds, I stirred and poured and dipped my brush into the creamy pink paint to lay the first stroke on the old black door. It was a streak of joy on darkness, and with it came inevitable levity. Stroke by stroke, I blotted out the depthless black, and with it, I erased my worries. Everything would work out. It always did. Jake would come around—he just needed breathing room. Space to see all my ideas in action, like the store. Before he'd hulked out of the shop the other day, he'd been genuinely struck by the money I'd made. For a second, I'd gotten through to him, and if I could keep it up, I knew I'd win him over.

I stepped back and took stock of the door, which was going to take a few coats. *Should have primed it,* I thought. The paint only went up as high as I could reach—a patch of black capped off my work. I'd need a ladder to fix it.

But when I turned to head for the shed, I ended up face to face with Jake, skidding to a stop an inch before tumbling into him.

Briefly, I wondered if a person's eyeballs could actually turn red if they got mad enough like in cartoons. If they built up so much pressure, they'd burst a blood vessel or ten just out of sheer rage.

Jake was the picture of magnificent fury, composed once again of squares. The hard line of his brows made the top, his jaw made the bottom, and somewhere in between, his flat lips opened and closed, making shapes that should have produced sounds.

I pulled out one earbud.

"... fucking *pink*? The store was fair game, but the big house? Frank rolled over in his grave the second you put that brush to wood. *Jesus*, Olivia. You have no fucking shame."

Blinking at him, I fumbled to catch up, noting how strange it was to be the same height as a giant, me on the porch and him on the steps.

"Are you serious? Are you seriously picking a fight with me *again*?"

Square shoulders rose, square pectorals heaving as he drew a breath like a billow. "Why are you doing this? Why can't you stop for one fucking minute and *think*? You didn't ask anybody if you could paint the door—"

"And who should I have asked to paint *my* door? The house isn't yours—Pop left it to me, and I can paint the door whatever goddamn color I want." I crossed my arms, forgetting the paintbrush was still in my hand until the wet paint soaked into my

T-shirt. Refusing to acknowledge it so as not to disturb my very powerful facade, I said, "I don't have to ask your permission. Not for this."

"How about the goats? How about the farm's expenses? How about posting all our business on the fucking internet? I just want to know why? Why do you think you have the right to slide back in here after ten years and rip this place apart?"

"Because this is my home. I'm trying to *help*."

He leaned in, his face the color of menace. "You keep saying that, but all you've done is—"

"Try? Work? I can't help if you insist on keeping everything the same, even this argument." The pitch of my voice climbed. "You don't want to save the farm—you want to push me away and pray everything works out. News flash, Jake—no one is going to save the farm except us. And that's gonna take change."

"You convinced me of change—I let you open the store, didn't I?"

"You *let* me?" I scoffed over him.

"But you won't stop. You can't leave well enough alone. It's like you've gotta scrawl your name on every surface you come across. Like you've gotta move everything you walk past until nothing looks right anymore."

My head cocked, my brows close enough to nearly touch as it dawned on me. "Is that what this is about?"

"This is about money."

"Are you sure?"

"Of course I'm sure," he snapped.

"You ... you don't recognize it anymore, and you're mad at me for ... for erasing your home?"

He shook his head, his eyes flicking to the heavens in a plea for help. "You think everything's that simple, don't you? You don't know me, Olivia. You don't know *anything* about me. So you'd best not assume."

Jake gave me his back and started to walk away.

I charged after him. "Oh, no. You're not gonna storm off and leave me here."

"Looks like I'm doing just that."

"Jake—"

"Leave it alone. You've done enough."

"I don't think I have. Please, stop."

His pace was such that I was nearly jogging.

"Jake, I understand it's not the same, but—"

"You don't understand shit."

I stopped dead, burning a hole in his back, and before I knew what I was doing, I chucked my paintbrush at him.

It hit him square between the shoulder blades at the exact spot my eyes were locked, bristles first. The second it hit him, he froze mid-stride. A pink smudge marred his white shirt, the mark disappearing as he pivoted to face me.

He glanced at my hand. "Did you just throw a paintbrush at me?"

I couldn't tell if he was mad or just curious, he'd said it so evenly. Mad was probably the safe bet.

"Well, I had to get your attention somehow." I folded my arms, my heart thundering with a strange mix of frustration and understanding. "This farm has been the exact same since you first knocked on that door ten years ago. That was the spot you first met him, isn't it? And I went and painted it all pink, which you hate on a regular day. But on that door, it was too much."

He turned his head to look off in the distance, thumbing his nose. "That color's stupid and has no place on the farm."

When the knot at his throat bobbed, it was all the answer I needed. My glare softened. I took a step toward him.

"I'm sorry," I said softly. "I didn't understand, Jake. I should have talked to you about it."

"Damn right you should have."

"But you can't keep doing this."

"Doing what exactly?"

"This." I gestured to the length of him. "Never once have you come to me with a problem and carried on an actual conversation with me. You just yell, insult me, and storm off." I paused, tracing the line of his profile with my gaze. "You don't want to hurt me—you're not cruel, even if you're bent on running me off. But you're hurting, and I'm the dog that gets kicked. We *both* lost Pop. I'm dealing with my pain by changing things because it's just too hard to see them the same. To remember. But you're seeing it all erased when all you want to do is hang on. Is that how you feel? Is that what I've done?"

His face turned to mine, his eyes hard and tight, his lips a line. "Stop it."

My brow quirked. "Stop what?"

"Trying to guess what I feel."

"If you told me, I wouldn't have to."

Those Herculean jaw muscles bounced as he considered. And when he finally spoke, it was clipped and as tight as the rest of him. "This is my home, and it's been my home longer than it ever was yours. You left when you should have stayed, when I asked you to, when we needed you. And now you've been here a month, and nothing is the same. *Nothing*. We've got strangers all over the farm. Everything's fucking *pink*, of all colors—who could take us seriously? You swooped in and touched everything, and when you leave, your fingerprints are gonna be all over this place. And don't look at me like that. Like you don't know for a fact you'll get bored and run back to the city. You know as well as I do that this isn't the life you want."

"How could you say that?"

"You did left once. Why wouldn't you do it again? If the farm was so important, you would have come back sooner."

Something in my chest ached so deeply, I couldn't breathe. "I was getting my degree."

A humorless laugh. "Sure, your degree. And then you went and got a job with your aunt without even coming home, without even considering that you might be needed *here*. Any excuse to stay away. You don't really want to be here, and the sooner you figure it out, the better it'll be for all of us."

My throat squeezed shut, and I swallowed to open it enough to speak. "I was wrong. I should have stayed when you asked. I should have come home after school. And every morning since he died, I've woken up with regret. I thought I had more time. I … I don't know that I can forgive myself for that, so I won't ask your forgiveness, either. But I'm looking you in the eye and telling you I *do* want to be here." I took a few steps toward him. "I'm here to right my wrong as best I can, and that means I'm not going anywhere."

"You can say it all you want, but I don't believe you. And deep down, you don't, either."

Gravity weighed me down, slumped my shoulders. "I'm so tired of fighting. I'm tired of holding myself together and running myself into the ground so I can avoid thinking about him. I'm so tired of arguing and pushing and being hurt by you." My voice broke, damn it. "All I want—all I want in the *entire* world—is for you to take a real look at what I'm trying to do and trust me. I wouldn't do anything to hurt the farm, and I wouldn't do anything to hurt you."

The tension in his face eased, his suspicion quieting just a little. "I know," he said after a beat.

"Then why are you punishing me?"

A flash of surprise streaked behind his eyes. "Punishing you?"

"For leaving. For changing things." I closed the gap between us, only stopping when I was close enough to touch his hand. But I stopped myself. "I don't want to hurt anymore."

His chin lifted, his eyes meeting mine. "I don't want you to hurt. I'm just …"

Scared. I heard the word hang in the silence.

And then I *did* take his hand. "Me too. But we have each

other. And if we can figure out how to work together, we'll turn this place around."

"How?" he asked quietly.

"Well, you have to trust me, like I said. You need to believe I wouldn't do anything that wasn't in the farm's best interest. Deep down, you know that, right?"

A nod.

"And you have to talk to me. *Talk,*" I repeated, "not yell. Not accuse. Not insult. *Talk.*"

A smile flickered across his lips. "You don't make it easy to keep my cool."

"We both have our work cut out for us, don't we? But the weight of the farm doesn't fall on you alone."

"It doesn't?" he asked, amused.

"I mean, like ninety-five percent of it is you," I joked, "but you're right—I need to consult you before I change anything."

"You should have been doing that from the start, you know," he noted wryly.

"So you could tell me no? Like the goats?"

"Which you went and got anyway."

"Because you didn't listen to me."

"Because goats are assholes."

"So are you."

An amused noise.

"And we have to agree—and we're going to shake on this, so listen close—we have to agree that we're going to hear each other out."

"Because I come to you looking for permission all the time?"

It must have been the way he was smiling down at me or the feel of my hand lost inside of his, but I became acutely aware of how close we were. I could smell hay and earth and sunshine on him, could feel his warmth radiating off of his body.

I rolled my eyes to cover. "One of these days, you're going to need me to sign off on something, and I'm gonna make you kiss my pink rain boots as a condition."

He groaned. I laughed.

"And we're going to compromise," I added. "Otherwise, we'll never get anything done."

A pause. A sigh. "All right."

"Okay," I said with authority, stepping back and extending my hand with no small amount of moxie. "Partners?"

Jake looked down at my hand, that hint of a smile on his face. When he took it, he met my eyes again. "Partners."

"Great! So about Fourth of July—"

"Goddammit, Olivia—"

"If I promise there will be no loud noises other than the crowd?"

His eyes narrowed.

"It's not a trick, I swear." I held up a hand and crossed my fingers. "Scout's honor."

With a chuckle, he undid my fingers and formed them in the Girl Scout salute. "It's not really convincing if you don't do it right." His eyes caught mine again. "How about you come to me with a list of what you want to do for the Fourth?"

"And we'll collaborate?" I asked too eagerly.

"If you want to call it that."

"And you won't fight me?"

"I won't fight you. Your ideas aren't all bad."

My face broke open. "That was almost a compliment. I feel like I won some kind of award."

At that, he full-on laughed, that sound I loved so much, even when I hated him. Warmth flickered low in my belly, and before I knew it, I'd launched myself at him, flinging my arms around his neck. He barely had time to catch me. I felt him chuckling through his chest, through mine.

"Thank you," I whispered next to his ear.

"I'm sorry," he answered.

I loosened my arms, signaling him to set me down, which was really a long slide down the length of his body. The honest remorse on his face at the apology broke my heart.

"I'm sorry too," I said.

"Now don't make me regret it," he joked.

I slapped him in the slab of granite he called a chest. "And I'll repaint the door."

He glanced behind me at the door, then back at me. "Leave it. I was wrong about Pop—he would have let you. He'd let you do anything you wanted, so I don't have any place to stop you."

A squeal that turned into a giggle bubbled out of me as I bounced like a little kid. "Thank you, Jake."

"You know what? Don't mention it."

I beamed.

"No, I mean it. Don't tell anybody—I'll deny it with my last breath."

With that little smile on his face, he turned, and this time I let him go.

Because I'd take what I could get.

And now that we'd be working together, he'd given me more than he knew.

PAJAMA PARTY

Olivia

"I'M JUST SAYING, BASED ON YOUR SOCIAL MEDIA, FARM life looks like it involves a lot of bullshit, literally and otherwise," my aunt said on the other end of the line.

"Is it weird that I'm enjoying it?" I asked as I folded my laundry.

"Yes. I mean, maybe not the big, hunky bullshit. I could probably find a way to enjoy him."

"I'm optimistic that we might have turned a corner. More bunny shit than bull. He's even helping me with our Fourth of July festival."

"I've been watching your Instagram. I'd say I was surprised at how well you've done with the farm's marketing, but there was no way you could fail. This is your domain, and you reign absolute."

"Trust me, I could have failed. I could still fail. I don't have long to turn a profit, and if Jake changes his mind again, he could make it impossible."

"And if you lose, you'll come back to New York?"

"That's the deal."

"I probably shouldn't root for him."

"You definitely shouldn't," I said on a chuckle.

"Would it be so bad, coming back?"

"Coming back would mean I failed the farm and Pop too. I don't know how I'd live with myself, Annette."

A sigh. "You're missed here. I didn't realize that you were the glue holding your team together. The last month has been a shitshow and not just at the office. It's been a long time since I've lived alone, since before you came to me. My next phase is cat lady, and I'm not sure if I love that look for me."

"I don't know. I could see it. Maybe get one of those hairless cats."

She made a disgusted noise. "They look like ballsacks with eyes, Livi. I'd never sleep again with one of those things lurking around my house."

A laugh bubbled out of me.

"What? I'm not an animal person."

"Oh, I know."

"Which is why you won't be surprised I think you should come back. Leave the farm to the farmers and come take a senior marketing position at the firm."

My hands paused over an open drawer of underwear. "Jill left?"

"She's moving to Seattle with her new husband, and I've got a spot to fill."

I was stunned silent for a moment. "That's a big career jump."

"Well, how else will I lure you back?" she asked on a laugh.

"Annette ..."

"Don't say no. Just think about it, okay? If things don't work out there, Jill leaves in October. The spot is yours, if you want it."

I didn't argue like I wanted to. Instead, I said, "Thank you. I'm honored, really. Jill has my dream job."

"For now. Just saying. I miss you, kid. You ... well, you're all I have left of Sarah. I didn't realize just how much you filled your mom's space in my heart until you were here. I wasn't ready to let you go. I thought I had more time."

My heart twisted in my chest. It didn't matter what I did—I was abandoning someone.

"So did I," I said quietly. "I miss you too. And New York. And people." She laughed, and the sound made me smile. "But I'm not coming back unless I lose."

"I'll take what I can get. You don't want to come back right now anyway—it's a thousand degrees and hasn't stopped raining for four days. Enjoy California while you're there. And that big, smelly jerk while you're at it."

"The one who hates me?"

"You know what they say—that line between love and hate is thin indeed. Maybe you two need to just bang it out."

"Oh my God." I giggled, closing one drawer to deposit some tees into another. "On that note, I have some goats to milk."

"Please, *please* record that."

"It's the same as milking a cow, and I know how to milk a cow."

"Somehow, I have a feeling your goats are going to be less willing."

"Then wish me luck."

"Good luck! Don't get kicked in the moneymaker."

"I love you," I said, laughing.

"I love you too, peanut. Talk soon."

We said our goodbyes, and I was left alone in my quiet room, missing my old life. For the first time since I'd come home, I felt the pull back to New York. The life I'd had there felt far away, like another person in another time. The hustle of the city, the bustle of a demanding job. Everything felt important, every choice, big or small. My old friends and colleagues were too busy and wrapped up in their lives to do more than text, leaving me questioning the depths of my relationships.

But it was the life I'd known for a long time, longer than I'd lived here, as Jake had so graciously pointed out. That Olivia had a promising career in the best city in the world, a speeding train that was going somewhere big. This Olivia had a career ahead of her that would never make her rich, would never gain her power or accolades. This career was a sack race that stuck close to home.

But this job was maybe the most important job of my life. And while it wasn't prestigious or elite, it was genuine. And the stakes were much, much higher. Decisions were a matter of survival, not only of mine, but that of the whole farm, human and animal alike.

When my laundry was put away, I grabbed the stack of custom-made pajamas I was going to put on the kids and headed out to the barn.

The goat pen was a hotbed of action. I'd bought five does and their kids, plus one buck for breeding, and all eight baby goats were leaping around the pen, chasing each other while I set up my phone to record. They stopped and rushed me when I stepped through the gate. Laughing, I took a seat on the stool and gave them a little love before picking one to put pajamas on.

"Look at you, Brenda," I called as she bounced off, bleating.

Within a few minutes, the kids were zooming around the pen in their new pajamas while the adults watched on like they were crazy.

It was so cute—even cuter than I'd imagined when I bought them—I got a little choked up.

"Are they wearing … pajamas?"

I turned to the sound of Jake's voice with a smile on my face, braced for a fight. "They sure are."

His skeptical expression melted when one of the kids took off like it had just been tagged it, and the rest ran in the opposite direction.

And Jake *laughed*.

He laughed from deep down in his belly, that free, easy sound so foreign from his lips.

It took him a minute to compose himself. "That is ridiculous. Absolutely fucking ridiculous."

"I know. I love it."

"Color me unsurprised."

"But do you know why it's funny?"

"Because you put clothes on goats?"

"The reason we laugh at animals is because our subconscious imagines they're human. Like, you see a baby goat in pajamas, but your brain secretly imagines a person in pajamas bouncing around a pen making goat noises."

He gave me a dubious look.

I held my hands up. "Look it up."

"Did you just come out here to dress up the kids for the internet?"

"First and foremost, I did it for myself."

A chuckle.

"And no. I was going to try to milk one of the goats."

"Then I'm right on time." With a smirk, he leaned on the fence.

I paused. "So you're just going to watch me?"

"It was part of the goat deal."

"That was in regard to clipping their hooves. You're not going to, I don't know. Yell at me for putting clothes on the goats?"

"No, because that is hilarious."

I shook my head. "I do not get you."

"Plus, we're working together, right? I figure I can trust you with pajamas." Before I could ask him some version of *what the hell*, he said, "Have you clipped their hooves, by the way?"

"No. Do they need it?"

He almost walked through the gate but paused. "Would you mind if I helped?"

"Since you asked so nicely, come on in."

With that little smirk on his face, he joined me. "I'm glad you didn't try yet. I was gonna let you figure it out on your own, but I worried you'd get hurt. So I took the liberty of getting you set up. Most importantly, this." He waved me to the fence that opened up to the yard, and in a space just beyond the barn stood a little platform with a wall on one side, two taller slats of wood that made a head catch, and a bucket on the other side.

"Is that a ..."

"It's a milking stand," he said, hopping the fence.

When I started to climb over to join him, he grabbed me by the waist and picked me up without even bending his knees.

"Lemme show you how it works."

I followed him to the device, which he explained to me in great detail. I was too busy puzzling over him to listen.

"All you have to do is slide this board over for her head to fit, then close it with this latch. And she can snack while you do what you need to. I made it a height that you should be able to reach her udder without hurting your back or anything."

"*You* made it?"

"Well, yeah. You think I was gonna spend a hundred fifty bucks on something I could make myself?"

I couldn't help but laugh. "Well, when you put it that way ..."

"I got you some clippers too. Couldn't make those."

"Who even are you?" I asked, smiling.

He rubbed the back of his neck. "I owed you. For ... punishing you."

"You didn't owe me anything, but I appreciate it. Especially the help. I haven't had time to YouTube hoof clipping, so I could use the advice."

"Then come on and I'll show you."

Back in the pen, he went from goat to goat, lifting their hooves so he could get a look at them, finally finding one who needed attention. I walked her out with a lead and to the stand, which she climbed on willingly when she heard the plink of feed in the bucket. In went her head, closed went the catch, and she nibbled happily, unaware that she was about to get handled.

Clippers in hand, Jake stepped up to the goat and lifted her hoof to show me how to clean out the muck and where it could be clipped. She was fine until he used what looked like heavy-duty scissors to trim off the outer ring of her hoof.

He tightened his grip until she quit fighting, explaining all the while how to hold her and what to do. And the why of it—domesticated goats didn't traverse the kind of terrain to wear down their hooves, and letting them grow over could change their gait and eventually cripple them. Or their hooves could get infected and make the goat sick. So he did the one, and then he passed the clippers to me.

I stared at the ass end of the jumpy goat, trying to hype myself up.

"You've got this," he said. "Just hang on to her and don't pick up her leg until you're at her side."

"All right." I took a step closer, putting my hand on her rump to reassure her.

Instead, her leg shot out like a hammer, nailing me square in the ribs.

I stumbled back, the wind knocked out of me again, though somehow I was still standing. It took me a second to realize that was because Jake was holding me up.

Coughing, I hinged over, my hand pressed to my burning ribs. "Holy shit," I wheezed.

"I shoulda gotten a different goat when I saw her jumpy, goddammit. I'm sorry."

I waved a hand and hobbled toward the barn.

"Hang on. Let me make sure you're okay."

Painfully, I straightened up, and with immense care, Jake pressed my ribs and side. I only winced a little, spending an exorbitant amount of energy keeping my game face on.

"Well, if it were broken, you wouldn't have been able to play it tough," he said. "Come on. Let's get you some ice and a bed."

I nodded, and he wrapped an arm around me to keep me steady.

BET THE FARM

"You gotta quit getting yourself hurt, Livi."

"Funny," I rasped, "since I only get hurt when you're around."

"You're right. My elaborate plan to get rid of you revolved around you getting trampled to death."

"I knew it."

"How about I clip their hooves for now. You can still milk them, though."

"Thanks for the permission. Are you gonna sell them since I can't live up to our deal?"

"Nah. Those kids in their pajamas are worth the trouble."

An unbidden chuckle slipped out of him. I thought he might be tickled. Tickled *pink* even.

When we made it to the house, Kit intercepted, fussing over me as I flopped down on the couch. She went for ice, and Jake knelt next to me.

"I'm gonna go finish up with Sharon and get her off the stand. You all right?"

I nodded.

A little smile brushed his lips. "Don't worry, farmgirl. You'll get the hang of it. Let's just hope you don't break any ribs while you're doing it."

My laugh turned into a cough.

"Thank you, Jake."

"I told you, I owed you."

"No, not just for the stand. For giving me a chance."

He glanced down, and I resisted the urge to slip my fingers into his dark hair.

"I should have done it from the start," he said.

"Either way, you're doing it now. Better late than never, right?"

"If you say so."

His hand rested on the cushion between us, and I covered it with mine. "I say so."

He looked up at me, our eyes locking, the connection

tangible. It lived in the tingling of my hand over his, in the beat of my heart, in the air between us, in the depth of his eyes. They were open, unguarded, a window to the man behind the wall.

"I've got you ice and some water, honey," Kit said as she rushed in, too busy with her burden to notice the way we flew apart or how quickly he stood.

"Here's some ibuprofen," she said, extending the pills. "And drink this."

I took the water and knocked the pills back, not realizing how dry my mouth was until the cool water rushed in.

"Where does it hurt?" she asked, searching my body with the ice pack in her hand.

"I'm, uh, gonna go get the goat," Jake said from his awkward position between me and the door.

I laughed again, but it hurt so bad, I was wincing within a breath. "You always get my goat," I joked.

At that, the tension in him eased. That little smile was back. "Do you ever take anything serious?"

"Not if I can help it."

With the shake of his head and the widening of his smile, he turned to go.

And for the first time, I wished he'd stayed.

PEW PEW

Olivia

I couldn't think of a single thing I didn't love about Fourth of July.

It was a day for barbecue and beer, swimming pools and suntans. Ice cream and popsicles and shorts with flip flops. It was sparklers and music and people you loved. It was a celebration of America's birthday, and for better or for worse, we loved her and hoped for a brighter future together. It was a day never short on happiness, wonder, amusement, leisure. Of remembrance and hope.

And this Fourth of July might have topped them all.

I'd been busy most of the day, but thanks to the addition of a few new women to the staff, I hadn't once felt like things weren't being handled.

Courtney and Kendall had jumped on the chance to help me plan the event and manage it today. Together, we'd booked two dozen local vendors for the market, and we'd hired a carnival to provide games and food, placing them as far from the livestock as we could get them. The brightly colored bouncy house, two-story blowup slide, human-sized hamster balls, and bungee trampoline had been packed all day. But the real star of the show was the massive inflatable Slip 'N Slide I'd found. To watch so many adults turn into kids again, giggling and belly-flopping, was some sort of magic.

We'd also scrounged up food trucks with everything from tacos to ribs to donuts and an ice cream truck to boot. Music played all over through a speaker system we'd set up, playing classic rock and honky-tonk with the occasional country song mixed in for good measure.

Fourth of July wasn't Fourth of July without a little Reba.

And so as dusk settled in on a very busy day, I sat on my front porch, watching all the smiling faces with a smile of my own. Jolene lay stretched out on her back next to me, gnawing on a rawhide pinned between her paws. Willie Nelson played in the distance, the sky a shade of deep violet. Naked bulbs stretched out in zigzags over the whole operation.

It'd cost a small fortune, but we'd made a moderate fortune. And what I hoped would be a new town tradition had brought the community together in a way I believed would last. I wanted our farm to be a permanent fixture in their holidays. Pumpkins in the fall, Christmas market and trees in the winter, Easter egg hunts in the spring.

If I was here that long. The way things were looking, I thought I might have a chance.

Ironically, that was in large part thanks to Jake. Before the door debacle, he'd said he'd stay out of my way when he didn't mean it. But this time, he'd stepped aside. It helped that I included him and didn't openly defy him—quiet defiance was still occasionally underway, though only with inconsequential things, which he deliberately looked the other way on. There was some grumbling, some money crunching, and some compromise, but he'd even gone out of his way to help me. This event was the big test.

For the first time, I saw the possibility of a happy partnership.

Movement at the edge of the crowd caught my eye, and from the throng emerged Chase Patton, hands in his pockets and a smile on his face as he strode toward me.

Warmth bloomed on my cheeks, my fingers moving to fiddle with a lock of hair. I'd seen Chase a few times, mostly at Buffalo Joe's when I went with Presley. Being around him felt like a cardinal sin. A Patton and a Brent, friendly.

But he was impossible not to like. I probably should have assumed whatever he said was some sort of trap, but I couldn't seem to muster up the energy.

Chase climbed the steps. "Hey," he said.

"Hey back," I answered.

When he leaned toward me, I froze, hoping to God he wasn't going to kiss me. At the last second, he winked, making for Jolene.

"There's my girl," he cooed, scratching her belly before glancing back at me. "Sorry—didn't see you there."

Laughing, I gave him a little shove. "I didn't expect to see *you* here."

"I wanted to see what you did with the place." He picked up Jolene and sat next to me, holding her like a baby to scratch her belly. "I'm damn impressed. I don't think this town's seen such a to-do in twenty years. And it looks like you've pulled people in from all over."

"The power of social media."

He chuckled. "Your Instagram in particular. I swear, I don't think I've heard Courtney and Kendall so excited about something since the cheerleading squad made the local championship. And let's be honest—the bar was low on that account. How do you come up with all that content? You're putting our team to shame. Not too hard, considering our team is one guy named Dan."

"I dunno. It's just second nature, I guess. Life amuses me, especially the awkward parts. So I take a cute picture, make a little joke. Ninety percent of it is unscripted."

"I hope so, because if you'd planned to get kicked by a goat last week, it'd be a whole new level of crazy."

"I still have a bruise," I said, lifting the hem of my tank to expose my ribs where the green ghost of a bruise still sat. "Sharon knocked the wind out of me—apparently, she wasn't the goat to learn how to clip hooves on."

"Sharon, Brenda, Barbara, Susan. Do they get together regularly for Avon parties?"

"Tupperware. And the occasional game of canasta. Linda is the top of the phone tree, though. Don't let Patty tell you otherwise."

He shook his head, rolling his lips to pretend to suppress a smile. "You're something else, you know that?"

"Why, thank you, sir. I generally shoot for tolerable to adequate, so it's good to know I'm hitting the mark."

"How about I buy you a drink and we'll see if I can't win you one of the big stuffed animals?"

"Don't waste your money. Those are just a scam, you know—unattainable."

With a clever smile, he said, "Nothing's unattainable if you try hard enough."

"Spoken like a true rich guy," I teased.

He hissed and rubbed his chest. "You wound me. I don't know if you know this, but I'm an ace, and I'm feeling lucky tonight." With an endearing smirk, he added, "Plus, who doesn't need a pink three-foot-tall stuffed kangaroo?"

"I mean, anyone who says they don't is either a liar or a bore."

Chase set Jolene down and stood, extending his hand. "My thoughts exactly." When I took it, he pulled me up to stand. "What'll it be? Darts at the balloons? Rings on rubber ducks?"

"Dealer's choice." I scooped up my dog, enduring a tongue bath for the time it took me to go inside and put her in her crate. She squeaked and yelped as I walked away, and my heart broke.

"I hate leaving her like that," I said when I reached his side.

"You can't bring her with you?"

"She's too little for a leash. I practically have to drag her behind me. No one is happy in this scenario."

"I suppose not," he said on a laugh as we headed into the crowd.

Mistakenly, I'd thought that once the sun went down, people would disperse to watch fireworks, but there seemed to be *more* people. So many that we were nearly separated—until Chase took my hand to lead me through.

His hand was warm and strong, a confident hand. A hand that held mine with a certainty that didn't require permission, somehow managing not to feel like an invasion, which it technically was. But this hand was soft where Jake's was rough and worn. This hand didn't swallow mine, just held it chivalrously. Our skin didn't spark, my mind wasn't consumed by the contact. In fact, I'd only noted the differences because the gesture made me think of Jake.

I frowned, blinked. Unlinked us when we made our way through the thick of it. Felt eyes on me and looked over to find Kit and Mack staring at me with narrowed eyes from the cotton candy line.

Offering what I hoped was a reassuring smile, I shook my head and wiggled my hand subtly, attempting to dismiss their misunderstanding.

Pretty sure it didn't work.

With a sigh, I followed Chase until we stood in the golden glowing alley of carnival games.

Chase studied them as if his decision would alter the course of the universe. He pointed a finger gun at the tin bullseyes.

"Fate has decided. There are the kangaroos. And they have pink, as suspected. Your favorite color."

"Shooting guns to win my favor?" My brow arched, my smile tilting.

He leaned in, shifting his eyes. "Think it'll work?"

"Doubtful, but don't let it stop you from trying."

With an easy laugh, he offered his arm. And when I took it, I glanced around, hoping no one saw me arm in arm with Chase.

"Embarrassed to be seen with me?" he teased.

"What? No. I mean …" I stammered. "You have to admit, it's weird."

"Only if you make it weird."

I rolled my eyes. "You know what I mean. Our families have been after each other for more than a century. Every Patton and Brent has been bred to hate each other. You can't pretend like it's not strange for you and me to be strolling through a carnival together."

"Unexpected, sure. But what does a hundred-and-twenty-five-year-old feud have to do with us? I'm not my father. He's tried to put this grudge on me my whole life, but I don't want it."

"Then what do you want?"

He didn't answer as we pulled up to the stall and handed the carnie a twenty. "Well," he started, bringing the BB gun to his shoulder to look down the sight, "I'll tell you what I didn't want. I didn't want to treat you like I did when we were kids."

My brain jolted when he fired. The BB hit the tin with a satisfying ping.

"I didn't want to go to Frank's funeral. Not because I didn't respect him—I did. But because I thought it was so disrespectful that we were there." He pumped, lined it up, hit the red-and-white circle right in the eye. "And I didn't want to try to dupe you into working with us like my dad wanted me to."

Pump. Aim. Ping.

My breath caught. "You … what?"

"He wants me to help acquire you. Told me he'd put me in charge of our Maravillo farm when he leaves for Washington in a few months, if I could manage it."

Pump. Aim. Ping.

"Why are you telling me this?"

"Because I thought you should know," he said as he pumped air into the barrel and took aim again. *Ping.* "And the more I'm around you, the less inclined I am to help him."

Ping.

"And what will he do when he finds out you told me?"

A laugh. "I'm not planning on telling him. Are you?"

I shook my head stupidly.

"I know you said you and me are never happening, and I know how much of that is to do with the fact that you can't trust me. So here's me being honest with you in the hopes you'll reconsider. My father wants anything he can't have. He wants to end the feud in the way my grandpa did and his father before him. But I don't want to see you hurt. And I can offer inside information and protection against my father. Just think what a long way it'd go in mending the feud if we had something?"

Shock was too mild a word. I stood there mutely as Chase pumped the BB gun and lined up a shot, trying to parse what he'd just said. Patton had set Chase on us, and he'd told me because he wanted to ... date me?

Nothing made sense. But one thing I knew was that his proposition was impossible, not only for what it would do to my family here at the farm, but because I didn't want him.

There was someone else I wanted, someone I'd told myself I could never have. Once upon a time, that might have been true. But not anymore.

I saw it in Jake's eyes, felt it in his touch. I'd witnessed his kindness, the gentle care that lived in him. It'd just all been buried inside layer after layer of armor. But with every day, I'd earned his trust a little more. And one by one, the layers had fallen away, leaving only the man he really was.

And that was the man I wanted.

The realization was a whip crack, snapping my consciousness to attention.

When I caught myself, I packed the knowledge away to address the problem in front of me.

"Chase …"

He unsquinted an eye in order to glance at me, his lips higher on one side. "You're not going to shoot me down while I'm in the middle of winning your favor, are you?"

I laughed, my eyes flicking to the striped awning. *Ping.*

"Oh shit. You are."

When I glanced at him again, he was still smiling, though now it was resigned. "I get it. I'm the enemy, right?" *Ping.*

"It's not that," I lied, hating to let him down. "I just … I have a lot on my plate. I only have a few more weeks to turn a profit on the farm, or Jake's going to get it, and I'll have to leave."

"Right … the bet."

"The bet," I echoed ominously. "At least it's friendly now. A few weeks ago, I didn't know that I'd get a fair chance. But after today, I think I'll have put a big dent in the margin."

"I can't imagine you've made enough to cover *all* the debt."

My brows drew together. "I was referring to the cost of starting up the store and what it took to put today together. What do you know about our debt?"

Chase shrugged and lined up another shot. "I mean, everybody knows Brent was in trouble. I don't know how much, just that the debt's there."

He was lying, but I didn't know why, nor did I know what exactly about. But I made a note to find out.

I changed the subject, not willing to discuss the farm's finances with him any more than I already had.

He fired the gun again and hit another bullseye. The carnie scowled at him.

"You'd better watch out," I said out the side of my mouth. "I don't think Reggie is amused."

A chuckle. "Told you I was an ace."

I turned to face his profile, leaning my hip on the rail in front of the booth. "The truth is, I'm so busy here that I don't have time for anyone else. Not until the matter of my inheritance is settled."

"So what I'm hearing is, there's a chance."

I laughed. "That's what you heard, huh?"

Reggie interjected with, "Which one do ya want?"

"The pink kangaroo, if you would, Reggie," Chase answered.

With a sigh, Reggie used his stick with the hook on the end and brought down a big, fluffy marsupial with outrageous felt eyelashes. He handed it straight to me, giving Chase a look.

We wandered away, heading toward the funnel cakes.

Chase was quiet for a minute. "So once you win the bet and Milovic's all settled, you'll have more time. And then I'm going to take you on a date." When I laughed again, he added, "In the meantime, friends?"

"Friends."

"Great. Then how about brunch?"

"You're relentless. Has anyone ever told you that?"

"A time or two. It's genetic. And anyway, friends have brunch. We can go to Debbie's Diner when Presley's working, if you think we need a chaperone."

I gave him an amused look and sighed. "Rain check?"

"All right," he said, stopping. He turned to me and extended a hand. "But you're gonna have to shake on it."

I shifted my prize to my other hip and took the offering, giving his hand a pump.

"Now let's platonically share a funnel cake before my stomach loses its voice."

With a laugh, I followed him to the line as he told me about a camping trip the Joe's crew had all gone on, but I only half listened, too preoccupied to do anything but smile at him.

Jake was right. Patton was after us, and he was using Chase to do it. I'd been used, but Chase had come clean before I was taken advantage of. He was honest in an effort to build trust. I'd seen a glimpse of that little boy who'd shared his dessert with me in the fourth grade. The kid who'd been a friend to me when I'd been left alone in the world. And I couldn't help but imagine we *could* be friends. Maybe his honesty would bring Jake around.

Jake.

My heart climbed into my throat and stuck there.

It should have felt complicated. I should have shied away from the thought. But instead, I found hope. I found possibility. I found the thrill and fear that Jake could be everything for me, if we could uphold each other's trust.

And if he felt the same way.

HEIGHTS

Jake

From my perch in the hayloft window, I could see all that Olivia had done in a sweeping panoramic.

Below me bustled what appeared to be the entire town and half the town next door, the hum of the crowd far enough away that I couldn't make out a single voice other than the occasional burst of laughter or a cheer from the direction of the carnival games.

I'd spent the day going about my duties—heifers needed milking regardless of the holiday—and for a while, I kept myself busy in the barn where I could keep an eye on the animals we allowed to be petted, ready to pounce should the need arise. But it never did.

Little kids and plenty of adults stood beyond the pens, cooing and smiling at the animals. Olivia had rented a tent, and we'd put up a temporary pen for the goats and the piglets with a farmhand inside to help the kids and make sure no one got bitten. The calf pens were busy with people bottle feeding them through the fences.

I didn't think there was an unhappy face in the whole place.

Other than mine, I supposed. But that was just how my face looked.

But even I couldn't muster up a complaint, seeing everyone so happy. The delight on their faces as they fed a calf or held a carrot as a baby goat nibbled on it. After work, I'd gotten myself cleaned up and wandered around. Picked up some barbecue, had a couple of beers. Within about an hour, I had enough peopling, so I'd put Bowie to bed, snagged a sixer, and climbed up in the loft to watch.

It had taken me a long time for me to get what the Fourth of July was all about. Mama and I never celebrated, and it wasn't until I moved here that I even participated. But I didn't see the magic in it—it made me feel like an outsider until I became a citizen.

Something happens to you when you stand in a room and pledge your allegiance to a country where you've always lived but never belonged. A door opened that day, and when I walked through it, the meaning of days like today changed. People tended to forget the hope that this country was built on, but when you *chose* this place, when you fought to be here, when you had to earn your life … it all meant so much more than hotdogs and fireworks. Days like today reminded me of everything I had to be thankful for. And all because of Pop and this farm.

I owed him everything.

I took a sip of my beer in an attempt to open up my throat.

I'd unknowingly skipped out on my refugee review when Mama died. I thought they'd take me, send me to Croatia. I didn't even know the language, didn't know a single soul. And if they'd deported me, I never would have been able to come back. So I ran. And since I missed the review, I was up for immediate deportation. Keeping me here required a fight with government lawyers, which are some of the best in the country. To win, we needed the best. And the best wasn't cheap.

Sometimes it felt like I'd be paying off that debt until I took my last breath.

I'd happily work my fingers to the bone to honor it.

The crowd below me contained faces I knew and plenty I didn't. Some I hadn't seen in years, some I saw every day. But there was a sense of unbridled joy that floated up into the trees and to the stars, and I caught it as it rose. I watched Olivia as she watched the sunset from her porch, unable to ignore the deep gratitude I felt for her, for all of this.

Sentimental but true. The last few weeks had run smoothly now that we were working together. Occasionally, she'd mention the bet, and I'd just make a joke and change the subject. Because the truth was, I hoped she won.

I didn't want her to go.

Granted, I still thought she was bonkers. She ran into everything she did full tilt, no hesitation. She had a thought, then acted on the thought with bravery like I'd never seen. I didn't think she was afraid of anything. Except maybe failing. I got the sense she wouldn't take that well.

It was just another reason to trust her. That drive in her almost guaranteed success.

She'd said we needed each other, but I didn't know that I'd understood completely when she first said it, tears in her eyes and puppy in her arms. But every day, I realized it more. Every day, I found new reasons to appreciate her. Every day brought with it a little more ease, a little more trust. Sometimes, I'd see her from afar and feel a jolt in her direction, like the tug of a string. Or we'd be sitting in the kitchen, eating whatever dinner Kit had drummed up, the two of us together rather than apart, like we usually were. I'd smile. She'd laugh.

She lit up from the inside when she laughed, and I found I'd do all sorts of things I otherwise wouldn't have just to hear that sound.

I hadn't forgotten she'd laughed me out of the barn when I

almost kissed her. Truth was, we were too different for anything but what we had. And I wouldn't jeopardize that, not with us only just starting to see eye to eye.

I'd been a fool to fight her so long. But she'd been right about everything, and I figured it was high time I said so.

If I had to guess, our proceeds between the festival, the farm, and the shop pushed twenty grand. It'd more than make up for what she'd spent to get us here with room to spare. We'd officially be in the green on her venture and set to make real money.

For the first time since I'd come to the farm, I saw the possibility of paying our debt down and turning this place around. And it was all because of her. All I'd had to do was get out of her way.

I watched her as the sun set, thinking about all I'd said, all I'd done. She'd stayed despite my punishing her, and if that didn't turn her away, I wasn't sure what would.

Until Chase Patton slid up to her. Next to her. Made her laugh. Before they walked into the throng, he glanced up, met my eyes with challenge I could see even from here. And then they disappeared into the sea of people. By that time, it was getting too dark to pick her out—her red hair was usually the equivalent of a fire alarm in a crowd—so I sat there, scanning the aisles in the hopes that I'd find her. That, and fuming.

The knowledge that she was with *him* set my blood boiling. Part of me wanted to truck ass in there to put myself between them. The rest of me knew I'd only look like an asshole, Chase ever the hero. Plus, I'd end up saying something to her I didn't mean and set fire to everything we'd built.

I'd hurt her enough with the weapon of my words.

But Chase could sell heaters on the equator. Finding a way to convince her to sell would just be another Tuesday to him.

She'll never sell. Trust her.

Thing was, I did trust her. I didn't trust *him*.

Tell her. Tell her who he is. Tell her what he is.

He was charming, that she knew. But showing his face around here was enough of an insult. I couldn't take him coming for her on top of it. How she could hang around with him was beyond me. I might have said Frank was rolling over in his grave for the door, but this? This would have killed him. And I was sure if anyone close to this farm saw them, they'd think the same.

I didn't know that Olivia disliked anyone other than me on occasion—everybody got a fair shake with her. Even Chase Patton, and that worm didn't deserve the favor.

They were gone the length of two beers. I heard their voices as they approached the big house, noted the ridiculous kangaroo hooked in her elbow, watched him kiss her cheek. Her laugh rode the breeze, and I hated him for summoning it. When he finally walked the fuck away like I'd been willing him to, he looked up at me again, and I swore I saw him smiling.

But the motion caught Olivia's eye too—when my gaze shifted back to her, she watched me with her head tilted. A small wave, and she deposited her burden on the porch before walking in my direction.

I took a long swig of my beer, figuring I'd need it.

She stopped beneath me, smiling up. "Got any more beer?"

"A couple."

"I'll be right up."

My stomach climbed into my rib cage when she disappeared into the barn, and I took a second to make sure everything was suitable for her. I didn't know why—it was a barn, for God's sake. But she had on cutoffs, and the hay would make her legs all itchy. So I set my open beer back in the case and grabbed a horse blanket off a hook nearby to spread it out at the edge of the gable.

Her head came into view as she reached the hayloft. "What are you doing up here?"

I shrugged one shoulder and grabbed a fresh beer for her, twisting off the top to a hiss of carbonation. "Just watching."

"Color me unsurprised. You're not a doer." She took a seat

next to me with a mischievous look on her face and accepted the offered beer.

"Please, I do more than you could manage in a day. I've seen you shuck hay."

At that, she laughed. "I really am bad at everything around here."

I jerked my chin toward the fair. "Not everything."

She brought the beer to her smiling lips and took a drink. I watched those lips a little too long.

"Not too shabby, is it?" she asked, appraising her domain.

"Nothing short of miraculous, if you ask me."

Her face swiveled in my direction. "Did you just compliment me?"

I chuckled and took a sip. "Don't let it go to your head, farmgirl."

"Have you ever met me? I am most definitely putting that in my Thank Bank for later."

"Your ... thank bank? You don't mean ..." I couldn't finish the sentence. I eyed her instead.

"My thank bank. Things I'm thankful for that I can rifle through if I'm sad."

"Only you." I took a sip so she wouldn't see my amusement.

She crossed her ankles and swung her feet a little. "It's scarier up here than I remember."

"When was the last time you were up here?"

She waggled her brows at me.

The night I kissed her a million years ago. "No. Really?"

"Really." She leaned back a little, propping herself on one locked arm. "I like it up here. It's quiet."

"Not tonight."

"Compared to down there it is."

"Which is why I'm up here."

Her gaze swept the crowd. "Seeing it from this perspective, it ... makes you feel both big and small, doesn't it?"

"It really does."

"You'll be happy to know we made a killing."

"Good. Now I only regret it a little."

She shook her head and bumped my shoulder.

"So are you gonna tell me what Chase wanted?"

Even in the dim glow from the lights below, I saw her flush. "Just to say hi."

"He win you that pink monstrosity?"

"As a matter of fact, he did, and please refer to her by her Christian name—Esther P. Higgenbottom."

"You should feed Miss Higgenbottom to the goats."

Her mouth popped open. "You take that back."

"She'd last all of twenty minutes before those bearded garbage disposals finished her off."

She swatted at my arm, and I pretended to flinch. "You're terrible, Jake."

"What do you even do with that thing?"

"Lay in her lap and let her tell me about her homeland."

"In the back of a carnie truck? Bet she's got some stories to tell."

"I'm eager to hear about her travels to exotic lands, so please, don't joke."

"I assume she was with you and Chase. Think I can get her to tell me what you talked about?"

"Oh, I think you know where her loyalty lies."

I let the bit go in favor of laying my full attention on her. "What did he want?"

"Nothing in particular." She squirmed and took a drink. "We're just friends."

"Does he know that?"

"He does now."

I stilled. "Did he come on to you?"

"Not in that *come on to you* kind of way, but he asked me out. Again."

A flash of jealous fury. I pressed it down. "Again?"

"And I told him no both times." She rolled one shoulder and looked out over the crowd.

"You don't think that's fishy?"

"Why would that be fishy? Are you saying I'm not hot enough to get his attention?" she baited, one eyebrow arched.

"No, that's not what I'm saying—"

A smile curled her lips. "Oh, so you *do* think I'm hot?"

I gave her a look. "He wants the farm, Olivia."

"His father wants the farm. Also, I take your avoidance to answer the question of my hotness as a yes."

"I never said that."

"You implied." She smiled sideways at me as she took a drink.

"The Pattons have been after the farm for generations. You really think Chase hasn't been brainwashed by his father?"

"Does it matter? I'm not going to sell to him."

"Are you gonna sleep with him?"

Olivia laid a hard look on me. "That is none of your business, Jake."

"My business partner sleeping with our enemy is absolutely my business."

Her chin lifted in defiance. "No, I'm not going to sleep with him. I know it's hard enough for you all to see me with him just as friends. I can't imagine what it'd do to poor Kit if I dated him."

"Chase doesn't date. Just so we're clear."

Her face tightened.

"He doesn't do honest, either. Chances are, he's sleeping with Amanda."

"Doesn't Amanda have a boyfriend in San Francisco?"

All I had to do was look at her.

She crumpled a little. "How do you even know that?"

"Nothing is a secret here. You know that."

But she shook the information off, straightening up. "It doesn't matter. We're friends."

"But why *him*? You have Presley. You have me—"

Again, one brow rose. "Because you've been so accommodating."

"You know what I mean. You have the girls you've been hanging out at Joe's with."

"Seriously, how do you know this?"

"Because she told Kendall, and Kendall is the biggest gossip in the tri-county area. She might as well have a bullhorn in her hand at all times, and she's been on every inch of this farm over the last couple of weeks. So why—of all the potential friends you have to choose from—why Chase?"

"So I can only be friends with women? Granted, you've got your fair share of toxic masculinity to overcome, but I didn't think it went *that* far."

A frustrated sound reverberated in my throat at her needling. "Chase isn't just any guy, and you know it."

"Okay, okay," she said gently, her hand resting on my bicep. "I'm sorry."

"It's fine," I grumbled. "But you still haven't answered me."

For a second, she was quiet, her attention sliding over to the pastures on either side of the drive where the people wandered.

"He's easy to be around, and he's ... well, he's not as bad as you've made him up to be in your head." She seemed to want to add to the thought but let it go. "Plus, it's nice to be wanted. That's all."

A mixture of anticipation and a rush of bravery wrested my heart, my lungs. "You don't want to be wanted by him. He'll only ruin you."

"It's nice all the same."

"He's not the only one who wants you."

Her face turned to mine. "He's the only one I know of."

"Well, I think we can agree there's a lot you don't know."

"You've been teaching me everything else. Why stop here?"

The air between us was charged, flecks of hay dancing in the air around us. "Olivia ..."

"Do you have something you want to tell me?" she asked quietly, closer to me than before. I didn't know if she'd moved or if I had.

"I …" My gaze caught on her lips, then my thumb as it tested the cushion. Her jaw was in my hand, I noticed.

"Yes?" It was a whisper.

The tension between us was unbearable, the fight in my chest at an impasse, a pair of locked horns. My mind was a void. Time was a vacuum. I stared at her lips.

"Oh, fuck it," she breathed, and then she was in my arms.

Our lips met with almost a bounce—hard from surprise, then soft in desire—as I gathered her up, felt the shape of her in my arms. Held her like a delicate thing, a precious thing, a thing to be treasured, this woman who could stop a thunderhead with a word.

I noted every detail of her with the obsession of an artist who'd seen a thing that would disappear. Her lips, soft and sweet—she tasted of sugar, did she taste like this everywhere? I needed to know. I needed to feel the press of our bodies, to mark how she fit against me with a familiarity I shouldn't possess. I traced her neck with my fingertips as our lips parted, a soft seam. I knew every line of her, knew without knowing the way the curve of her waist would fit my hand. I knew her mouth, not from the clumsy kiss so long ago. I knew it because she was mine.

Mine. The word was a rush of thunder, a roar in my ribs, the knowledge pure. I couldn't fathom how I hadn't known. How I'd missed something so plain, so clear.

With a shift, I rolled us, fitting my hips against hers, pinning her with my lips, with my hand on her face. A long flex against her, and she mewled.

You can't have her.

I broke away with a pop of surprise, staring down at Olivia. Pale skin, eyes closed. Rosy cheeks, lips plump.

You can't keep her.

I rolled off of her, staring out the window at the oak trees, scrubbing a hand over my lips.

This was a mistake. As right as it felt, I knew it was wrong. We were partners, and if we did this, I'd drive her away. Somehow, I'd lose her too.

"Jake?" she said. Her hand found the small of my back.

"I ... I'm sorry. I shouldn't have—" I scrambled to my feet.

She shifted to sit, her face bent with confusion. "What do you mean? What's wrong?"

"I can't ... we can't ..." I raked a hand through my hair and headed for the ladder. "I'm sorry."

"I'm not. Please, come back and talk to me."

My feet were four rungs down when I chanced a look at her. "I can't."

"Is this about the bet? Is it about the farm?" she asked frantically, moving to crawl in my direction with rejection all over her.

I stopped. "No. Or not exactly. But we can't do this. You know we can't. I shouldn't have kissed you—"

"I kissed *you*."

I shook my head and started down the ladder. "It shouldn't have happened. Goodnight, Olivia."

"Don't say goodnight to me, asshole," she said with a rough voice and tears in her eyes as she threw a handful of hay at me. It rained down on me, sticking in my hair and fluttering down to the floor.

I jumped the last few rungs, hurrying for the back of the barn where I could cut to my house without her seeing me again. I didn't want to hurt her any worse than I already had. But I couldn't pretend like if I did what I wanted with her that it'd be casual. And I couldn't pretend like it wouldn't kill me when she left me here like anybody with a brain knew she would.

So I stormed across the property in the dark like a thief.

She didn't follow me.

But I wished more than anything she had.

F IS FOR

Olivia

I LOOKED LIKE SHIT.

It was a fact, not negative self-talk. My face was puffy from crying all night, and no amount of scrubbing would loosen up the mascara from my lashes, not without losing a hefty portion in the process. It'd been calcified by my tears.

I wished I were kidding.

Pop's office was warm that afternoon even with the windows open, my neck dotted with sweat and my hair piled on my head. I'd been in here for a few hours going through Pop's things, digging through his drawers in search of treasure. And I found quite a bit, everything from a tiny Holstein cow from a farm set I'd had as a girl to one of his wooden snuff boxes. A pair of six-pound scissors that could have decapitated an intruder sat on the leather desk pad next to a handful of unexpectedly fascinating rusty nails.

Essentially, Pop's office was a gigantic junk drawer.

Of course, when I opened up the file cabinets, I discovered records going all the way back to a ledger from the late 1800s. I pulled the most recent set when I found some of my drawings stuffed haphazardly into the folders and promised myself I'd go through them.

Jolene was going to town on an old rope she'd discovered under his ancient glass-doored bookcase, and I eyed the scissors, wondering what part of Jake I should cut off first.

I relived the shame I'd felt last night as I climbed down the ladder with hay in my hair, bleary-eyed and miserable and desperate to be alone. The house had been silent as a tomb until Jolene heard me and started howling, not stopping until she was in my arms. And with that, I was up the stairs and facedown in bed until the sun came up.

Well, that wasn't exactly true. I lay on my back too, staring at my ceiling with tears in my ears. There was also a stretch where I watched out the window as everything wound down, the lights going down and gear loading out. Courtney had said she and Kendall were on it, and I'd put all my faith in them because I didn't know if I could get out of bed to smile my way through the rest of the night.

So I'd spent most of the day wandering around, hoping to run into Jake after the supreme rejection he'd laid on me. The time it took me to milk Alice was occupied with rattling annoyance with the whole affair. Like *me* having to kiss *him*. Or that we had *literally* been a millimeter from a *literal* roll in the hay before he rejected me. While I dewormed the goats—which wasn't as gross as it sounded, though no one enjoyed the process—I was just mad. Mad at his stupid, manchild, *I'm sorry, but I can't use words* line. Mad at his stupid mouth for kissing me back like it did. Mad at his hips and the python between them that he'd promised but didn't deliver.

But when I came inside without seeing him—thus giving me a place to actually dump my rage—my emotions dwindled down to sadness alone. Because I wanted Jake and not just for the hayloft. But he'd made it clear how he felt about me. About us. He'd left me crying in the barn with nothing but a halfassed apology and no explanation.

And I wanted an explanation.

Jolene and her rope went all blurry when my eyes filled with miserable, frustrated tears. So I got myself up, stuffed my feet in my rain boots, and marched toward the big barns. Somebody would know where he was.

White-topped barns stretched out in rows across a wide spread of land, bracketed by pastures. Each herd—between thirty and fifty a pop—had their own interior barn with access to grass and extended time in the pastures. I caught sight of a couple of our guys, one of them pushing a wheelbarrow. I must have been a sight, storming through the yard in sweat shorts, my boots, and my hair a mess, because they both stopped and stared at me like I might bite them.

Depending on whether or not the wind changed, I might have.

"Hey, Joey—have you seen Jake?"

They glanced at each other and had a silent drawing of straws.

Joey lost. "Heifer check. Barn F."

F for fucking jerk. I was already stalking in that direction. "Thanks."

"Don't tell him I told you," he called after me.

I gave him a thumbs-up without looking back.

You'd think that the vet would be the one to do heifer checks, but it was really the job of the overseer to make sure the upcoming calves were faced the right way—a task learned early. The vet had enough to worry about than checking the entirety of the pregnant herd. I'd only done it once—my arms weren't quite long enough for me to be of much use.

When I rounded the corner into the partitioned portion of barn F, I was met with the most satisfying thing I'd seen all day—Jake's face against a heifer's ass with his arm buried up to the shoulder in a cow's vagina.

F for funny.

I snorted, covering my nose with my hand when a couple of farmhands gave me a look.

At the sound, Jake's eyes snapped to mine, and the hard eye contact stopped all illusion of being professional.

Laughter bubbled out of me as Jake gave instructions and they shifted the calf inside.

"What do you want, Olivia?"

I rolled my lips and bit down to try to stop my laughter.

"I'm kind of busy here."

"I can see that." I paused, contemplating my next move. "I don't know if I can say what I need to say with your hand up Gertie's lady parts."

Another hard roll of his eyes.

"I mean, you are *inside* of her. She's literally never seen so much action."

"Jesus, Olivia," he grumbled.

The farmhands snickered. Jake cut them a look.

"Seriously. Artificial insemination is about as anticlimactic as it gets, but this? Pretty sure you just got three cows over there pregnant."

One of the guys cleared his throat to cover another chuckle.

"It's indecent, Jake. Honestly."

"Are you gonna tell me what you need or just stand there making stupid jokes?"

"You really want me to tell you now?" I folded my arms in challenge. "Right now, in front of Gertie and everyone?"

"I really want you to go away."

"Fine. I need to talk about how you manhandled me in the hayloft and then ran off without an explanation."

The room was still other than for Gertie, whose jaw was working a mighty lump in her mouth.

"You asked."

Jake expertly removed his hand from the cow—only *light*

slurping, squishing sounds—and peeled off a shoulder-length glove.

He jerked a chin at the farmhands. "Put Gertie out to pasture and bring me the next one in five minutes."

Their gazes bounced between us, still suppressing smiles as they did as they'd been told, leaving us alone. From other humans, at least.

"Five minutes, huh?" I snapped. "Glad to see you're devoted to the conversation."

"You make it so easy when you act like a teenage boy," he said from the sink.

I chewed up the space between us, talking all the way. "Why? What the hell are you doing? Why would you do that to me?"

"You kissed me," he reminded me.

"You kissed me back and threw me into the hay like you were going to take me right then and there. And then *poof*—you were gone. And I want to know why."

"This is stupid, Olivia."

I paused, watching him wash his hands. "This conversation or kissing me?"

"Both," he said, turning off the water with a squeak.

My lungs emptied. "Wow."

He shook his head, his lips pursed, frustrated.

Well, me too, buddy.

"We can't do this."

"You said that last night. But you didn't say why."

He turned to face me, dark from brow to boot. His hands hung low on his hips, and I almost looked down, my heart fluttering at the thought.

"I don't understand why I have to explain. We're currently stuck in a game of tug-of-war for the farm. All we ever do is fight—"

"That's not true. We've been better—"

"Nothing about us makes sense."

"Who said anything about making sense?"

He shook his head and glanced off, his jaw flexing. "We're not doing this. It's a bad idea, and you know it. We have dire things to address, and it's hard enough to work with you without complicating it any more than it already is."

I let out a sharp breath through my nose, my eyes leveling him. "Why do you always get to decide? You decide everything, and I'm just supposed to follow your biblical law without question. Maybe you're right. We don't make sense. I'd never lower myself to be with someone who has so little respect for my thoughts and feelings."

"Now come on—"

Angry tears filled my eyes, the pitch of my voice climbing. "Just because *you* don't have any feelings doesn't mean no one else does. Maybe it'd be easier for you everyone else kept it to themselves, but guess what? Life isn't easy. And I'm not willing to put up with some jackass who can't use his words just because he's a goddamn good kisser." I pointed at the front of the barn where the backward shadow of the letter F stood. "F is for *Fuck You*, Jake."

I turned on my heel and pushed out of the barn, nearly running into the guys who'd just left. But they were nothing but blobs of color behind a curtain of tears.

T-R-O-U-B-L-E

Olivia

IT WAS MY TURN TO AVOID JAKE, AND I'D DONE A KICKASS JOB at it, if I did say so myself.

I stayed out of his domain, and he stayed out of mine. He spent his days with cattle, and I spent mine working on my marketing schedule for next month. The biggest focus would be the newsletter, which I'd grown exponentially every week since we'd opened the farm to the public. Everyone who joined the newsletter on our website was issued a coupon for fifteen percent off in the store. I'd done half a dozen giveaways on Instagram with best-selling goods from the shop in exchange for their subscription. Our profits were up, and that fact didn't require Jake to believe in it to be true. But the trouble was, I didn't know exactly what I was working against when it came to the farm's debts.

My last conversation with Chase had left me curious. If he knew the extent of our debts, everyone knew. Except for me. I couldn't make sense of the numbers, and Ed didn't do much to help beyond some cursory explanations that did little to clarify what I was looking at.

BET THE FARM

So once I stopped fantasizing about braining Jake with a crowbar, I threw myself into organizing Pop's office.

Which was where I found myself that night.

I'd eaten two meals in his office, both delivered and tidied up by Kit, who'd eyed me with a dubious look on her face and no small amount of concern. But she didn't question me, just let me organize the collection of randomness that was this room.

It was after ten that night, and the last hour had consisted of a hundred yawns and a crawl through what I had left in Pop's file cabinet. Determination drove me to keep going—I was too close to being finished to quit now. So I leaned into the filing cabinet from my office chair with an aching back, putting the files I'd just gone through back where I'd found them and exchanging them for the very last set.

They'd been buried in this drawer since who knew when. I'd thumbed through them before I started, searching for anything that stood out, but it'd seemed like just a whole bunch of the same thing.

But when I landed on a thick file titled *Jake* stuffed in the very back, my heart stopped.

I held my breath as I swiveled in my chair, my eyes never leaving the folder. I set it down. Opened it.

My eyes moved too quickly to comprehend all they saw, my hungry hands flipping the pages.

Immigration papers flew across my field of vision. Legal letters and court notes. Lawyer invoices. Release paperwork from immigration holding. Copies of the first mortgage. Government forms. And all of them wore Jake's name alongside Pop's.

I reached the end of the stack. Flipped it over. Started again, slower.

They weren't in any sort of order, so I put them in stacks by date. First the release paperwork from ICE—a year after I'd left, Jake had been placed in custody. They'd taken him from the farm, and some legal documents showed that Pop had hired a big immigration lawyer out of San Francisco to get Jake back.

The paperwork applying for the mortgage on the farm was just a few days later.

Legal receipts totaled tens of thousands—near two hundred thousand, I gathered from some sloppy, scribbled math I jotted on the back of the folder.

I sat back in my seat, staring at the number.

Pop had mortgaged the farm for Jake.

They'd taken Jake, and Pop fought for him with every penny he had. All of his equity. The safety of the farm. His legacy and his life's work.

He'd put all his money on the boy he barely knew and for no other reason than because it was the right thing to do.

And the farm had never recovered.

My throat closed up, my nose stinging and vision blurry. All this time, I'd thought Jake was just being stubborn. That he didn't want me here because I was an outsider, that he didn't want change because it made him uncomfortable. And while all that might be true, there was a bigger reason, a reason beyond me.

This farm's debt was his, and he'd carried the weight of that burden for so long, you could see the toll it took on him once you knew what you were looking for.

Everything slid into focus like I'd twisted a telescope lens. I replayed fights, relived conversations fresh as daylight. No one had told me. And why would they have? I was seventeen—Pop wouldn't have put the weight of the farm's finances on me at that age. He wouldn't have troubled me with the news that he'd sponsored Jake's immigration, knowing it would have worried me, especially when coupled with the questions I'd surely ask about money. I would have come home the second I was able if I'd known. And he'd known that too.

Jake's silence was warranted. I imagined that with the state of our finances, he carried an undue share of responsibility and shame, and I wondered just how he'd punished himself for it over the years. Especially now, with Pop gone and me here. Invading.

Spending what little money we had on a whim, changing things without realizing what I was doing, without understanding how I was hurting us.

Hurting him.

I scooped up the papers and slapped them into the file, clutching it to my chest as I hurried out of the office. I slipped my feet into my rain boots with my heart beating so hard, the file trembled gently from the rhythm.

The screen door slapped the frame behind me, but I was already down the stairs and on a path straight for Jake's house.

I didn't know. I didn't know. I didn't know, my mind echoed with every set of footsteps across the yard and up to his door. My knuckles rapped sharp on his screen door. I swiped tears from my cheeks, looking greedily into his living room for any sign of him.

Bowie barked, the sound of his nails slipping on the hardwood growing louder as he approached.

"Slow down, buddy," Jake said on a chuckle from somewhere beyond my vision.

He was smiling down at Bowie when he came into view. But when he looked up and found me, he stopped, his smile falling. I didn't care about his flat lips or any of the sharpening squares of him at the sight of me. It didn't matter. Because now I knew.

Nothing was what I'd thought it was.

Slowly, he started toward me.

"What do you need?" he asked. It wasn't quite rude. It wasn't friendly, either.

"Can I come in?"

He glanced at the bundle of papers clutched in my arms. "What's that?"

"Please, can I come in?" I couldn't seem to say anything more, my voice wavering. My brain had devolved to single-thought processing.

Jake's lips went from flat to turned down just a little. But he pushed open the door and held it so I could enter.

I flew through the threshold and past him, whirling around as soon as I was inside.

Puzzled, he turned to face me. "What the hell's gotten into you—"

"I found the papers," I blurted.

"What papers?"

I shoved the folder into his chest—if I spoke, I'd burst into tears.

He looked down. Took them. Angled them out for inspection. Understanding hit him.

When he met my gaze, his eyes churned with sadness, regret. Pain. "Where did you find this?" he asked quietly.

"Pop's office."

Silence. Then, "So now you know."

"Why didn't you tell me? Why didn't Ed tell me?"

"That the farm's debt was because of me? I asked Ed not to tell you—it's not his job anyway. But I figured you'd find out sooner or later."

I frowned. "They came for you. Pop helped you. You—"

"I ruined the farm."

"No—"

"*Yes*," he shot, instantly furious and arching over me. "All of this is my fault. He should have just let them send me away, but he wouldn't. He wouldn't let it go, said the farm would bounce back. It never did, so he took out the second mortgage. And now it's up to me to fix it."

"Not you. Us."

A dry laugh. "All you've done is put *us* in the hole. Sure, you're making it up, but there's no getting *this* back." He held up the file before slapping it on the table near the door.

"All this time, and I had no idea," I said with an air of wonder, unfazed. "I would have done everything differently if I'd known."

"I don't want your pity."

He brushed past me, but I grabbed him by the arm. He stopped.

"Jake, please," I begged gently. "Please don't walk away."

His nostrils flared when he looked down at me, but his eyes still broiled with feeling he wouldn't acknowledge. I wondered how long he'd been ignoring it. His whole life maybe.

"I'm not here to blame you for anything—I don't. You trying to stop Pop from helping you was useless, and we both know it. I'm not upset with you or with Pop ... I'm proud of him. He saved you, Jake."

"I know what he did."

"Please," I said again, urging him to turn, putting us face to face. "For one minute, please don't fight me. I came here to tell you I'm sorry. I'm sorry for the horrible way I've treated you—I didn't fully understand what this place meant to you. I'm here to say that I wish I'd known so I could have done more helping and less fighting. What I've done is so much worse than change the farm—I've put more financial strain on top of what you believe is your debt alone. But you don't have to do it alone anymore—I'm here, even if you hate me."

"I don't," he said, his voice rough.

"You don't what?"

"Hate you."

I shook my head at my feet. "You don't have to do that. It's all right."

"I don't hate you, Olivia. You drive me crazy, but I don't hate you. I've wanted you since I first met you. I've wanted you and covered it up with a fight. I've wanted you and denied it to myself. I'm tired of fighting it, Livi. So tired."

My gaze lifted to meet his, but I was too surprised and affected to speak. He stepped closer. I wanted him closer still.

"But you don't belong here." His eyes hung on my lips. "You're bigger than all this. And when you figure that out, you're gonna leave."

"How many times do I have to tell you I'm not going anywhere before you believe it?"

"I don't know if I *can* believe it."

"Because you don't trust me?"

"Because I don't think you know better. You *think* you're never going back to New York, but how could you know for sure? I haven't gone more than a hundred miles from this farm since I knocked on the door. I don't think anyone could argue where my home is. But eventually we're going to lose our shine, and you're going to leave, just like you did before. And then what?"

My throat closed with a painful squeeze. "So you'd rather have nothing than take a risk?"

His lips rose on one side. "I don't know if you've noticed, but I'm not exactly a risk taker."

"Maybe it's high time you tried it. Frank Brent risked his whole farm for you."

"And look at how that turned out."

"You're here, so I'd say it turned out pretty well."

He watched me, his brows together in curiosity. "How can you defend me after everything I've done? I've said things I don't mean and shouldn't be forgiven for."

"You're right. I should go." I pretended to turn, then smiled up at him when he chuckled.

"How do you always do that?" he asked, searching my face. "How do you take every hurtful thing that happens to you and twist it into something good? You've always done it, even when we were kids. Frank used to tell the story of your little pink suitcase you rolled up to the house with after your parents died. About how you dried your tears and put on a smile and unpacked your teddy bears. How you went a whole year and only wore pink because it made you happy. You have a Thank Bank, for God's sake. You should hate me, but you kissed me. You came here even to apologize when it's me who should be apologizing."

A hard swallow did little to rein in my tears, but I said, "I mean, I'll take an apology if you're handing them out."

Another laugh. "God, I am so sorry, Olivia. I'm sorry for every unkind word, every push, everything. But I don't deserve your forgiveness."

"Are you asking me to not forgive you?" I teased.

"Would you think less of me if I said it'd be easier to accept rejection if I asked for it?"

"No, I'd say it was pretty on-brand. And so would my inability to do anything but forgive you."

He shook his head with a pained sort of wonder etched on his face. "Why?"

"Because you're more than you believe you are. You're worth more than you know. But I see it—I've always seen it, even when you try to prove otherwise. This place, Pop—they're a part of you, and they're a part of me. All I've wanted is to prove my worth. To earn your trust. I'm not leaving, Jake. Where would I go? What would I do when part of me will always be here? I don't have to *make* good of everything—there *is* good in everything. I just have to find it. I've always known there's good in you too, if I was patient and persistent enough to get past Mad Jake."

His hand slipped into my hair, my jaw in his palm. He lifted my face so he could peer down into it. "But if I'm not mad, there's no way I'll be able to stay away from you."

The squeeze in my chest tightened at the admission. "Then don't stay away. Don't listen to Mad Jake. Nobody likes him anyway."

A laugh of surprise floated out of him, his chin tilting and eyes closing for a split second. "I'm not a fan of him, either."

"Don't fight anymore," I plead. "Don't fight me. Don't fight what you want. If you let go, you'll just float on what comes. It'll carry you instead of you pushing in the other direction. This fight, the one you've been fighting since I've known you … it's killing you. There's no way to be happy when all you do is buck against what you have. You have me, if you want me. Are you willing to walk away from that happiness? Or do you doubt I can make you happy?"

"Never. Not for a second, even in those stupid boots."

My heart flung itself into my sternum, and I smiled at him to cover my nerves. "See? You even like my stupid boots. You think my boots are cute *because* they're stupid, don't you?"

"Why do you always think you're right?" he asked with a smile that told me I was absolutely right.

"Because I usually am. It's just math at this point."

A chuckle. A look of deep longing.

"I won't hurt you, not on purpose."

"I know. You couldn't hurt a rabid bunny rabbit, not on purpose." He pulled me closer. "What if it's me? If you don't leave, I'll still lose you somehow. I'll drive you away without meaning to because I just don't know any better."

"I'm tougher than I look. I've taken it this long and I rose to the occasion. You can't scare me off, Jake. Because I understand. I know the why of it. Don't get me wrong—you'll still get in trouble, but I'll always forgive you."

He didn't respond, just watched me with that deep longing on his face.

"You still think it's a bad idea?"

A nod. And then, "I just don't know if I care enough to say no."

Relief and possibility and utter joy lit me up. The door from apart to together opened. All we had to do was step through the threshold.

"Kiss me," I said. When he didn't, I added, "It's inevitable—you said so yourself."

He looked down at me again, his smile fading into something hotter, something darker. "It's all I've thought about since I kissed you in the hayloft."

I stepped into him, erasing the space between us. "Another gentle reminder that I kissed *you*. Which is why it's your turn."

Jake caught my chin in his thumb and forefinger, angling for my lips. "I don't have a clue how much trouble I'm in, do I?"

"None whatsoever, but do it anyway," I joked.

And with a passing smile, he did.

The last kiss we'd shared was hot and hard, a frantic, fleeting moment. A meteor streaking through the night sky, burning out in the atmosphere.

This kiss was altogether more.

It was a press of lips, both timid and firm, his mouth against mine, both unsure and absolutely certain. I could feel the fight leaving him with every flex and release of his lips, with every sweep of his tongue. I felt the moment he gave up the ghost. It rode a deep inhale through his nose, lived in his tightened grip on the back of my neck. His body curled around me, and he was everywhere—every slide of his hands, every heavy breath another consumption. We were as close as we could get, our bodies flush, mine held in place with his arm snaked around my back.

I stretched up on my toes to thread my arms around his neck, wanting to be level with him where I could appreciate the sweet heat of his mouth. A squeeze closed the circle of my arms, and he took the cue, picking me up by the ass. My legs wound around his waist to lessen the burden, and I held on tight when he blindly turned us, the world spinning before he marched us toward his bedroom with a hand out.

I heard the thump of his foot opening the door, felt gravity shift as he laid me down. He took advantage of the spread of my legs to press his length against me. When his hand trailed down my leg and found my rubber rain boot, he chuckled into my mouth and broke the kiss so he could reach the heel of one. I watched him as he pulled off the first, then the second. He was lit only by the rectangle of glowing light from the threshold. The silhouette of his long body as he reached over his shoulder and pulled off his shirt. The line of his profile, the light kissing the rolling curves of his shoulders, his biceps, the swell of his pecs and square planes and deep valleys of his abs.

The vision was gone when he descended again.

His skin radiated heat through my tank, and every brush of skin-to-skin contact triggered a frantic wave of desire. My legs locked around his hips again, my hands roaming his chest, his waist, the curious mounds of muscle on his back, but my attention was fully engrossed in charting the path his hand made on my body. His fingers on my neck, his thumb along my collarbone, the sweep of my tank over my shoulder so his fingertips could taste the curve without interruption. The graze of my breast when he trailed down my ribs tightened my legs, set a whimper in my throat. At the sound, his hand stopped, backtracked, brushed the curve as I willed him to touch me.

He granted my wish with his palm cupping my breast, testing its shape. Learning the feel of me in his hand. Thumbing the peak with nothing between his skin and mine but a slip of cotton. At the sound of the moan low in my throat, I earned an answering sound and a squeeze that shot a bolt of electricity to the place our hips connected.

And I lost my patience. I'd gone too long without him, without this, to appreciate anything short of naked.

I tugged at the hem of my tank, and he leaned out of the way, watching his hand slide up my torso as my skin was revealed, pausing when my breasts were exposed. I was too busy pulling it off to notice he'd stilled, his eyes drinking in what they found. For a handful of heartbeats, I didn't move, only watched him watch me. And then I reached for him.

His lips found me first, then came the glorious press of his flesh against mine. I fumbled for his belt, pushing his pants over the swell of his ass. I felt him before I saw him, the weight of his length resting between my legs. With a satisfied sigh, I slipped my hand between us, held him in my palm as best I could, learned the shape of him with hungry fingertips. Another moan from him, a flex into my hand.

That sound—the sound of his pleasure—the feel of him against me, and my core pulsed once against nothing, anticipating him. And then it was him who couldn't wait.

A shuffle and a yank of my shorts, and there was nothing between us at all. He settled his hips between my thighs, kissing me still as his hands roamed, circled, stroked. And his lips followed. He rolled to his side, our legs tangled, gaining access to my neck, the dip of my throat, the tight peak of my nipple with the warmth of his mouth, his hand holding my breast where he wanted it. My hands didn't stay still either, finding his length again. I couldn't think with his mouth on me like that, with his fingertips that wandered south again, tracing the curve of my ass, my hip before slipping between my legs to return the favor.

And then there was nothing to do but hold him in my hand and feel his in me. He traced the rippling flesh between my thighs, taking his time with the tip of my desire, knowing where to stay by the unrecognizable sounds I made. I felt the creeping tingle of heat spread from low in my belly, up to my heart. Racing up the column of my neck, down my arms and legs, and I leaned back, laying a hand on his heaving chest. Because this was not the way I was going to come, not the first time.

He didn't stop as I panted up at him, my lids fighting to stay open as my purpose flitted in and out of conscious thought, which had been slim to start.

"Mmm, wait," I whispered.

His hand paused in its track. Mine found its way back to him.

"This. Not that," I mumbled, shifting to bring a knee up and angling him for me.

That goddamn smile. "Let me get a—"

He started to move for his dresser, and I stopped him with a stroke and the shake of my head. "Safe. And if you don't fuck me right now, I'm going to come without you."

It wasn't a lie, and he didn't fight me, just kissed me with those smiling lips and let me do what I would. I charted the line of my core with the tip of him—the kiss stopped. He breathed against my lips, his hand gripping my hip as the cleft of his crown slid over that aching peak, then down again, to the dip that longed to be filled by him.

With a long, slow flex, he slid into me.

I sighed, rolling my hips, arching my back until only his crown remained. And I took him again until he was fitted in me, grinding to press that place, the key to my pleasure.

A moan, and he rolled us onto my back. I urged him closer as I raced to the edge, wanting to feel the weight of him pressing me into the bed, wanting to feel all of him as my senses climbed, my awareness rushing to the point where we connected. I wanted him, all of him. His pleasure and his pain, his trust and his heart. Because no one would care for him like I could. No one could heal him like I would, this broken man with everything to give and no one to give it to.

I felt the longing, the need, the relief in him with every thrust of his hips, with every drag of his lips against my skin. He wanted all of me too.

As far as I was concerned, he could have me.

A hard thrust and a shift. I was caged, my pulse quickening. Lungs locked, chin tipped to the sky, eyes pinched shut.

And with a fatal flex, I came unraveled beneath him in a long, sweet shudder.

But he didn't slow. Didn't stop. Rode the rhythm at the pace I'd set, but with new intention. He rose so he could see me through hooded eyes, braced himself with one hand so he could grip my waist in the other. I could feel him close in the force of his thrust, in the surge of him inside me. He gasped, buried in me, pausing for a frozen heartbeat, and he came with a deep moan and a new, slow retreat and advance, drawing out his pleasure as if to feel every inch of me with every inch of him, strictly for appreciation's sake.

He didn't collapse, didn't roll over, but lowered his body onto mine slowly, bracketing my face with his hands, his fingers in my hair.

And he laid a kiss on me that shook the stars.

A long admiration, a sweet adoration, a praise to a thing we wanted, we needed.

Each other.

He pulled away to look down at me, to sweep my hair from my face, to trace the lines of its shape with his gaze, with his fingertips.

And I smiled. "If I'd known this was what I was missing, I would have made you kiss me a long time ago."

His laughter was a deep, rumbling sound in the cavern of his chest. Another kiss, this one brief.

"Stay the night, and you'll regret not making me kiss you the second you got off that plane."

Turned out that for once, he was right.

BOSSYPANTS

Jake

The sun was barely over the horizon, my room touched with shades of violet that would soon be buttery yellow, and Olivia Brent lay snoring softly in my arms.

I found it extraordinarily hard not to laugh.

She was naked as sin, our legs entwined and her arm draped over my waist. I'd woken with us just like this, though I'd leaned back a little to get a look at her face on hearing her snoring.

God, she was gonna be annoyed when I told her.

I couldn't wait. In fact, I almost woke her up just to fuck with her about it.

Her other arm was somewhere beneath her pillow, her cheek smushed up against the downy fluff and her lips parted just enough to see a sliver of teeth and the dark promise of her mouth behind them.

I almost woke her for that too.

But I couldn't bring myself to disturb her. Her hair was a mess of copper tangles—my fault—her skin creamy white. The covers rested in the bend of her waist, her breasts bare. My eyes stopped their roaming at the sight of the pale pink of her nipples, the peak smooth and soft. A rush of blood headed south at the thought of bringing them to attention.

Hell, maybe I'll wake her up after all.

A shift, and my lips pressed a kiss to the space between her breasts, brushed the curve, closed over the nipple I'd admired. She mewled sleepily, her hips flexing in my direction.

I abandoned my place in favor of another warm, welcoming space I'd acquainted myself with into the small hours of the morning. Beneath the sheets, the shape of her was dim, but I found my way just fine. She rolled onto her back, spreading her legs in invitation, her hand stroking my face, my hair, with infinite care.

In the haze of the morning, I couldn't seem to remember how it hadn't always been just like this. The time before last night was nothing but a memory, a faraway, forgotten dream. What a fool I'd been for not spending every minute I could right here, with her in my mouth, with her sighs in my ears, with the warmth of her waiting for me.

Now that I had her, I couldn't fathom her leaving—abandoning the farm wasn't on the list of probable outcomes. All that work I'd done to push her away had been to spite myself, and I wondered how I could hate myself so much that I'd ignored the gift of her.

I paid homage to one of what I suspected were many gifts that came along with her until she wriggled away and flipped over, redirecting me with an outstretched hand between her legs. Chuckling, I kissed my way up her back until what she wanted was in her palm, then diving into her slick center. I watched her, my hands guiding her by way of her hips, her face pressed into the bed in profile and lips parted with desire.

God, what an idiot I'd been. I could have had all of this, all of her, stupid fucking rain boots and everything. I couldn't even pretend to hate them anymore. In fact, I couldn't find a thing to be unhappy about. I'd made up every excuse to keep her away, and she'd erased them all, first by calling me on my bullshit, then with a kiss. Now with the rest of her. It was impossible to remember what the hell I'd ever been so mad about when buried to the hilt in her.

When she reached between her legs to feel me, my eyes rolled back in my skull, my lips pursing to stifle a moan. The sweetest sounds escaped her—I didn't know if I'd burgeoned or she'd tightened, but the pressure was so tight between us, I couldn't breathe. She came with a rush, a throb echoing from deep within me before I followed, spending all I had inside of her.

Her back prickled with sweat, and I tasted its salt as we sank to the bed and rolled to our sides. I curled around her, kissed her shoulder, the bend of her neck.

She hummed her approval.

The honest to God truth was that I'd thought she'd be more reserved in bed, but she was just as free, willing, open as she was in the rest of her life. She lived with a sense of abandon, a fearless life so heavy with hope, it was impossible to get her down. She was unstoppable, a necessary force of nature as potent as the sun.

I envied her that.

When she sighed, I could hear her smiling.

"Can you wake me up every day like that? I'd like to retire my alarm in favor of your mouth."

"I think that can be arranged. Should I make the *beep-beep-beep* while I do it?"

"Not if you want to keep me," she said on a laugh.

"Scratch that then. Want to go up to the big house and get breakfast? Let Jolene out?"

Olivia yawned. "She's probably torn up every pair of shoes in the house."

"Too bad you wore your boots over."

"You *love* my boots."

"I'd love to burn your boots, but they'd stink the place up for a week."

Giggling, she rolled over with a look on her face that did something warm and painful to my insides.

"What are you doing today?" I asked, already calculating when I'd be through with my day. When I remembered lunch, I was almost what you'd call giddy.

"Well, I have brunch at Debbie's, and I need to work on my promo plan for next month. Should definitely take some new pictures. That sort of thing."

"You going to see Presley at Debbie's?"

"I am. It's even more crucial now that I have all this tea to spill."

"Good thing you told Chase to fuck off, or I'd be worried."

Her face flattened. "Seriously?"

"What?"

"We're friends," she began, but I cut her off.

"You can't just *be friends* with Chase Patton."

Her face screwed up in anger. "You can't tell me who to be friends with."

"I can when it comes to him."

She huffed. "This is part of the problem—you won't even consider giving him a chance. Don't you see that I could mend fences? I could be a bridge. This old feud has to end, and this could be the way to do it."

"He just wants to fuck you."

"Jake!" she shot, shoving me in the chest. "Jesus!"

"I've known him longer than you, and I've seen him at work. He wants to fuck you and get a foot in the door here—you have to see that."

She was downright pissed, pulling the sheets to her chest as she sat up, glaring at me. "That is a horrible thing to say."

"Liv, I'm sorry if it came off wrong—it was an insult meant for him." I stroked her arm with my chest all twisted up, encouraged when she relaxed by a small margin. "What I mean to say is that you can't trust him."

She gave me a look. "You say that about everybody. You've said that about me."

"I was wrong about you. I'm not wrong about him."

Leaning in, she cupped my jaw. "Jake," she started gently, "You trust me, right?"

A single, willful nod.

"After last night, do you think there is *any* chance of me running off with Chase Patton?"

My eyes narrowed. I shook my head.

She smiled, satisfied. "Right. So I'm going to brunch *with Presley*, and when I get back, I am coming straight here, taking off my clothes, and getting into your bed where I will stay until you come in for lunch."

That earned her a smile—she'd been imagining lunch together exactly like I'd been. Naked. "Fine. But just for the record, I don't like anything that puts you and Chase in the same sentence, never mind building."

"Duly noted. And you're going to let me be friendly with Chase."

I watched her. "The Pattons capable of more than you know, and Chase is a trained liar. They want the farm. Just remember that for me."

"I promise. As long as you let me be a diplomat so we can put this whole thing to bed once and for all."

One of my brows rose. "I'd rather not involve Chase in any discussions involving beds, either."

"To pasture then."

"Better."

She leaned in to give me a tender kiss that turned into a breathless one. When I broke away, she was pinned under me.

"I thought you were hungry," she said with a smile.

"Oh, I am."

So I took my fill in the hopes she would ease my fears with the devotion of her body.

And it almost worked.

CALENDAR BOY

Olivia

I FLOATED TO THE DINER LIKE A CLOUD.

Not riding on top of a cloud, as one usually imagined. Not in a cloud, oblivious to the outside world. I was as thoughtless as a fluffy white cloud drifting across the horizon with a smile on my face and not a care in the world.

Jake and I had parted ways only after a very long, borderline disgusting display of affection. When we'd walked into the kitchen for breakfast half dressed, Kit took one look at us, squealed, and burst into happy tears. Jake looked terrified at Kit's state, seeing as how it was fifty percent directed toward him. His eyes were a couple of ping-pong balls, his cheeks a little flushed, his back straight as a ruler. I wondered if he'd ever brought a girl home like this to meet everyone and decided by the level of Kit's excitement that the answer was no.

But when the majority of her joy blast had been exhausted, she went back to the kitchen, and Jake and I had sat at the island, smiling at each other like a couple of dummies.

It was basically the best day ever.

We'd taken a shower together, and once I was dressed, he'd sent me off with *that kiss* and a long list of things to talk to Presley about.

I hated that Jake hated the thought of me being friends with Chase, but there wasn't any way around it. We'd all been bred to hate each other, and deprogramming from that was no small task. Jake was probably a lost cause. But Chase and I had a rapport. I wasn't so stupid to think he didn't have *any* ulterior motives, but I believed he was genuine after coming clean and offering inside information. He'd come to me if he heard anything, I was sure.

I'd been playing devil's advocate with Jake for months, but it'd taken us sleeping together for me to convince him to let me try to make peace.

Hopefully, it wouldn't take *that* to get Chase on board. If he had designs leading that direction, he was going to be real disappointed—and maybe end up with a broken nose, if Jake happened to find out.

I hadn't even told Jake what Chase had said about his dad and James Patton's designs, not wanting to give Jake any more fodder for the grudge.

Jake, Jake, Jake.

I smiled at nothing and sighed like a teenager as I slid into a booth at Debbie's.

"Well, what's gotten into you?" Presley asked from my elbow.

She looked adorable in her little blue uniform that was straight out of the '50s, starched collar and name embroidered on the breast and everything. In revolt of any sort of uniform, she rejected the '50s hair, or even a conventional hairstyle. Today, it was two little buns on top of her head like teddy bear ears.

One of her dark brows made an elegant arch, and her lips rose on that side in amusement.

"Jake," I said, mirroring her expression.

Just like that, her face fell open. "*What?*" She slid into the booth. "I'm sorry ... *what?*"

BET THE FARM

"Well—we almost banged in the hayloft on the Fourth."

She shook her head, blinking. "Rewind. Start over."

"Banging might have been preemptive, but given another five minutes, it would have happened if he hadn't run off like a jackass. But then ..." I leaned in. "Did you know my grandpa mortgaged the farm to keep Jake in America?"

I didn't think her eyes could open any wider, but they did. "I knew Frank helped him, but I didn't know he had to borrow off the farm to do it. Jesus."

"Well, I found all the paperwork last night, and I ... I didn't understand him, not until then. So I marched over there and told him as much. Let's just say, I didn't make it home last night." I waggled my brows. "I got the Roman candle I was denied on the Fourth."

She made a face. "Ouch."

I giggled. I was officially someone who giggled at leisure. "He blew it up like—" I made an explosion sound and gestured to my hips.

"Oh my God, stop," she said on a laugh.

"It was all *blam, blam, blam.*"

"That's it—we can't be friends anymore. I'm embarrassed for you," she said on a laugh, pretending to leave.

I grabbed her arm and pulled her back.

She narrowed her eyes at me in confusion. "I'm still trying to put this together. You. And Jake."

I nodded, grinning with my lips together.

"You hate each other."

"Turns out, we super *don't* hate each other. Like *at all.*"

"Yeah, yeah, I think they've even got it in the back." A laugh puffed out of her. "If you had a thought bubble over your head, it'd be full of doodly hearts. I do not even know what to do with you right now."

"How about getting me a coffee?"

"I'm not your servant, ma'am," she said too loud as she stood.

"You can't talk to me that way." As she headed to the back, she cut me a smart look and said to Mr. Wheaton at the soda bar, "She can't talk to me that way."

He chewed his bacon, unfazed.

Immediately, my mind wandered back to Jake.

I daydreamed about what he was doing. Maybe he had the puppies with him. I wondered if he had a shirt on, and for once, I hoped he didn't. Maybe he was feeding a calf with a bottle. My insides turned to goop at the thought. In my fantasy, I conveniently left him shirtless.

This, of course, wasn't a thing he would be doing, but I put all that energy into the universe to manifest it anyway.

I sighed again with that dopey smile on my face, so preoccupied with my imagination—Jake conveniently slipped into something more comfortable, which turned out to be a pair of very tight boxer briefs—I didn't see Chase until he slid into the booth where Presley had just been.

With a jolt out of my reverie, my cheeks flushed hot.

He wore an amused expression. "Where were *you* just then?"

"Oh, nowhere in particular." I glanced around to see if anyone was watching. They were. "What are you doing here?"

"Breakfast, same as you. Mind if I join you?"

"If I say no, will it get weird?"

"Probably," he said with a smirk as he unfurled his napkin roll.

When I laughed, I sounded like a stranger.

Maybe Jake was right. God, I hope he wasn't right.

Swiftly, I changed the subject. "You'll be happy to hear that Esther P. Higgenbottom has found some prime real estate in my bedroom. She can see the whole farm from the window."

"Lucky her. That's a view I wouldn't mind myself."

I was pretty sure he didn't mean the farm. I made that weird laugh sound again.

Presley saved me, her weapon of choice in hand. She slid

the coffee in front of me, her eyes on Chase and the fake waitress smile on her lips. "What can I get you to drink?"

"I'll have coffee too, and the eggs Benedict."

"Done." She extended a hand for his menu. "And for you? We're having a sausage special—two for the price of one."

Her tone coupled with the expression on her face was so suggestive, I gave her a *quit fucking with me* look and snapped my menu shut. "I think I'll have the Benedict too."

She took my menu. "Oh, you're gonna love it. The sauce is *super* hot and creamy today." She winked and made the okay gesture with flair only a perv can pull off.

Chase watched us, clearing his throat to cover a laugh.

"She's insufferable," I said.

"She really is. How'd the Fourth end up?"

With me dry humping Jake in the barn. "Really well. We made enough that even Jake couldn't argue."

"That's a first."

"Tell me about it. How's ... everything at Patton?"

He shrugged. "Same old. Dad's been out of town overseeing the farm in Washington, so he's left me in charge."

"And how do you like that?" I took a sip of my coffee.

"Is there any liking it? If I'm honest, the farm's depressing—all that cattle looking miserable in the milking stalls, getting pumped and pregnant until they're ground chuck. Too many to pasture, too many to let roam, just living their lives shoved tail to nose in a barn. But I've been raised for this since I was in utero. Not much to do but eat the shit sandwich."

I frowned. "That's terrible. Your cows."

"Not my call. I learned very young that nothing mattered but following my father's direction, especially if I wanted my inheritance. Which I do. Very much."

"Maybe one day, you can change things."

A dry laugh. "If I'm lucky. But I have a feeling he's going to outlive us all, and if I change a single thing, he'd haunt me."

"Let's hope not," I said with a small smile.

"I'm glad you've figured out how to turn a profit. Maybe you'll be able to get the finances straight after all."

"How do you know about it?" I asked, unable to keep my curiosity to myself.

"My father makes it a point to know everything about everyone."

"Ah."

He watched me for a second. "You know I'm not like him."

I nodded, taking a sip so I didn't have to answer. I wanted to believe he wasn't, but imaginary Jake monkey screeched from my shoulder, calling for caution.

"Anyway, I don't want to talk about that."

"What do you want to talk about?"

Presley walked up with his coffee. "How about pancakes? Do you both like pancakes?"

"Who doesn't like pancakes?" Chase asked.

"They're the original dessert for breakfast food," I added.

"Please, discuss," she said.

My phone buzzed in my pocket, and when I pulled it out to send the call to voice mail, I saw it was the big house's number.

I frowned. "Sorry, I have to take this." I hit the green button and brought the phone to my ear. "Hello?"

Kit was hysterical, her voice shrill and quivering. "Livi, there's a fire. There's a fire—you've gotta come. The hay field is gone. It's gone, Livi—*gone*—and it spread to a pasture where the teenagers are, and those calves we just moved—"

"I'm coming."

"Hurry."

"I will."

I was already out of the booth. "There's a fire on the farm," I said against the pain in my chest. It felt like a bomb had gone off in my rib cage.

Presley's hand covered her mouth. Chase tried to stand.

"No, please don't. I can't show up with you."

A somber nod from him, and I was flying out the door.

The radio was off, the windows cracked, and my thoughts were jumbled up and frantic. I couldn't hear anything past the ringing in my ears as I flicked through scenarios. I could see the smoke billowing all the way from town, as white as the clouds it reached for.

The ten-minute drive felt like an hour, and when I pulled into the drive, I rumbled down it faster than I should have, skidding to a halt in front of the house and cutting the engine. I didn't think to grab the keys as I ran in the direction of the staff, including Kit, who ran for me.

I didn't see Jake.

"Oh, Livi," Kit cried, bursting into a fresh bout of tears. "The crew, the calves out there, the firetrucks pulled through, and I just can't believe how fast it caught. It was so fast," she rambled.

My hand was on her arm, but my eyes were on the crowd. "Where's Jake?"

"He went with them. All those calves ..." She dissolved into tears.

I took off running for the truck.

Kit called after me as I sped in the direction of the smoke, leaning over to open the glove box, digging blindly for a bandana I kept there for when I wanted the windows down. When I reached the pasture, I slammed the brakes hard enough to drift.

I couldn't get to the huddle of trucks fast enough. A dozen farmhands were herding the young cows, trying to keep them calm. Their eyes were ringed white as they stamped and stomped and ran in every direction, and the crew all stood in loose lines on either side with shirts and bandanas tied around their mouths and noses, yelling *H'ya!* and *Get on!* and whooping with their arms out. Thank God none of the cattle were fully grown—it would have been expoentially more dangerous.

When my bandana was tied, I sprinted for Mack, who stood next to the firetrucks, as spooked as the calves.

"Mack!" I screamed, panting. I took him by the shoulders, met his eyes, waited for recognition.

"Livi, you can't be here."

"Neither can you. Go to the truck. Where's Jake?"

Mack's chest heaved. He glanced to the fire. "Some of the calves were penned in. He went to get 'em."

"No," I breathed.

"He got three out, but there are a couple more."

I stared at the wall of smoke and flames. "Go get in the truck, Mack."

"What's that?" he yelled, cupping his ears.

My gaze snapped to him. "Go get in the truck! Take it back to the big house," I yelled back.

A nod, and he was gone.

For a moment, I stood there, frozen by indecision. With the cattle in a stampede, I'd only endanger the farmhands and myself if I ran in. And the fire … there was no knowing, no seeing, no finding him.

There was nothing to do. So I stood there, dragging labored breaths, staring at the fire while I prayed to every god I knew that he'd appear.

"Miss, you've got to get back." A firefighter took me by the arm.

"He's in there."

"I know," she yelled back. "Your man doesn't listen for shit."

A laugh surprised me, tears rushing to my eyes too fast to notice until I felt them hot on my cheeks. My smile faded instantly.

"You've got to get him," I yelled.

She shook her head. "It's not safe."

"I fucking know it's not safe—that's why you need to go get him!"

"He'd only go back in." She tried to step me back, but I shook loose.

"I'm not going anywhere," I said with such ferocity, she conceded.

She glanced over her shoulder at the fire. "The grass is short here, and we got to it before it got out of hand. It's gonna burn out quick. Stubborn as he is, he'll get out."

"Millie! Grab a shovel and go with the guys!" someone called from the fray.

With an understanding nod to me, she ran off.

I didn't know how long I stood there, poised to run into the mayhem. Looking back, I thought it was only a few seconds. It' felt like a year.

He was a shadow first, emerging from the smoke like a ghost. Smudged with soot from top to toe with a shirt tied around the bottom half of his face, he charged out of the fire as fast as he could with a bucking calf in his arms.

I ran for him, meeting him just as he set the calf down at the mouth of the chute funneling the animals into the next pasture, and she ran off, screaming bloody terror toward the barns.

I flung myself at him like a rag doll, boneless and crying.

He caught me, squeezing me so hard, my ribs ached. His breath was labored, his trembling so intense, my teeth rattled.

He didn't let me go for a long, long time.

When he did, it was on the heels of a yelling firefighter, shooing us toward the fence like the cattle. Jake took my hand and towed me to the fence, lifted me over, climbed over himself, and we edged back, turning to stare at the carnage.

Neither of us could breathe. We just watched the pasture burn.

"How did this happen?" I asked after a long while.

"It started with a bale in the hayfield, and the whole field went up in a handful of minutes. It crossed the fence so fast, we didn't even get here in time. Not until the herd was nearly surrounded. Bunch of us ran in, scared them out. Jimmy got knocked over. I think he broke his arm." They'd become flat, distant sentences as he stared at the fire. "It coulda been worse. We hosed down before we got here, second we saw the fire. But a couple of the little ones wouldn't go. They just ... stopped. I brought two of them out, but the third ..."

My breath hitched. There wasn't enough air. Panic tightened my ribs.

Jake's eyes snapped to me, sharp with adrenaline. "Liv. Livi, breathe."

I dragged in air, tugged off my bandana, hinged as my vision dimmed.

Jake grabbed me and ran for the barn.

"You're all right," he said with a calm certainty. "I've got you. Everybody's safe, and so are you. Okay? Hold your breath."

I tried.

"That's it. Hold it again."

I tried harder.

"Good girl," he panted.

A whistle split his lips, and I heard a truck slide to a stop. He set me down in the bed and climbed in after me, pulling me into his lap as we took off.

"I ..." I gasped. "I'm sorry."

I lay cradled in his arms, staring up at the vision of him cast against endless sky as we bumped and bounded toward the big house. A smile tugged at his lips.

"Are you apologizing for having a panic attack?"

I chuckled and closed my eyes, nuzzling against his chest. "I stopped too," I rasped, my throat raw from smoke. "Like the calves. I just stopped."

"If you'd come in after me, I would have yelled at you like you have never been yelled at before, Olivia."

"I thought you ... I didn't know if you'd ..."

His arms tightened. "I know. I shouldn't have gone back, but I couldn't leave them."

My eyes were still closed, the smell of smoke in my nose because it was all over him. "In a few hours when I can breathe, we're gonna talk about how you just ran out of a fire with a baby cow in your arms. Shirtless."

A raspy laugh rumbled out of him, and he kissed the top of

my head. "You're not making a calendar out of me. I don't care how much you beg."

"But you rescued a *baby cow*. I don't know how you can turn your back on the millions we'd make." A dry cough shook me so hard, I couldn't say anything else.

"Don't talk. You can convince me later."

I leaned into him. "Don't ever do that again."

And he held me closer, saying soberly, "I won't."

THE WINDING PATH

Jake

THE DAY WENT BY IN A BLUR.

When we reached the house, I deposited Olivia into one of two ambulances, staying with her while they checked her out, though they insisted on looking me over too. Other than being scuffed up, I was fine, as was she. She'd caught her breath, settled down.

Scared the shit out of me.

Wasn't hard in the moment. I'd been razor sharp and looking for danger to throw myself into.

When the EMTs released us, we hopped back in the truck and headed for the barn where we'd put the cattle.

It smelled of smoke and fear. The herd was wide-eyed and jittery, snuffing and braying and in constant motion. One of the guys had the good sense to leave a tractor running outside the barn, blotting out the noise in the hopes we could get them calmed down. One of our girls, Pinky, sat on a post, singing Led Zeppelin at the top of her lungs with a hose in her hand, spraying a fine mist on the stock. The herd was dotted with snouts up and long tongues extended to taste. Miguel watched them, making notes on a clipboard, waiting for them to calm down before venturing in.

We'd only lost the one calf—a miracle—a hayfield, and a pasture. The patch of land was a smoldering blight, a mark we wouldn't erase for some time. We'd lost months' worth of hay. But the truth was, it could have been much, much worse.

Flashes of the fire shot through my mind without warning. The smoke stinging my eyes, filling my nose and mouth. The crackle and roar of flames, the scream of the heifer I couldn't save. And I was thankful for Olivia at my side. For the unexpected moments when she'd slip her arms around my waist and hang on to me, tethering me to the present. But we operated as a team, the two of us rolling through the farm, taking stock of everything to make sure we had the whole picture.

We checked our grain and hay stores. Rounded up the farmhands and hauled them back to the big house. Kit stress-made a thousand sandwiches and made it her life's work to feed every mouth on the property. We brought out tanks of fresh water, made sure everyone was all right. I watched Olivia make her way through the haggard pack of farmhands and their loved ones with tender care, hugging them and handing the guys wet towels, making sure they had something to drink. I called in the other half of our crew—the livestock still needed tending to—and after a good long while, we watched the last of those who had weathered the day head home.

It was dusk by the time Olivia and I had done all we could. I tucked her into my side as we walked toward the big house in an exhausted, drawn silence. We hadn't left each other's sight since she'd found me at the fire.

"Don't go home," she said as we approached her porch.

"I wouldn't even if you told me to."

A chuckle. We parted as we climbed the stairs, but I snagged her hand so I wouldn't lose the connection.

Jolene and Bowie barked their way to the front door when they heard us, bounding out the second they could to stand on their hind legs and scratch at us, tails wagging and faces begging to be picked up. So we did.

Kit rounded the corner of the kitchen, wiping her hands on the towel slung over her shoulder.

"Everyone all right?" she asked, her face twisted up with worry.

"Everyone's fine," Olivia said wearily.

"Good," Kit said on a sigh. "I hope you're hungry. I made enough lasagna to feed a small country."

I chuckled and glanced down at Olivia. Her face—nuzzled in Jolene's neck—was smudged with soot, darker at her hairline where she'd missed when she tried to clean up. Her hands were streaked with black on the blonde of Jolene's fur.

"I think we need to get cleaned up first," I said.

Kit nodded once. "I'll leave half a tray here and gather up the crew to make sure their bellies are full."

"How many did you make?" Olivia asked.

"Five pans. The big ones," she said sheepishly. "But go on. Go wash the day off and get some rest. I'll be here in the morning, and you know where I am if you need me."

"Thank you, Kit." Olivia's voice was rough from exertion and damage from the smoke. "For everything."

Instantly, Kit's eyes brimmed with tears. "I am just so relieved you're all right." Before either of us knew it, she flung her arms around us and held us close, kissing our cheeks. "Don't ever scare me like that again."

The puppies wriggled from inside the Kit sandwich, prompting her to let us go. I didn't think she would have otherwise.

"Okay," she said, dabbing at her eyes with the hem of her apron. "Okay," she repeated, this time a little stronger. "Now go. Shoo."

We abided as she chased us up the stairs, setting the puppies down when we reached the top. They scampered off toward my room, but we went the other way, to the bathroom. I closed the door behind us with a snick.

We were a filthy mark in the pristine white of the room, from the white honeycomb-tiled floor to the shiplap walls. Olivia crossed the long space to the iron claw-foot tub, reaching in to turn the shower on.

I pulled off my shirt and tossed it in her hamper. She stopped in front of the mirror, assessing herself as she unraveled her hair from the hasty braid she'd thrown it in.

"God, I look terrible."

I moved to stand behind her, taking a long look at the two of us. Her hair, bright against the dingy tinge to our skin. She came up to my shoulder, though mine were almost twice as wide as hers. She seemed so small next to me, the delicate shape of her sparking a protective flame in my heart.

"You couldn't look terrible if you wore hillbilly teeth, shaved your head, and put all your clothes on backward."

A laugh as she finger-combed her hair. "That's oddly specific."

I assessed our state in the mirror. "I keep forgetting we didn't clean up."

"At least you got a fresh shirt."

"I mean, I *did* run the other one through a fire."

"I didn't say you weren't excused."

I reached for the hem of her shirt and pulled. She lifted her arms to let me, and I took great pleasure in watching her curly copper hair tumble down her back. Once free, she leaned back against me and met my gaze in the mirror.

"I don't ever want to live a day like this again."

"Me neither. But it would have been a hundred times harder if you hadn't been there with me."

"Well, I *am* your business partner," she joked.

But I turned her around, held her face with all seriousness. "Not because of that."

"I know," she said softly. "I don't think I've ever been so scared as I was waiting for you walk out of that fire."

"I don't think I've ever been so relieved as I was when I saw you on the other side," I admitted.

A smile brushed her lips. "Two days ago, you'd rather have kissed Sharon the goat on the lips than kiss me."

"Not true," I corrected as she reached for my belt buckle. I kicked off my work boots, and she kicked off hers. "I wanted to kiss you for longer than I'll ever admit out loud, so don't ask."

"I bet you pulled all the girls' pigtails in elementary school. I bet you were that boy girls are told to excuse for being a butthole because they like you."

"Did you just say butthole?" I asked on a laugh.

"I said what I said." She shimmied my jeans off, and I dropped hers.

Once free and clear of clothing, I walked to the tub to check the temperature. "No, I didn't pull any pigtails."

"Braids then?"

"No braids or ponytails, either. I barely talked to anybody."

"This doesn't surprise me."

I took her hand and helped her in, following when she parked herself under the stream with her eyes closed and her face tilted to the ceiling. At the sound of the metal rings on the curtain rod, she sluiced the water from her hair and opened her eyes, trading places with me. When the hot water hit me, I nearly melted down the drain.

"You had friends, though. At school. Right?" Small, soapy hands scrubbed their way across my chest.

"We moved a lot. Just went wherever Mom could find work."

"She cleaned houses?"

I nodded, reaching for the shampoo and dispensing a dollop. "Outside of Philly." I dragged my fingers through her hair and gathered it up, lathering it on top of her head until it was a ridiculous tower of foam and red curls. "Seemed it was always something. Jobs wouldn't stick. We'd get evicted. We had to take whatever we could get."

"Which meant lots of schools."

I wound a curl around my finger and placed it artfully at the peak of shampoo mountain. "About the time I made a friend, we'd move again. By the sixth grade, I gave up trying."

"Raise your arms," she ordered.

Smirking, I did. When her hands slipped into my armpits, I flinched.

"Oh my God, are you ticklish?"

She wiggled her fingers, and I grabbed her by the wrists, laughing.

"*You are!*" Her hands darted out like cobras.

"Stop it."

"If this wasn't the worst day, it'd be the best day of my life." She giggled as I fought her off.

"You are so weird." I laughed.

"Why, because I want to wash your armpits?" She'd moved around so much, her whipped hair sagged sadly, the curl slipping into her face.

"Yes." I grabbed her by both wrists and held them in front of her, the two of us laughing like idiots.

"The indestructible Jake Milovic is ticklish. It's a beautiful day for mankind to learn you have a weakness." Soap ran down her forehead toward her eye, and she slammed it shut, blowing up the length of her face with her bottom lip to try to stop it.

"That's what you get." I let her go and swiped the soap away before drawing her into my chest. "Come here." I turned us around slowly and put her under the stream to rinse out her hair.

"God, I am going to tickle you so much, and you're never gonna see it coming." Her eyes were closed, her lips smiling.

I tilted her head back to get her hairline. "I will end you, Olivia."

"Oh, it's gonna be so good," she mused, ignoring me. "In the middle of the night when you're dead asleep. Bam! You've got your hand up a heifer's vagina, bam! Ninja tickling, coming at you like *hi-yah phrlebrepthhhhh*," she spat when I forced her face under the water.

"Told you not to mess with me."

She was too busy laughing to sling a comeback. Instead, she swiped the water from her face and switched places with me again.

When she composed herself, she looked up at me with velvety brown eyes, bar of soap rolling around between her hands. "After today, I couldn't imagine I'd ever laugh again, but you proved me wrong. You're good at that."

"I'm good at all kinds of things."

She slid into me, smiling slyly. "You are." But her smile faded, the weight of the day heavy behind her eyes. "I couldn't do this by myself. Any of it. And I can't imagine running the farm with anyone but you. I'm sorry you've been so alone."

I stroked her jaw, not knowing what to say.

"Did you read Pop's letter?"

I shook my head. The letter had been sitting on my dresser since I'd gotten it. I couldn't bring myself to open it, knowing it was the last thing he'd ever say to me.

"In mine, he said he gave us both the farm because he knew we'd need each other. At the time, it felt like a cruel joke. You didn't need me."

"I did," I said quietly, pain striking like a match in my chest. "I needed you more than I knew. I needed you even though I didn't want to. I was just too stubborn and foolish to admit it."

"Good thing I was too stubborn and foolish to walk away."

"Good thing."

It was all I could say without saying too much, so I kissed her to rid us of words for a moment.

She disarmed me completely, exposed me entirely. I often found I said too much, showed her more than I intended. She was quite possibly the only person left on God's green earth who understood me. She understood me when I didn't want her to. Sometimes when I didn't understand myself.

She was a person I could share my life with. I'd been sharing it for months already. Owning the farm together, we'd share it for a long, long time whether we wanted to or not.

My breath hitched at the thought that someday, we wouldn't want to.

And the realization of what that implied hit me like a freight train.

But for once, I didn't run. I held on to her, emptied my heart into that kiss, into her.

Because of all the paths my life could take, I knew the one that ended with her was the brightest.

DRIVE SHAFT

Olivia

"All right, you ready?" Jake asked from the grass beneath me.

"I'm ready," I assured him from my perch in the tractor.

"It's not like driving a car."

"Yes, I know."

"It's gonna be loud."

"Jake. I grew up on the farm. I've been on a tractor."

"Yeah, yeah—I know." His face did not know. "Okay. What speed are you at?"

"Low," I recited.

"And you're not gonna go out of first gear."

"Nope."

"Then turn the key, honey."

"Thank you, dear," I said and fired the engine. The rush at the rumble and thunder shook me, the sound louder than I remembered. Laughter bubbled out of me in my exhilaration, and I bounced in the squishy seat, my cheeks high and flushed.

"Okay," he shouted, barely audible over the engine. *"Push the clutch and put her in gear."*

Grinning, I did what I'd been told, and the tractor lurched forward. A squeal shot out of me, my hands white-knuckled on the wheel. When I glanced at Jake, his face was open and bright with laughter I couldn't hear.

The last week had been a little slice of heaven.

Without discussion or decision, we'd slipped into a natural, easy cohabitation. It was just understood that when we weren't working, we were together. And even sometimes when we *were* working, we were together.

I'd learned more about the inner workings of the farm in a week than in my whole life. I'd been all over the property with Jake as he oversaw operations. I'd driven an RC car in the bull pen to distract them while Jake and a couple of the guys mended the fence. I'd marked cows for checkups with neon-green chalk at Jake's and Miguel's direction. We'd wandered through herds of breeding heifers, checking the stickers on their flanks that changed colors when they were in heat.

In turn, Jake had run around with me, picking up orders for the shop and unwillingly becoming my photographer for social media. He took direction much better than my tripod. And to my absolute and utter delight, he'd even let me take some pictures of him. The brawn of our operation got way more engagement than anything I'd ever posted.

This was unfortunately not enough encouragement for him to green-light my calendar.

Unsurprisingly, I had not given up the ghost.

The rest of the time, we were just *together*. The logic center of my brain did its best to remind me that being together this much, this fast, was dangerous. But the logic center of my brain was a drag.

I was convinced that nothing that felt this good could possibly hurt me.

The farm continued to perform, and we'd expanded our tours to Wednesdays and Fridays last week with the shop open the same hours. My debt had been paid in full a couple weeks ago, so everything we made now went straight into the mortgages.

The matter of the fire hadn't been resolved, not with the fire department labeling it arson and as such, dooming any help from our insurance. Jake was certain it was the Pattons, but he was the king of conspiracies. A fire in a hayfield seemed too small a scale for corporate warfare, beyond its lack of imagination. Many a heated discussion had occurred over the subject. Neither of us were convinced. But it didn't matter. It was behind us. And things were looking way up.

I bounced and bumbled, giggling as I crawled forward. *"I wanna go faster!"* I shouted at him.

"What?"

"I said, I wanna go faster!"

"No."

"You are the poopiest of party poopers."

"Huh?"

"I said—"

Jake hopped onto the step and grabbed the handle on the frame of the roof. *"You call me a pooper?"*

I shrugged dramatically, my eyes on the pasture in front of me. *"Call 'em like I see 'em."*

This time, I heard his laugh. It was the best sound in the whole world.

"Take it to second."

My face shot open. *"Really?"*

"Really. Eyes on the road, ma'am."

I was giggling again, and I threw it into second, which was fast enough to almost go ten whole miles an hour. *"Where do you want me to go?"*

He leaned in and pointed to the winding line of trees on the other side of the pasture. A creek split the trees, one of the water sources for the cattle.

I turned us in that direction, bobbing my head as I yelled, "*They see me rollin'—they hatin'.*" When I earned a chuckle, I said, "*Mooooo, bitch—get out the hay.*"

I got a full-blown belly laugh for that one.

He reached around me, and I shifted so he could slide beneath me.

"I'll take you for a real ride," he said in my ear, shifting the levers as I settled into his lap. "Hang on."

A lurch, then a second, and we were flying over a stretch of green grass. Well, as fast as we could go in a tractor, at least.

I'd only just finished laughing when we reached the trees, my hand on the top of my sun hat so it wouldn't fly away.

I sighed when he cut the engine. The silence was loud, my ears ringing and my body still vibrating.

"What are we doing here?" I asked. "Am I yelling?"

"A little," he sorta yelled back, patting my butt in his lap. "Come on, I'll show you."

I climbed out of the forest-green tractor carefully, but Jake had all the grace of a jungle cat as he exited with a slide and a leap. He reached for my hand, smirking at me.

"What in the world did you do?" I said on a laugh, hanging on to my hat again as he towed me toward the creek.

"Really, Kit did most of it," he answered, sweeping boughs out of the way to reveal a picnic basket on a plaid blanket.

I gasped like a big, squishy mush and ducked in.

He'd found the perfect little patch of grass next to the bubbling creek, and by the look on his face, he knew just how perfect it was. I wondered how long he'd looked for this spot, and my heart melted like a candle.

I whirled around and stretched up on my toes, angling for a kiss. "I love it."

"Good," he said and pressed his lips to mine.

And then I was off, hopping on one foot so I could pull off a rain boot, then the other. They didn't even match my sundress, but he'd told me I couldn't wear sandals, so I'd opted for the rain boots as a joke.

He chuckled behind me and knelt on the blanket to start unpacking our food, and I tiptoed into the frigid water, relishing the feel of the smooth stones pressing the soft arches of my feet. I kicked the stream, watching beads of water fly into the air.

Looking down, I stepped on one of the bigger rocks, then another, using them as a bridge to the other side. When I looked up, he was watching me with that look on his face he'd given me so many times lately.

Smiling, I hopped back toward him and sat next to him.

"Ooh, is that Havarti?"

He turned the wedge of cheese over in his hand to look at the label. "Guess so."

I sighed. "I miss Havarti."

He hissed a swear and threw the cheese back in the basket. "How'd I forget that? Once upon a time, that was one of my favorite things to tease you about. Stupid Pinterest."

I tried to stifle a smile. "You went on Pinterest?"

"Don't make it worse. It said charcuterie, which I told Kit. There's meat and grapes and crackers in there too. It also said wine, but I figured whiskey was more our speed." He reached into the basket, and in his hands were two crystal glasses. A bottle of whiskey followed.

"You did good." I leaned in and kissed his neck as he continued to unpack. "How'd it go today? I'm sorry I was too busy to come with you. I'd rather have been in the barn than stuck inside on my computer."

"Went fine. We have a handful of heifers sick in one of the herds, but Miguel doesn't seem worried about it. The fire marshal came by with an update on the investigation."

I stilled, cracker in my hand. "Did they find out who did it?"

"No—the update was that there was no update."

My shoulders slumped. "I just can't help thinking it was a farmhand smoking after banging his lady friend or a Wiccan ritual or a psychic doing a seance or something."

"A seance?"

I shrugged and popped the cracker into my mouth, saying around it, "Anything's possible, Jake."

"A seance with gasoline?"

"Probably not," I admitted. "I should ask Chase."

He gave me a look. "No, you shouldn't."

"You are such a stick in the mud."

"And a pooper too, apparently."

"Every party's gotta have one."

"Do you think if Chase was somehow involved that he'd tell you?"

My nose wrinkled. "Probably not. But maybe if I don't flat-out ask him, he'll give me a hint. It couldn't have actually been *him*. He was at the diner when it happened."

"Which isn't at all suspicious." He handed me a glass with a finger of golden whiskey in it.

"You're suspicious of everyone."

"Which is why nobody can get to me."

"I got to you."

There it was, that little flicker of his lips that only happened these days when he didn't want to smile.

"Well, you're special."

"Thank you," I said primly, straightening my dress over my thighs.

He raised his glass, touched it to mine. We took a sip.

"So," I started, "is there an occasion we're celebrating? Or did you just want to tease me with forbidden dairy?"

"No occasion. I knew we'd be out here with the tractor, and I thought you'd like a picnic."

"Enough to *Pinterest* it." I pressed a hand to my heart.

But he laughed. "You're the worst."

"*You're* the worst."

"You're welcome for teaching you how to drive the tractor, by the way."

"You let me drive for like four seconds before you took over. I mean, it tracks, but still." I took a sip and reached for another cracker. "Think next time I can get to third?"

"Ooh, I like it when you say it like that. Sounds dirty."

I set my whiskey down on the cheese board and crawled toward him, saying in a fake sexy voice, "Want me to grind your gear shaft?"

He leaned back a little, his legs stretched out in front of him, that smirk on his face. "I really do."

I climbed into his lap, straddling him. "Put your key in the ignition and rev her up." I shimmied my shoulders, still using my ha-cha-cha voice.

A laugh as he put down his glass. "That's the best you've got?"

"Why, do you have better?" I flicked open the top button of his plaid shirt.

His hands slid up my thighs to cup my ass. "Hop on—I've got a full load."

I undid another button. "Not bad. When was the last time you had your shaft lubed?"

"About the same time I had my ball bearings checked."

I nibbled my smiling bottom lip, working on unfastening the rest. "Lucky for you, this is a full-service shop."

"Good. Maybe you can figure out what to do when I show you how I handle curves."

"If you were a car door, I'd slam you all night."

He volleyed, "What are the chances of me popping your clutch?"

I laughed, burying my face in his neck. "Okay, that's a good one. Um … oh, I've got one. Wanna jack me up and check out my undercarriage?"

"Been thinking about it all day." His hand slipped under my hem and to my ass. His smile fell. "Fuck, Livi, you're not wearing panties?"

"No. It made riding the tractor *real* interesting."

He sat up, held me around the waist, tipped me back. Kissed me deep and long. When he broke away, I lifted to my knees to get his pants out of the way. He took the moment to slide his hand up the tender flesh of my thigh, arresting my attention.

"I've never felt lucky," he said, his voice rough.

My hands stilled. I peered into his face until he looked up at me.

"Never," he said with somber sadness. "How'd you do it? How'd you make me feel this way?"

My chest ached, heavy with emotion I couldn't acknowledge, that we couldn't speak without jinxing it.

So instead, I said, "So there was this seance ..."

And then he was laughing with adoration on his face. I held his jaw, lifted it. He wound his arms around my waist and pulled me to him.

"I don't think it's just me or you," I said. "I think it's us. I don't know where it came from. All I know is, I don't want to lose it."

He lowered me onto his lap, cupped my neck, brought his lips to mine in silent accord, and kissed me.

I didn't know how I could have kissed him so many times and still be surprised. He put on an unfeeling front, convincing everyone around him that he didn't care. But the truth was, he cared so much, it nearly broke him. He'd never say it. But I felt it in the way he kissed me, in the way he touched me. It was a kiss always on the verge of longing, as if what he had would slip away. It was with a sense of presence, as if he needed to be here—right here—so he could remember every moment when it was gone.

He kissed me in such a way that exposed him, and what I saw broke my heart. It triggered some deep and aching desire to be everything he needed, to give myself to him so he'd know love was real and that he deserved it. Because I didn't think he knew.

I made it a point to show him.

I hoped I already had.

My hand found its way between us, finishing its abandoned job to free him. Guiding him to meet me. Fitting him just inside of me. Letting gravity do the rest.

Our foreheads pressed together when I was seated, my body squeezing him, his throbbing in an echo. On trembling legs, I rose and fell, his face in my hand, our gazes locked. And then he pulled me down for a bruising kiss, guiding the rest of me with his free hand on my hip.

My body rolled against him, his lips breaking from mine to trail down my neck, my chest, pulling my strap over my shoulder to expose my breast to him. On I went, through the gentle graze of his teeth on the delicate flesh of my nipple, through the feel of his hands on me, desperate for skin. On I went, seeking pressure, seeking release. Harder I rode when he lost the wherewithal to touch me, his lips parted and panting against the flesh of my neck. He was close—I could feel it in the grip of his fingertips, in the swell of him inside me. I cradled his face, pulled back to see him, watched him until I was blinded by the hard burst of my desire. And watching me come was too much to stop him. A flex, a groan deep in his throat, and he grabbed my ass and took what he wanted, how he wanted it. And I gave it freely.

He lowered me slowly, wrapped his arms around me, buried his face in my breasts. And I cradled his head in my arms, kissed the top of his head. He listened to my heart beat.

And I wondered if he knew it was his.

RED AND BLUE

Jake

THUMP, THUMP, THUMP, THUMP.

Olivia popped out of bed like a sleepy-eyed jack-in-the-box, scaring the shit out of me. I blinked at the clock. One thirty. Her room was silent other than the soft ping of rain on the windows.

"Was that the—" she started before another *thump, thump, thump.*

"What the fuck?" I muttered, flipping back the covers.

Olivia slid out of bed in the dark, reaching for her silky robe.

But I was already padding down the stairs, flipping on the porch light when I reached the door.

My heart jerked at the sight of Mack, wild-eyed and frazzled on the other side. His hair was damp, the shoulders of his Carhartt jacket dark from the rain.

I pulled it open with a whoosh. "What's the matter?" I asked gravely.

"Th-the stock, Jake. We're missing a herd."

Instantly, I was awake. "What do you mean, missing a herd?"

"Just that. Number fifteen, every animal gone."

I swore, raking a hand through my hair. "Wait here."

The door was shut with a slam before he responded, and I was halfway up the stairs in a heartbeat. Olivia stood at the top, peering down at me.

"Missing?" she breathed.

"I'll find them," I promised as I passed her, pressing a kiss to the top of her head.

She followed me into her room, flipping on the light as I tugged on my jeans. "I'm coming with you."

"Just wait here. I don't know what we're dealing with."

"If you really believe I'd just sit here by myself, you don't know me at all."

I would have chuckled if I wasn't so worried. "All right, but wear something warm."

"Sure, Dad," she said from inside the sweatshirt she was getting herself into. She'd already put her jeans on.

Once my shirt was on, I hurried down the stairs, stuffing my feet into my boots. Olivia was behind me, pulling her hair into a bun when I opened the door again.

Mack waited on the porch as I'd asked, his face bent with worry and his hands deep in his pockets. I didn't stop, just marched out the second the door was open for my truck.

"Tell me everything." I climbed in and started the engine as he talked, Olivia sliding in between us before I took off for the barns.

"Jimmy was on rounds tonight, said everything was the usual until one of the other herds got out. Animals were restless, noisy—one of the barns on the other side of the farm was open, the cows put to pasture. And while he and a couple of guys were gettin' the animals rounded up and back in the barn, somebody let herd fifteen out to their pasture. They're gone."

"Where the fuck did they go? Forty one-ton cows don't just disappear. How long was Jimmy gone?"

"Maybe a half hour. Half the guys followed the gates to the pasture. There was sign of the livestock, but nothin' was left of them except hoofprints, tire tracks, and a thousand pounds of bullshit."

Olivia and I shared a look.

I turned down a dirt road that headed in the direction of the empty pasture. Headlights glowed in the distance.

"I assume you called the police?"

"They're on their way. I came straight to get you."

For a moment, we drove in silence but for the gravel beneath my tires and the ping of rocks against the undercarriage.

The fire. The missing livestock. And just a few weeks apart.

If I hadn't already been convinced the fire was sabotage, this would have done it.

The gate to the pasture had been left open, and I rolled in, heading for the cluster of trucks and ATVs. There wasn't much action, just the lot of them standing in the headlight beams, looking stiff and worried. I noted tire marks, big ones. Duallys with double tire tracks inside wider sets so deep, they made six-inch ruts toward the gate. Somebody had let the cows into the pasture where three, maybe four trailers waited to haul them off. I followed trails of hoofprints to the huddle of vehicles, parked, exited the truck. Stalked into the group and looked around.

Their expressions were a mix of concern and shame.

"I'm sorry, Jake," Jimmy said, his baseball hat twisting in his hands, one in a cast. "I didn't think to leave anybody back when we wrangled the loose herd. I should've only called a few guys to help me and left the rest on watch. I just … I didn't think to—"

I clapped a hand on the kid's shoulder. "It's all right," I assured him. "You did just what you were supposed to. Anybody find anything?" I asked, scanning their faces.

One of the guys spoke up. "Three trailers hauled them out. Cut the bolts at the back gate by the road, drove right in."

I looked toward a dark pasture, too angry to meet anyone's eyes.

If we'd chipped the cattle, we'd have found them with a phone call. But we hadn't had the extra funds for the sizable expense. We were too busy trying to keep our equipment running smoothly and up to snuff.

At the loss of an entire herd, that expense didn't seem so steep after all.

In the distance, a storm cloud lit up from the inside, a rumble of thunder meeting us a few seconds later. The lot of them were silent, waiting for my direction.

I wished I had some.

"All right," I finally said. "Anybody see anything?"

They shook their hung heads.

"Jimmy, grab one of the guys who helped with the other herd and stay here with me to talk to the police. The rest of you, head back to the barns. I want two of you making rounds without stopping on ATVs and get a couple of guys together to check the other barns. Mack, go on back up to the house and show the cops where we are when they get here. Take my truck." I tossed him the keys and turned to Olivia. "What do you want to do? Go with Mack or—"

"I'm staying," she said grimly.

"Figured," I answered with a halfhearted smile. "All right, go on. Paul, if you need more hands, call the list until you get somebody. And send somebody to find me when the livestock commissioner gets here."

"Yessir," he said, and they broke off, heading for their rides.

One by one, headlights swung around and disappeared, leaving us standing in the rain. I wandered away, my eyes on the tracks in an attempt to read them, wishing they could speak.

We were being targeted, and I wanted to know who the fuck would be so stupid. Because there would be all of hell on my heels when I found them.

I stopped at one of the trailer tracks, staring at the tread. It was perfect, the tires brand new if I had to guess by the depth and sharpness of the pattern. If it was three trailers, they'd have to be big—forty feet, or they wouldn't have been able to carry the whole herd.

This was no small operation. It was organized, with insider knowledge of our farm, the pastures. An operation like this would know our stock wasn't chipped.

They knew too much.

Olivia stepped up next to me, sliding her hand into mine. "Our cattle …"

"I know."

"Who would do something like this?"

It was a rhetorical question, but I looked down at her with an answer all the same. I didn't even have to say their name, and she knew.

"Why would the Pattons steal our cows?" she asked with indignation. "They can't keep our heifers or we'd know."

"Would we? How so?"

"Couldn't … well, won't the police be able to check their livestock numbers? See their herd grew?"

"They have cattle moving in and out of that farm every day. A snap, and that'd be explained. They'll sell the heifers though, probably to a rustler. Off the books. There's no getting them back, and there's no proving the Pattons are out for us. But that doesn't change the fact that they are."

"That isn't a fact, Jake. We don't have any proof—just your hunch."

"I'm gonna find proof. First the fire, now this. What's next?"

"Jake …" she breathed, looking up at me. "The sick heifers."

I stilled. The handful that had been sick just a few days ago had multiplied, then again. We had clusters of cases in a few other herds—all of the herds quarantined—and Miguel had been running tests nonstop to try to figure out what was wrong. He'd tried a handful of remedies without luck. All we'd done is cross possibilities off the list without learning anything new. But if we knew it was some sort of interference, we could narrow it down.

I pulled my phone out of my pocket. Called Miguel. Told him I'd meet him in his office once I was finished with the police so we could do some more searching, considering sabotage as the primary cause.

Sirens wailed in the distance as I put my phone away, and when I looked in the direction of the sound, I could see their lights shining blue, purple, red. Olivia wrapped her arms around my waist, and I held her close, watching the lights over the top of her head without seeing anything.

"What are we going to do, Jake?"

"Everything we can," I answered.

I only hoped it would be enough.

I scrubbed a hand over my face, glancing at the clock.

The night had been unending, the sun rising on the forensics team busy around the barn and in the pasture. I'd left Mack with them in favor of partnering with Miguel to talk through what might be wrong with our stock.

So far, no luck.

"It just doesn't make any sense," Miguel said from behind his computer. "None of my panels turned anything up. I'm waiting on some results—viral, mineral—but everything I can check for is negative. If I knew it was viral, that'd be one thing. I even called a few buddies of mine to see if they had any ideas, but I've done it all. Until I lose a heifer. An autopsy might help diagnose."

That grim thought hung in the air.

Olivia entered with two cups of coffee and an exhausted expression on her face. She set one in front of Miguel and handed the other to me before taking a seat next to me. She said nothing.

Miguel leaned back in his chair, his brows threaded together.

"I don't know anything about how it was contracted, but I don't think it's contagious—since quarantine, there are no new sick cattle in the herds, only from the barns. The best I have to go off of is red urine—it's the only visible symptom other than general lethargy, decreased appetite. Could be their kidneys. It's not blood. No natural causes like beetroot or clover would last for an extended period. It's not urethral. I just …until I get more test results, I'm stuck." He closed his computer. "We've got four herds in quarantine and a hundred sick cows within just a few days."

"So there's nothing we can do," Olivia said. She didn't ask.

"For now, no."

She sagged. I felt the weight of it all dragging me to the ground, and I stood, defying it.

"Then we need to get some rest," I said, reaching for her hand. A nod, and she stood, leaning into my side. "Have Kit wake us if you need anything."

Miguel nodded. "I will."

And we dragged ourselves back to the house.

"I don't know if I'll ever sleep again, Jake."

"Me neither. But I bet once we clean off and get in bed, it'll find us."

"I just don't understand." Her voice quivered.

"I understand just fine. Pretty sure we all know who would do it and why."

Olivia skidded to a stop, her flushed face bent and her eyes shining with tears. "Stop it. Just stop it. You've convinced yourself the Pattons are obsessed with you, but I think it's *you* who's obsessed. It doesn't make any sense, Jake—why would they damage the property they want to acquire? They're smarter than that, aren't they?"

"Jesus, Olivia. Don't be naive—they'll do anything to take this farm down. They'll do whatever it takes to ruin us just so they've done it. They don't need any reason more than that."

"But there's no proof that they're sabotaging us. Yes, they

want to put us under, but we can't just run around accusing them of something without tangible evidence, now or ever. Name *one* thing they've done that's done real damage."

I didn't answer. I was too busy trying to figure out how to tell her the Pattons' greatest sin.

"See? You can't even tell me *one*."

A fire of rage and regret and shame rose in me like a wildfire. I could feel it in my lungs as they sawed the crisp morning air. I could feel that fire in my skin, steaming and flushed.

"They're the ones who reported me."

Confusion flitted across her brow.

"To ICE. You want to know who really put Pop in the hole? It's them."

Realization struck her, her eyes widening.

I gave her my back, paced a few steps, dragged a hand through my hair. Turned to her. "They figured it out and called immigration. This, after years of stealing our business and generations of fighting. But they stopped when Frank bankrupted himself to save me. Then all they had to do was wait for us to fall apart."

Her lips parted. "I ... how did you find out?"

"Because Chase Patton can't keep his fucking mouth shut. You know nothing stays secret around here, and the second he told Kendall, the whole school knew. Are you satisfied now? Have I convinced you yet?"

"That's not fair."

"What's not fair is that you don't trust me on this," I shot. "You think I'm just a stubborn fool. But never once have I called it wrong, not until you. Then again, you make it a point to buck expectations, don't you?" I shook my head and looked off, my teeth grinding hard enough to squeak. "Frank's gone, and they've figured *you* for our weak spot. They're going to choke the life out of us and break in, and you're the only avenue they have. You own half of this, Olivia. And they want it."

"Jake," she said quietly as she approached.

I stared at a nick in the side of the big red barn.

"Jake, please."

Her hand on my arm was a balm on my wounds. I looked down at her, finding peace in the bottomless brown of her eyes whether I wanted to see it or not.

"I'm sorry. I'm sorry they did this to you. To the farm. The only thing to thank them for is keeping you here so I could find my way back to you."

My throat tightened. I pulled her into my chest so she couldn't see my face, too tired to put on the mask.

"I believe you," she said after a minute. "I think we should make sure the police know who we think is interfering."

A dry laugh. "You forget the Pattons run this town. Every corner of it, the sheriff included. Won't do any good."

"We'll figure something out," she promised. "Get some outside help. Find irrefutable evidence. I have to believe it's going to be okay, Jake. It has to be. I don't … I don't know how we'll …" Her words dissolved into tears.

But I knew one thing she'd said was true—she needed to believe it was going to be okay. And I might not have been able to do much, but I could give her that.

"You're right," I said before kissing the top of her head. "We'll figure it out."

And it was on me to figure out how.

DEAL WITH THE DEVIL

Olivia

AHUNDRED TWENTY SICK CATTLE.

Thirty-two dead in three days' time.

Kit's face was drawn as she finished arranging the basket piled with sausage biscuits I was to take around to the crew.

"Miguel should hear something on the tests today, right?" she asked, her eyes on her hands.

My heart sank even lower than it already was. "He got them this morning. Nothing."

"I just don't see how that's possible," she huffed. "These labs don't know what they're doing. They're supposed to be giving us answers, not a bunch of zeros. Somebody has to help, and they're the professionals."

"I know. But all they can do is give us data, and the data doesn't show *anything*. Miguel's running another round of mineral and toxin tests on the stock as well as the water, hay, feed. The FDA was here yesterday, for God's sake. We're in danger of being shut down, so we've got to figure it out—and soon. We've checked the fields for any signs of interference, but it could be anything, Kit. Somebody could have tampered with the soil, planted something in a corner that'd hurt the herd to eat. Put something in the water that we couldn't detect with our own tests. Let's just hope this round turns something up, because no one seems to be able to work out what's going on."

"I'm just so mad," she said, her voice trembling as she used too much force to stack the little sandwiches. "And scared. After everything, now this. It just all feels too big, too hard." She sniffled and pushed the basket in my direction.

"I know," I said with my insides in pieces as I walked around the island to give her a hug.

She held on to me like she'd fly away if she let go.

"What are we gonna do, Livi?" she asked quietly. "How are we going to survive?"

"We're going to keep on trying," I said with hope. "We need money to replace the cattle we lost and keep ourselves up and running, and we haven't tried the one place that happens to have a safe full of it."

"The bank?" She leaned back to meet my eyes. "Livi, are you going to try to take out a loan? Mortgage the farm again?"

"I already applied. I have an appointment this afternoon to find out if we got it."

Her eyes widened with hope. "Do you think they'll give it to you?"

"All I can do is cross my fingers."

"Then I'll cross mine too."

"Oh, and Kit—don't tell Jake."

She gave me a look.

"It's not like that. I just knew he'd say no. If I get it, I'll tell him. If not, he'll be none the wiser."

Kit drew a long breath and let it out in a sigh. "I hope you can pull it off. If anybody can, it's you."

The banker across the desk wore an expression of pity as she pushed my folder of financial paperwork back at me.

"I'm sorry, Ms. Brent. But on looking at your statements, returns, and debts, there's no equity to draw off of. There's no collateral."

"There has to be something we can do," I insisted. "Our farm has to be worth something."

"Given your outstanding debt, we can't in good conscience lend you the kind of money you need. I really am very sorry. Your farm is a staple in this town, and your grandfather was a cornerstone in our community. But at the end of the day, the math has to work out. And I'm sorry to have to be the one to tell you that in this case, it just doesn't."

I swallowed back bile and nodded my head, reaching for the folder with shaking hands.

"Is there anything else I can do for you?" she asked, knowing good and well this was the *only* thing she could do for me.

"No, thank you," I said as I stood. "I appreciate your time."

We shook hands. She walked me to her door. I left her behind me, trying to tamp down tears, but the closer I got to the sliding doors of the bank, the less control I possessed. I couldn't see past the curtain of tears, the futility of our circumstance a sledgehammer, and I'd been driven into the ground.

I have to get out of here. I have to get out. I have to—

I slammed into a blurry figure who caught me before I ricocheted off them.

"Olivia?"

When I blinked, fat tears fell without even touching my cheeks, revealing Chase Patton.

He looked down at me with worry all over his face. "What's wrong? What happened?"

I shook my head, desperate to get away. "I'm fine, thank you."

"You look fine," he teased gently.

A wan smile. "If you'll excuse me ..."

"You're really not going to tell me?"

He asked the question with such care, I wavered. But at the

remembrance of what he'd done to Jake and our farm, my back stiffened.

"Why should I tell you anything? You're the reason our farm is in trouble."

"How so?"

"Jake told me what your father did. The cost of Jake's freedom was our farm. And if you all hadn't turned him in, we wouldn't even be here right now."

He glanced in the direction of the offices, then at my black dress, this time worn to a funeral for hope. Understanding passed across his face.

"Is it that bad?" he asked. "I heard your cows were sick—"

"Well, aren't you well informed? Please, don't keep me here any longer. I'm humiliated enough as it is."

Chase shook his head, looked at his shoes. "I'm not the kid I used to be."

"No, now you're the grown-up version of the Patton asshole."

"You don't understand ..." He paused. Glanced at the ground. Shook his head. "I'm the one who told my dad about Jake when I heard at school. All because I thought it'd please my father, and it did. I got the pat on the head I wanted and ruined your farm. It was my fault. But what I didn't know then was that James Patton is never satisfied and he never will be."

I glared at him. "What do you want from me, forgiveness? Because that's not mine to give. And you don't want to know what I think of you right now."

"I've laid awake nights like people do. Most people think about inconsequential things—something they said carelessly, an embarrassing moment, a childhood bully. But I think about how many lives I did or could have ruined with that one little scrap of information."

"Good. You should be ashamed of yourself. I hope it keeps you up for the rest of your days, Chase Patton."

"Let me try to make amends. Can I try to make it right?"

"Your words are worth less than dirt, so I doubt it."

"But what about money?"

I closed my mouth, swallowed what I was about to say so I could take a confused moment to parse what he'd said. "I have no use for Patton money."

He pulled a checkbook out of his back pocket and opened it. "How much do you need?"

"You can't buy your way back into my good graces. And I'm with Jake now—if there was no chance of it happening before, now it would end up with you in traction."

Ignoring me, he did his best to scribble in the checkbook without something solid to write on. "A hundred thousand enough?"

"I cannot fucking believe you," I said under my breath before turning.

But he grabbed my arm. "Olivia, please."

Something in the way he'd said it stopped me. I whirled around to face him. "I don't understand what you're doing. We won't partner with Patton Farms, and you can't have me. So what's your angle?"

"There's no angle. You'd be clearing my conscience, and I'd be setting something to rights that I broke a long time ago. Two hundred thousand," he said as he wrote each number and signed it with a scratching swoop of his pen. He ripped the check out and handed it to me.

I stared at it.

"No strings. Just ... think about it. Okay? Talk to Jake. If you want me to sign some sort of release, I will. This is money my father has made on account of *you*, money he gave to me to do what I would with. It should cover the cost of Jake's immigration."

I shook my head but didn't speak.

"*Take the money*," he urged. "None of this would have happened if not for me—you said so yourself. You need help. I can help you. Take the check and make sure the answer is a hard no before tearing it up. That's all I'm asking. Because if you couldn't get money here—"

"There are other banks."

"Doesn't matter if you're upside down on your farm. Nobody's going to lend it to you." When I still didn't take it, he added, "Pay me back someday, if it'd make you feel better."

I stared at the check for a moment longer, weighing my options. A loan from a Patton was blasphemy. But a peace offering? Maybe we could work something out, if we covered our asses with legal paperwork. If I could get Jake on board.

It was the biggest *if* I'd ever put my money on.

Reluctantly, I took it, sliding it into my folder of paperwork. "The answer will likely still be no."

"So what I'm hearing is that there's a chance for a yes," he said with a gentle smile.

"Hear whatever you want. Thank you for the offer. It's ... too generous."

"It's not enough, if you ask me."

I wanted to believe him. I wanted to cash this check right here and now and go home to tell Jake I fixed everything—we could pay down our debts and replace any cattle we lost. Provided no more got sick. And the FDA allowed us to stay open.

"I really have to go," I said, backing toward the door.

"I understand. Let me know if there's a way I can help. Even if it's my public humiliation for your boyfriend's sake."

A smile drifted across my face and away at the thought of Chase in tighty-whities, standing on Joe's bar, singing Britney Spears. With a nod, I turned for the door again, and this time, I made it out without intrusion. Once in Pop's truck, I tossed the folder onto the bench seat like it was an envelope dusted with anthrax.

The weight of decision fell heavy on me, and I bucked against it, anxious to escape.

There was no money for the farm with the exception of the

check in my folder, and it'd come from the pocket of our enemy. As much as I wanted to believe Chase, as wonderful as it'd be for everyone to join hands and sing "Kumbaya," we couldn't be further from peace and happiness.

I tried to imagine what Jake would say. I tried to imagine what we would do with that money and without it. Sell off cattle? Downsize? Let our staff go?

My stomach turned, and panic rose.

The ride home was a blur. When I pulled up to the house, I snatched the folder and marched inside, tossing it onto Pop's desk before heading upstairs to change. I pulled on my boots. Tied a bandana around my head. Opened the door and hustled for the red barn.

Nothing like a little manual labor to burn off your angst.

The barn smelled of hay and feed and the tang of animals. Motes of dust floated in light slicing in from the windows, and for a moment, I watched them dance. How nice it would be to just float lazily in the sunshine, carried around by whatever current grabbed you.

When I stopped by the animals' pens to say hello, they greeted me with sounds of recognition. Or hunger. Maybe both.

I approached Alice last.

"Hello, and how are you?" I stroked her head. When we met eyes, she chuffed like a train. "Want a milking?"

I reached for the bucket and stool, but before I had them, Alice lay down. Her face was upturned, her eyes searching.

Frowning, I made my way back to her, kneeling to pet her. "What's the matter, girl?"

Dread rose, bubbling up from my belly to my esophagus. Again, she chuffed and laid her head in my lap.

"Oh God," I breathed, searching the hay for the only sign the cattle gave that they were ill.

I found it too quickly, the pinkish ring of hay that told me what I didn't want to know. Then another.

No.

The twist in my chest hurt too badly to speak or breathe or think. I just sat there with Alice's head in my lap, my mind a screen of static until something finally broke through.

Jake. Find Jake.

Before I had the chance to move Alice's head, Jake's voice sounded behind me.

"Where'd you go in your funeral dress just now—" He stopped.

Tears nipped my eyes, my vision blurring when I met his gaze.

"No. Not Alice."

I nodded.

"Jesus," he said, rushing to kneel at my side, somehow managing to hold me with a heifer's head in my lap.

"How did she get sick?" I asked around hitching sobs. "She's not even with the herds."

"I don't know."

"It doesn't make sense. Nothing makes sense." Fear and hysteria gripped me, pinching my lungs until my fingertips tingled.

"It will. I'm going to find out what's going on. I promise."

"You can't promise that. And what happens if we don't? What if we *never* find out?" I pulled back to look at him, falling to pieces without anyone to catch me. "It got to the red barn, Jake! Alice hasn't been anywhere near the sick cows, and look! Look at her!" Both of us did. "What if all the cattle get sick? What if we lose everything we have?"

"I won't let that happen," he insisted.

"What happens if you can't stop it?"

The question hung between us.

"We have to start thinking about what happens if this doesn't go away. Where's the threshold of loss? How long until we're bankrupt or worse? If this keeps going like it is, we won't be able to replace the cattle. And then what?"

He watched me, his brows low, his eyes dark. "Then we'll figure it out," he ground out.

"And what if we *can't*?"

"What exactly are you getting at?"

"You're too stubborn to consider any outcome but success. You think you can overcome anything by the sheer power of your will. But you can't make something from nothing. You can't just *decide* it's going to be okay. It's time we thought about what happens if it isn't. And the fact of the matter is, we can't do this alone."

"We can sell off stock. Downsize."

"We don't know how many cattle we're going to lose—we might not have anything left to sell."

"The bank then. Another loan—"

I shook my head, my tears choking me. "I tried. That's where I was—the bank. They won't give us any more money, Jake. We don't have the capital or the equity to save ourselves. Without an influx of cash, we'll never make it. And the more stock we lose, the deeper our debt." When I tried to take a breath, it hitched in my chest. "I ran into Chase today, and—"

He backed up. Stood. Looked down at me. "If you propose Chase Patton help us, I swear to God, Olivia, we are through."

The ease with which he'd thrown something so serious at me left me gaping. "You would leave me just for suggesting something?"

"If that something is rolling over for the Pattons, then yeah. I would. Because that would mean we fundamentally disagree on the most sacred point—loyalty to this farm and everything it stands for. Not to mention that *they* are the ones who did this to us."

"What else do you suggest we do? I don't want to do it either, but I'm out of ideas. Who else has the money to help us? If not them, *who*? Chase might be our only option. You were right—the Pattons were after us. James Patton sent Chase to infiltrate, and Chase told me. He didn't lie, didn't try to sneak around me. He came straight out and *told* me, just because it was the right thing to do."

He glared down at me with all the anger and all the betrayal of the apostles finding Judas. "When did he tell you?"

"Fourth of July—"

"You've known this for weeks?"

"I ... I didn't think—"

"No. You didn't think." His chest heaved. "I thought we were on the same page. You don't know me at all if you think I'd ever consider shaking hands with those thieves. And I guess I don't know you either, not if you'd keep this from me. Not if you'd suggest we take money from a Patton." He drew himself up to his full height, his face shutting me out like a door blown closed by the wind. "I'm not taking their filthy, tainted money. You kept the truth from me—the Pattons have been after us this whole time, just like I said. You knew, and you *defended* them. If you think Chase doesn't have an angle, you're a sucker and a fool. But worse than that—you trust him over me. You'd choose his word over my wishes."

"I'm choosing the farm over pride, not him over you. You're just too blinded by your grudge to even *consider* he's not the evil you've made him out to be."

"And you're too gullible to consider he's full of shit. He's got you eating out of his fucking hand, Olivia. If you think that a hundred-and-twenty-year-old feud is all of a sudden dead and that taking money from the Pattons is a solution, you haven't been paying attention." He shook his head, ran a hand through his hair, his eyes on the ground for a long moment. "You say you're loyal to the farm. To me. But if that were true, you'd never have uttered those words. You'd never have opposed me on the matter of the Pattons."

He turned to leave. I scrambled up from beneath Alice to catch him, touching his arm.

"Jake, let me explain—"

He shrugged me off with a jerk so sharp, I nearly tripped. He didn't look at me, just kept stalking toward the barn door.

"I understand just fine," he said coolly. "You've done enough damage for a lifetime, Olivia. No amount of explanation will change t hat."

I stood in the middle of the barn and watched him until he disappeared. My cow lay sick and dying behind me, our farm caught in quicksand, our future slipping away.

He'd cool off, I promised myself. We'd talk just like we always did. We'd work together. Talk about what-if. Find a solution. But we couldn't do it without help, not if things got even a little worse.

In the moment, I fully understood why anyone would sell their soul to the devil.

I would have signed in blood right then and there.

THERE'S A SNAKE IN MY BOOT

Jake

I'D HAD A LOT OF LONG NIGHTS, BUT NONE LIKE THIS.

For the first time in weeks, I slept in my own bed, alone. If the loss of her next to me wasn't enough to keep me awake, it would have been the replay of our fight in my mind.

I couldn't make it stop.

Bowie jumped on the bed when he heard me stir from the thin sleep I'd managed. He charged for my face like a rocket, tongue first. Just when I wrangled him, he wiggled out of my arms, returning with a stuffed turkey leg. So I did as he'd asked—I took it, chucked it, and listened to him scramble off in its direction.

In my rib cage sat a cinder block, crushing my heart and lungs, radiating pain in thudding waves with every aching heartbeat. Everything was wrong. Olivia not being here. The things I'd said and the things she'd said back. The cattle. The farm. Frank's absence.

Frank would have known what to do. But I wasn't half the man he was. I had no idea how to handle what had been dumped in my lap, not until we had answers. I didn't know what to do about my suspicions about Chase, either. My instinct was confrontation, one I'd also spent some time fantasizing about. Many scenarios played out in my mind that involved my fist and Chase's ocular cavity. His nose was also a hit in the fantasy reel—I knew the sight of his broken nose and the bottom half of his face covered in gore would satisfy many, many things in me.

I'd settle for a confession, but that was about as likely as successfully fitting bicycle tires on a tractor.

Or me apologizing to Olivia.

My Olivia. Deep down, I knew she was trying to help, trying to be reasonable. She was looking for solutions. But she was sniffing around in the very last place she should.

How it was even possible that she could consider it was beyond me. Endlessly, she'd ignored my warnings.

Even after I told her what they'd done to me, to the farm. To Frank.

What she'd suggested was unforgivable. That she thought for one second that I'd ever comply was unconscionable. One thing was unmentionable, just one—the Pattons. But over and again, she'd pushed me in that direction, knowing I'd only dig in my heels and push back.

And then there was the matter of her lie. She'd known for weeks that Patton was actively after us and hadn't told me. The only reasons I could figure were that she either had feelings for Chase or she didn't trust me.

I didn't want to walk away from her. I didn't want to be anywhere she wasn't. I'd been cruel to her, said things I shouldn't have, things I didn't mean. The last thing I wanted was for her to leave here. To leave me.

But I'd thought she understood how deep the division between our farms ran until she disregarded what I'd said and felt, called me stubborn as if this were just a matter of me being obstinate. And my wound was so deep, I couldn't see her. Not right now. I couldn't keep having the same conversation, the same fight. I was too tired, and there was too much at stake.

And so, it was what it was.

I flipped back my covers and got out of bed, making my way to the kitchen with Bowie nipping my ankles, his turkey leg abandoned in the threshold of my room. He was as bad as a toddler—his toys were strewn around the house, pulled from their basket and distributed evenly across the square footage. In the kitchen was a tennis ball, which I threw into the living room in order to buy myself a second to make coffee.

Today would be another whirl. Alice had been quarantined with the other cattle and checked out by Miguel. We'd ended yesterday with a total of thirty-two cows dead and no end in sight.

It was all too much.

Regardless of what Olivia said or did, the Pattons were the only people who would go to such great lengths to burn us down. It was true—I had no proof. But it was time for a reckoning. Even if I couldn't shake anything out of Chase, I'd feel twenty pounds lighter if I could unload it all on him. If I didn't do it soon, I was likely to explode, and what would the farm do with me in globs and pieces all over the barn?

But before I dealt with Chase, I needed to deal with the farm's rounds.

I pulled on clothes while I waited for my coffee, pouring it into my Thermos when it was through. Stomped my feet into my boots and headed for the barn with the jingle of Bowie's collar behind me.

Almost all of me was tuned to the big house as I passed it, looking for motion or a streak of red hair with a contrary tug-of-war in me. I wanted to see her. I didn't want to see her at all. I was afraid of what I'd do if I did. Whether I kissed her or picked a fight, it'd be the wrong thing to do, and I couldn't face the choice or its consequences. Not until I had some time and a full night's sleep.

When I pulled open the barn door, Bowie shot in and ran straight for the goats to tease them as he did, the asshole. Alice's stall was painfully empty, and it seemed like every furry face in the barn was pointed at it. But I made my way around the pens and horse stalls like Olivia and I usually did together, making sure everyone had feed and hay and salt licks. Saying hello and petting heads. Kit would bring pig slop and take the chickens' eggs. Stalls would be mucked and horses groomed by one of the crew.

Bowie barked his little bark at Brenda the kid, who'd once nearly brained him with her thick skull. Sometimes I wondered if he remembered, as relentlessly as he pestered her, running into the pen to nip her haunches before hauling ass right back out before she could catch him. If Jolene were here, she'd just chase Bowie like a hype man, giving him the glory while she offered moral support.

Felt awfully familiar.

I passed the pigpen, checking the feed trough that supplemented the slop. But I stopped dead when I got close enough to get a good look at them. Because they weren't pink—they were yellowing.

Jaundiced.

A bullet of thought fired through my brain. I moved back to the goats, climbing in to check one of the doe's eyes, gums, between her legs. Yellowing, all. But the horses were fine. The other animals also showed signs, but the chickens were unaffected. Very few illnesses could jump animals. But these animals all had one thing in common with the sick herds.

Their water came from our old water mill. All but the chickens.

I turned on my heel and took off for my truck.

As Bowie and I rushed to Miguel, I was a rumble of thoughts. Worries. Accusations. Because while it was possible that particular water source had been naturally contaminated, it was highly unlikely. Two years ago, we'd replaced the underground

DON'T FORGET TO SELL IT

Jake

The Patton estate was straight out of either a *Better Homes & Gardens* magazine or hell.

The five-thousand-square-foot farmhouse was the cheerful color of a robin's egg, with white trim and wooden shutters. The wraparound porch was touched with hanging chairs, rocking chairs, topiary plants, flower boxes, and the yard was a manicured marvel of understated class.

Bunch of rich-people bullshit, if you asked me. As fake and curated as the Pattons.

The elder Patton's dually was missing from the drive, conveniently absent through our farm's trouble. He was holed up in Washington at their new headquarters, since it seemed the Pattons had outgrown the town that made them. But Chase's spanking new Ram sat tall and hefty in the driveway, which was good.

He was exactly the son of a bitch I was looking for.

Rage vibrated through me like a struck tuning fork as I exited my truck and stormed to the front door, furious that I had to ring the doorbell and wait like a civilized man rather than rip the door off its hinges and hunt him down like I wanted to. Movement from inside, and the door opened.

I hated his fucking smile. I wanted to see it half toothless and bloody from a split lip and freshly bare gums.

"And what can I do for you, Milovic?"

What thin control I had on myself failed. I reached in, grabbed him by his pressed shirtfront, and pulled him out only to slam him against the siding.

"I know what you fucking did, you sack of shit."

A flicker of confusion behind his eyes. "Is this about Olivia?"

I snarled. "Why? Did you do something to her? Because I don't need another excuse to break your neck, Patton."

He didn't answer right away. "What do you think I did?"

"Sabotaged my farm. The fire. The missing cattle. The goddamn copper in our water mill tank. I know it was you."

"It wasn't me."

Again, I slammed him against the wall. "Don't fucking lie to me."

"I'm not," he said with a flat earnestness. "I swear to God, I'm not lying."

My jaw ached from strain, my eyes wildly searching his for the truth.

"I don't want your farm put under," he said. "I want to help."

A bitter laugh left me, my throat burning. "Help. You think you're so fucking smart." I leaned into him, pressing my fists into his chest. "But if you think you can get in that easy, you're dumber than I thought."

He shoved me, and I let him go by choice, happy to see the creases from my grip marring the pristine cotton of his button-down.

His blue eyes were somehow both ice-cold and aflame. "If you think I'm not already halfway in, then you're dumber than *I* thought. And I already thought you were pretty fucking dumb."

I paused. "*In* how?"

"Ask your girlfriend. Better yet, take a look in the folder she had at the bank. That's where she put the check I wrote her."

A cold rush raced down my arms and legs. "Liar," I growled, squeezing my fists at my sides so I wouldn't hit him.

Head cocked, he assessed me. "Your farm is coming undone. You're about to lose everything. Olivia has the good sense to see that, but I can't say I'm surprised you don't."

"You did this," I said through my teeth. "You took down our farm, hobbled us so you could acquire it. And you expect me to just roll over and let you have it? You know me better than that."

"I'll say it again—I didn't have anything to do with it, Jake. I wouldn't do that to Olivia. You? I wouldn't think twice. But not her."

Again, I felt that prickle in my gut that said he was telling the truth. "Then who? Because I can only think of one other person."

A heartbeat, and Chase's expression shifted. "You think—"

"I *know*. If I went out to your barns, would I find my herd? Or did you and your daddy already sell them?"

He shook his head, put a hand out. Nothing in his posture was aggressive, which pissed me off.

I wanted to hit him real bad, but I was no animal.

"How many cattle?" he asked.

"Forty heads. Three trailers' worth."

He scrubbed a hand over his mouth, his eyes bright with calculations. "And it started a couple weeks ago?"

"Three." My fists loosened. I watched him.

He thought a second longer before shaking his head. "It couldn't be. Dad wants your farm, but not like this."

"You mean to tell me he hasn't been using you to do his bidding like the tool you are? Olivia already told me you *were* working on her."

"Sure, but I told her I wouldn't take part in it anymore, and I haven't. I don't know anything about the trouble at your farm, Jake."

My eyes narrowed in suspicion. If he knew anything about it, he'd be slithering around me just to watch me squirm. The man in front of me was shocked and concerned. And playing dumb had never been Chase Patton's style.

"How'd he get all this past you?"

He sobered. "Dad has been nudging me in Olivia's direction, sure. But he came to me just after your fire and ... *fuck*. I should have known."

"Known what?"

"Known better than to believe he actually gave a shit about your farm. He came to me, talking about how rough you were having it since Frank passed. Said he wanted to help and wanted me to figure out how. But our overseer—you know Garrett—he's been acting funny. You know, shifty. He and Dad have been Velcro lately. I'll catch them talking, and they shut up the second I'm in the room. And I might know something about your stock—"

I took two swift steps in his direction, arching over him. "Chase, if you know where my cattle are, you'd better fucking tell me *right now*."

He squared up, but his face was more gentle warning than outright aggression. "Let me do some digging. It's just a hunch. Let me see it through."

I drew an inhale through my nose so hard, my nostrils flared. "I'm coming with you."

"You come with me, and I'm not gonna find anything. In fact, if anybody sees you here, you might blow it."

"Let me help give you a good story."

Before he could ask what, I popped him in the eye.

He doubled over, hand to his eye. "*Fuck!*"

I shook out my fist. "They can't help but believe you since I gave you a black eye."

"You fucking asshole! Jesus, I'm trying to help you!"

"You already did," I said with a wry smile. "Haven't felt this good in days."

He growled. "Get the fuck out of here. I'll be in touch."

"My pleasure."

My smile faded as I walked to the truck where Bowie waited, panting out the window at me. I'd just been handed two surprises, one good and one bad. Chase might know where my herd was, and that was hope I'd lost.

The bad sat in a folder in Olivia's possession.

I didn't want to believe she'd accept such an unholy piece of paper. That she'd consider cashing it. This was where she'd gotten the idea to ask the Pattons for help. Where she'd driven a wedge between us.

How long had she had the check? How long had she been sitting on it without telling me? Could it have been weeks?

I hated that I didn't know—and for more than knowledge's sake.

I didn't know that I'd believe whatever she told me. Not after I'd given her my trust, only to have her make a deal with the devil behind my back.

My heartache was complete—I felt it from brow to boot.

I didn't trust her, and I could never be with someone I didn't trust.

No matter how much I loved her.

BELONGING AND OTHER LIES

Olivia

My fingers fiddled with Alice's crop of hair as we sat together on the hay bed floor of the medical barn that afternoon. Miguel had hooked her up to an IV, administering some medicine with a long and forgettable name, and told me to keep my chin up. We'd caught it early enough that there was a good chance for her.

The rest of the cattle wouldn't be so lucky.

Most of them had advanced too far to save. Some had been affected by the poisoned water just before quarantine and were at the same stage as Alice—those we could maybe help. Over the days, as new water had been pumped into the tank, the copper solution had thinned out, resulting in lower numbers of new cases. And size mattered—though there were sick cows across the herds, the smaller they were, the faster they died.

We'd lose some barn animals too. But now that we knew what we were dealing with, we could act, and acting was always preferable to the hell of endless, helpless waiting.

Now the farm could move on.

BET THE FARM

It was the first bright spot I'd seen since Jake walked away from me in the red barn. Had it only been a yesterday? It felt like a week.

The long hours of the night had passed here with Alice, and I spent the time thinking. Thinking about all he'd said, all the ways he'd hurt me and how I'd hurt him. The ways he'd been right and how he'd been wrong. Maybe I had been naive. Maybe Chase had no good in him, despite what I thought. Maybe I *was* a sucker and a fool. Or maybe Jake was wrong.

All I knew was that we'd hurt each other again. He saw me as a liability, and I saw him as a roadblock. Here in a bit, when he'd had a little more time to stew, I'd find him so we could talk. We'd be fine, so long as we both apologized and found a way to communicate.

Hope sprang, sparkling and bright, at the thought. And I put all my focus on that in the interest of willing it to fruition.

That hope was dashed by a blood-red slash when Jake walked into the medical barn.

If I hadn't known what'd happened by the grim calm on his face, I would have figured it out from the slip of paper in his hand.

My heart lurched and my stomach sank, my gaze hanging on the check.

His steps were long and measured as he approached, looking down at me like a furious god. "Have anything to tell me?" he asked quietly, darkly.

"I can explain," I started, scrambling to my feet.

His eyes followed me as I rose. "I don't know that there's a way you could explain this one away, Olivia."

He was so calm, so sharp, I didn't think I'd ever been so afraid of what he'd say. The wild, angry bear could be met with a roar. But this I didn't know how to fight.

"He just gave it to me yesterday—"

"You should have told me the second you came home. Just

like you should have discussed it with me before you tried to put the farm up for a loan."

"After you said … when you said …" I stammered. "What was I supposed to do, chase you down and hand you two hundred grand from the Pattons? I was never going to cash it, Jake."

"I don't believe you."

A hot flush bloomed on my cheeks, the sting of my nose warning of tears. "You don't actually think that I'd—"

"When you accepted this scrap of bullshit, you betrayed me, this farm, and everyone who depends on it. Which is apparently everyone but you." He crumpled up the paper and dropped it. "And again, you lied. You didn't tell me about the money—I had to find out about it from *him*."

"Do you *honestly* believe that I wasn't going to tell you?"

"You've kept things from me before. Why not now? It tracks—you've been pushing for peace with the Pattons since you got here. Since Pop's funeral. This is what you want, it's what you've wanted for a long time, but if you'd been *here* instead of leaving us all those years ago, you'd know just how grave that mistake was. I told you I'd figure all of this out, but you didn't have any faith. Instead, you ran off to the bank to try to borrow off the farm without even mentioning it to me, and then you accepted a check from the devil. Be honest, Olivia—you don't trust me anymore than I trust you, or you would have come to me with the loan, the check, the truth about James Patton and his intentions. If we don't even have trust between us, we don't have anything."

"What are you saying, Jake?" The question trembled.

"You're dangerous, Olivia. You are a danger to this farm. You're the weak spot, just like the Pattons figured you for, and that check proves it. If you'd just fucking gone home, none of this would have happened. The sick cattle, the fire, the missing stock—it was all a scheme to steal the farm through *you*. And you let it happen."

"That's not fair," I said softly, painfully. "I tried to tell you."

"Not very hard."

For a long, pregnant moment, we stared at each other.

"Tell me what to do, Jake. Tell me how to make it right."

He shook his head. "There is one thing in this world I hold above all else—loyalty. I believe you think you're helping. I believe you think you have the answers. You told me you'd never hurt me on purpose. You'd never hurt the farm on purpose, either. But here we are, and both are broken, thanks to you. And the good you've done was erased when you put your faith in the fucking Pattons over me."

"And you're so scared to trust anyone that you'd push me away, accuse me of sabotage. I *do* trust you. How was I supposed to throw that check away when we need it so desperately? It warranted a discussion, at least. But I should have known. I should have known you'd throw it back at me when you *know* I would never betray you."

"I can't do this."

I paused. "Do what exactly?"

"Fight you. Forgive you. Let this go. I can't do it, Olivia."

My lungs burned, my breath still. "Don't say that. You can't mean it."

"Have I ever been anything but honest with you?"

"No—"

"No, I haven't. Unlike you."

"Where does that leave us? What do we do?"

He met my eyes with white-hot pain and betrayal. "I don't know."

I stilled. Read the writing on his face. Felt the ground tether me, felt the weight of gravity across my skin.

It was over.

Whether I'd intended to or not, whether I was right or wrong, I had breached the trust I'd earned, the trust he'd given with such rare faith. I knew it was bad, but I believed there was a path back to each other, even if it took time and mending.

But that was all gone the second he'd found that check on my desk, and I couldn't say I blamed him. Not knowing him as well as I did, which, despite his insistence, was very well.

His eyes shone, his jaw set. But behind his anger, I saw his pain. I saw the fight in him as clearly as I could see my own.

Tears welled, blurring the room and the betrayal on his face. For that, at least, I was grateful.

He turned away, leaving the barn.

And he took my heart with him.

MUTUAL ASSHOLERY

Olivia

"I DON'T LIKE IT." PRESLEY STOOD AT THE END OF MY TABLE at the diner with her arms folded and her eyes narrowed. "I don't like it at all, starting with whatever this is." She gestured to me. "When was the last time you showered?"

"Tuesday? No, Monday. I think."

"If you have to think that hard, it's been too long." She slid in across from me and leaned on the table, braced by her forearms. Her shoulders made an *M* that matched her eyebrows. "He just … walked away?"

I nodded and smoothed my hands over my hair, deciding to retwist it in the four hundredth bun I'd put it in since it was last washed. "It's been three days, and the only thing I've managed to do is cry buckets and buy a plane ticket back to New York. Everything is fucked."

She tried for an encouraging smile. "It must be, throwing the F-word around so casually. Good thing Cilla's not here."

"How much of that money actually goes in the jar?"

"Who knows. I think she's hiding a cache of quarters

somewhere behind her pile of stuffed animals like a squirrel." She paused, her face softening. "When are you leaving?"

Instantly, tears threatened to spill. "Monday."

"I hate this."

"Me too."

"There has to be some way to get through to him. There has to be some way to convince him to see your perspective."

"Maybe before, but not now. That was it, the last straw. I should have thrown the check away. I should have gone straight to Jake."

"Why, so he could yell at you? Listen, I think Jake's a great guy, but he can be a real asshole."

"I know. But so can I. Mutual assholery."

"You're not an asshole."

"I pushed and pushed him, listened to Chase when I shouldn't have. I didn't tell him that James Patton was after us. With a feud this deep, with this many years between their family and ours, there's nothing to consider but the people who have been here all the time I haven't. We could have figured out another option for the money, or at least tried. I could have backed Jake up, but I didn't. I suggested he join forces with the enemy, and what's worse—I took their money."

"Fear makes people say and do things they don't mean. Like the prospect of losing the farm, your home, Alice—of course you'd consider taking the money. You didn't mean any harm. It's sort of like how when Jake is afraid, he turns into a raging butthole."

"But that's the thing. Since we got together, we haven't fought—I'd earned his trust. Then I went and threw it in the fire."

She sighed. "You haven't seen him at all?"

"Just once and from a long way away. Even from across the property, I could feel how angry and hurt he was. He just got into his truck with Bowie and drove away. A couple of times, I sat on the back porch and watched for him to come in after work, but he never showed. I figured he probably saw me there and waited me out."

"I can't believe he hasn't even spoken to you."

"It's better this way, really—I don't know what would happen if he did, but I can't imagine it would be productive. I'm through being hurt by him, and I'm through hurting him. I just need to go before I break anything else."

"But you'll come back, right?"

"Of course I will. I'm still running my half of things. I'll just be heading it up from New York."

"What about the bet?"

"It's off. It's been off for a long time, I think. It's easier this way. I can do what I've been doing from the other side of the country and leave this part of it to him like I should have from the start. Anyway, this means you can come see me. I can take you to Zabar's and Central Park and do all the touristy things you want."

"I'd still prefer you here."

"Me too."

"Excuse me, Presley," Mr. Blalock said from too far away to be polite. "If you're through with your conversation there, I could use a top-off." He wiggled his mug at her.

"*Yeah, yeah, okay, all right,*" she muttered before standing. "I'll be back in a second."

I looked down at the spread of food on my plate and felt sick. I'd had to force myself to eat, which wasn't easy—my mouth was so dry, no amount of water could satisfy it. Food was either cardboard or mush. And the hollandaise sauce on my eggs did *not* look appetizing today.

I pushed my plate away and felt a manic tug in my gut to leave. To run away from the table. This town. The farm.

Jake.

I reached into my pocket for a twenty and left it on the table, waving to Presley on my way out the door and mouthing, *I'll text you.*

She looked worried, but her hands were too full of dirty plates to do anything but let me go.

A hard swallow didn't open my throat. A sniffle didn't dispel the tingle of my nose. And as I pulled out of the parking lot and onto the road, I was left too alone to fight.

First came the tears on a wash of despair. Then came the sobs that shook my shoulders as I hung on to the wheel, unable to wipe the streams of tears from my face without losing control. They ran without interference down my cheeks to cling to my jaw until they were heavy enough to fall. I reached a pull-off and drove in, throwing the truck in park, curling in on myself.

My face dropped to my hands.

I let go of the tenuous hold I'd had.

The path of my life had taken a hard turn when Pop died, re-routing all traffic here, home. I'd thought this was a permanent place for me. That the road ended here, at the end of a long drive lined with ancient oaks. Maybe it would have.

But now it was time to go.

What I hadn't told Presley was that I'd been frozen out by most of the farm. Only the barn animals and Kit were still sympathetic, but I saw the hurt in Kit's eyes, the same betrayal written on everyone's face. The cattle were blessedly safe, that particular problem solved. But on the matter of The Money, there was only one problem.

Me.

It was a long time before I pulled myself together, taking a good portion of that time to feel sorry for myself and mourn all my losses, all the way back to my parents. I'd been thinking about them a lot, Pop too. About how I didn't realize that my life had been missing *this*. The farm. It was a piece of me that had clicked back into place the second we pulled into the driveway.

I knew what it was like to not have a home. But I'd found it again here, after ten long years adrift.

But the anchor had been pulled up and stowed, and it was time to float away again.

By the time I got back to the house, I'd composed myself, though a glance would tell whoever looked that I'd been crying. My plan was to hurry inside, climb into my bed, and empty myself of whatever tears might be left. I could hide there for a little while before heading to the store to show our new shop girls how to do the inventory. It would be fine. Everything would be just fine.

I'd convinced myself that was true until I saw Jake walking out of my front door.

Breathlessly, I parked the truck, and he watched me with blazing intensity hot enough to fry an egg. For a moment, I wondered if he was here to talk, *really* talk. Otherwise, he would have sent Mack to relay any messages. The fantasy played out in my mind—an apology, a declaration. Happy tears and his lips against mine.

I pushed the thought away as I climbed out, though I couldn't let go of a little ember of hope.

God, has he even blinked? I wondered as I climbed the porch stairs.

"Hey," was all I could think to say.

"Hey." His voice was gravelly and raw as he looked down at me.

I hadn't known just how much I missed him until he was right here, tearing me to shreds.

"I … I'm sorry. I didn't know you'd be here," he said, breaking my heart just a little more.

With a small smile, I said, "You live here too. It's just … well, I thought you might want to talk."

He didn't answer right away. His brows ticked a little closer together, a war behind his eyes. "I don't know what to say."

"Me neither."

A long beat.

"I think …" he started, trailing off. "I wondered if I could handle seeing you."

My heart jerked. "Can you?"

"No."

I pursed my lips, biting down to stop myself from crying. "Because you hate me."

"Because it hurts too bad." He paused. "I told you once, I could never hate you."

"I didn't think that was still true."

"It is. That's why it hurts."

I tamped down my emotions like sails in a storm, the edges flying away before I could secure them. But I didn't cry.

"I think you should take the deciding share," I said with more strength than I felt. "Just take control of the farm. You're the only one who really knows what to do with it."

Again he looked down, his Adam's apple bobbing. "I don't want anything else."

"You say that, but—"

"I don't want anything else, Livi."

My shoulders sagged. He wouldn't even let me give him what he was owed. "If you change your mind—"

"I won't."

A chuff of laughter through my nose. "No, you wouldn't. Once you make your mind up about something, there's no going back."

The faint smile on my lips faded at a shift of context. He only looked torn.

The moment broke with a stiffening of his back. "I'd better get back to work."

"All right," I answered, watching him move for the stairs.

Stop him. Say something. This is your last chance.

"Jake," I called after him a little too loud.

He stopped and glanced over his shoulder, and I was devastated by his beauty, by that deep and constant river of pain that rolled through him. And I knew it was useless. Fighting would only hurt both of us worse.

So I gave him another truth, one he already knew. "I'm sorry."

He stood, poised to either walk away or climb back up the stairs and to me.

But he only said, "Me too."

And then he walked away, and that final ember of hope went with him.

This farm couldn't function without Jake. I was replaceable, inconsequential to the work he did. I gave nothing to this farm that someone else couldn't provide, but Jake was the beating heart of this place.

To lose him would mean losing the farm's motor.

The time to fight had passed. Trying to make a stand now would only drag the battle on and on until we were both bloody and ruined. But I had no doubt he would win.

As he should. Because where else would he go? Some other farm, to leave his home behind simply because he couldn't look at me without reliving his pain? I had a job waiting for me in New York. I had a life there to fall back on.

I realized with a cold wash of reality just how right he'd been about me, just not in the way I'd thought he meant. This farm was Jake's entire world, and I always had a plan B. There was always a safety net for me where he had none. His ferocity in defending this place was born of something deeper.

It was everything he had.

The truth dawned on me like sunrise from the gallows. If I stayed on, I wouldn't be helping the farm at all.

I wouldn't be helping Jake.

I'd be breaking everything I loved.

There was only one thing I could do.

And with tears on my cheeks, I turned for the house to make the call that would do it.

JUST ONE FAVOR

Jake

T WICE IN MY LIFE, I'D EXPERIENCED SUCH LOSS THAT A PART of me broke, the fault leaving a sharp, craggy chasm in me, too deep and wide to bridge. The death of my mother and then of Frank.

Today marked a third.

I walked away from her shaking, too overcome to think, too overwhelmed to do anything but sink into my loss and hope I didn't drown. I wanted to turn around, to gather her up in my arms, to kiss away everything that'd happened. To beg her to forgive me. To let myself forgive her.

But I couldn't. Not if I wanted this farm to survive.

What a dumb idea, coming up to the house. Here I'd thought I had a firm grip on the reins, and one look at her had set me on a wild gallop. All I could do was hang on until I mastered myself.

Somehow, she still managed to surprise me.

She'd tried to give me the majority share, though she didn't argue, didn't try to convince me, knowing it wouldn't do any good.

The two of us together were trouble, and the two of us trying to run the farm through that trouble seemed impossible, not without destroying it and each other in the process. How I felt about her was irrelevant—there was no trust to hold us together. Everything about her hurt. How I loved her. How she'd betrayed me. How she loved me. How she'd disregarded me.

Nothing had been the same since she'd come home. Not the farm. Not me.

It'd happened like it did in my nightmares—she swooped in, left her touch on everything. There were whispers of her everywhere. Even the fucking pink door to the big house.

Bowie came running out from behind the red barn, tongue lolling and ears flopping. But at the sound of heavy, clanging metal, he stopped and stiffened, his eyes trained on the back entrance. Mack wandered out behind Bowie like he was caught in a trance, his eyes wide and mouth gaping as he stared in the same direction as Bowie. Confused, I turned to the sound and adopted the same expression.

Three duallys clanked and rumbled toward the barns, pulling forty-foot trailers full of cattle.

Chase was behind the wheel of the first, his elbow hanging out the window and a hotshot smirk on his face.

A gasp from my side caught my attention, and when I looked down, there was Olivia, slack-jawed and breathless, smiling with big, shiny tears in her eyes.

"Oh my God. Is that ..."

"I think it is."

We took off in a jog toward the barns where Jimmy had pulled open the gates to let the trucks in. We got to them as they were parking and made for Chase's truck.

He popped out of the car window, leaned on the roof of the truck, and waved.

"Why does Chase Patton have a black eye, Jake?"

When I gave her a look, she sighed, her eyes flicking to the cloudless sky.

"You looking for these?" Chase called.

I dragged my gaze over the sight of our cattle back in our farm.

"How in the fuck?" I asked in wonder.

"Well"—Chase jumped down and walked over—"we have an empty facility in Redding we're renovating, and its barns are empty. I had a hunch—if he stole them, that'd be where he took them." His levity hardened to stone. "I can't fucking believe him."

"I can. Jesus, look at them. I never thought I'd see them again." I shook my head to clear it and turned to Chase, extending a hand. "I don't know how to thank you."

Chase took the offering with a clap and pumped once. "There's one thing you can do."

"Anything."

"Don't call the cops."

I withdrew my hand and glared at him. "You can't be serious."

Chase sighed, hanging his hands low on his hips. "I am. Not because he's my dad and we might get shut down, but because there's another way out. One that will not only get rid of him, but it'll give you all the cash you could ever want for."

Olivia and I exchanged a glance.

"I know you don't trust me," he added, "but I went against him for this. I don't know if you have any idea what the consequences of that will be, but do me a favor and hear me out before you call."

I met Olivia's eyes in search of an answer and found it before turning back to Chase.

"All right. Let's hear it."

A LITTLE BIT OF THIS

Jake

Two days later, James Patton glared at me from across the substantial depth of his opulent desk.

I glared right back. Difference was, I wore just enough of a smile to make him mad.

"Are you gonna tell me what this is all about, or are we gonna lock horns in silence?" he asked.

"I know you're behind what's happened on my farm."

He didn't even flinch. "I don't know what you're talking about—I haven't even been in the state."

"I know your overseer had one of his guys start the fire. I know the names of the guys who stole my herd. And I know your overseer himself poisoned my water supply."

At that, he laughed, a big, hearty sound. "That's cute, kid. Real cute. You got any proof of that?"

I opened the leather folder in my lap and withdrew the first of many papers, flipped it in his direction, and slid it across his desk.

"I have an affidavit here, signed by several of your farmhands who have agreed to testify that you paid them to sabotage our farm in court. And to the police. And the FDA."

Amused, he picked it up. But the second he started reading, his smile faded, then turned down. "Nobody'd believe any of these guys, and I hope you know you just got every one of them fired."

I shrugged. "Pretty sure I know of another farm that'll take them."

A tinge of red climbed out the collar of his tailored shirt. "You can't prove shit, Milovic."

"You mean to tell me you're so confident that *none* of this worries you?"

"No police officer in the county would hear you out. Not a single person in that station would ever accuse me of thieving. What the hell do I need your ratty cattle for? Why would I give two shits about Frank's farm?"

"Because it's the one thing you could never have. Because you wanted to succeed where your daddy, his daddy, the one before him failed. You thought you could wiggle your way in through Olivia, but she's as good as gone." I pulled out a handful of photos. "But fine. All right. Let's say I can't prove it. Think the FDA will have a hard time figuring you out when I call in a tip?" I tossed the pictures on his desk.

The blotchy red reached his jaw. "I don't know who the fuck you think you are, but—"

"Look at the pictures, James."

"Don't tell me what to do, you little shit."

"*Look at the pictures.*"

Tiny muscles flickered next to his nostrils as he tried to maintain his composure. But he looked. And when he did, *all* of him went red.

I tsked, enjoying his discomfort. "Cipro? I thought you were better than that. Patton Farms, pumping their cattle full of illegal antibiotics. No wonder your heifers are so fat and healthy."

Furious breaths sawed in and out of him, his chest rising and falling too hard and fast. A prickle of sweat beaded at his hairline. I wondered if he was hyperventilating and fantasized about him passing out right here on his desk.

"One call, and the FDA is here, testing your milk."

"What do you want?" he asked through his teeth.

I pulled two packs of papers out, handed them over. "The papers in your hand include a number of things—documentation I'll be sending the police for my missing cattle, the fire, and the losses from the copper poisoning. Behind that, you'll find a lawsuit for damages and our filings for formal police charges. The last is a settlement contract."

He skipped the first two and went straight for the out.

"The terms are simple enough. You will leave town indefinitely and hand the creamery to Chase. And you'll pay us—"

"Three and a half *million* dollars?" he spat. "You're out of your mind, son."

"We can get ten in court. And with the benefit of seeing you in prison."

"You can't fucking tell me to move—"

"These are the terms, Patton. You've got your shiny, new headquarters and a house being built up in Washington, if I heard right. You're going anyway. I'm just suggesting you go now and stay there."

For a long, silent moment, he stared at me with the cold, assessing glare of a predator. "You're smarter than you look, 'specially for an illegal."

I ignored the jab, not interested in wasting energy correcting him. "So what's it gonna be? The quantity of antibiotics you have suggests all of your livestock will test positive. And what then? What'll you do when you've lost everything and the town where you started turns their back on you?"

He sat back in his leather chair with that hard expression still on his face. "Never figured you for an extortionist. More of a by-the-book type."

"If I had my way, you'd already be in jail. But I owed somebody a favor."

"Must be some favor."

"So what's it gonna be?" I asked, unwilling to give him anything that would implicate Chase, that stupid asshole.

"I need some time to consider."

I shrugged, my head cocked in mock disappointment. "It's now or never. But if you don't want to sign—"

When I reached for the papers, he grabbed them. "I haven't answered you yet, boy." He pulled his reading glasses out of his shirt pocket and put them on without breaking our eye contact.

I sat, still and silent, watching him as he went through the papers one by one, the terms of the settlement last and longest. My heart was a jackrabbit in my chest, my mind chanting *sign it* in the hopes of manifesting my request.

A humorless chuckle from across the desk. "You even figured out how to make it look like a legitimate business deal."

"Had to figure out how to cover for the cattle you stole, didn't I?"

"As much as I could beat the shit out of you right now, I'm impressed."

"Maybe that'll stop you from underestimating me again."

His eyes flicked from the contract to me, and I noted a sense of approval on his features. And then he signed.

When he tossed the pen on top with a clank, he said, "Shoulda asked for five. I'd have given it to you."

"This is more than enough to meet our needs. Initiate a wire, and we'll put all this behind us. It'll be nice for the next generation to do what yours never could."

His laugh boomed. "What's that, be a bunch of pussies?"

"Get along."

"Exactly." He opened his laptop and started typing. "I just want to know one thing."

"I'm not telling you who ratted you out."

He watched me for a beat. "At some point, I'm gonna find out."

"Well, you let me know when you do. I'll buy you a drink."

Again, a chuckle, touched with respect. It was a strange feeling to be even distantly respected by someone you hated so much. A sweet sort of sour.

And I enjoyed the taste until I was three-point-five million dollars richer.

The pop of a champagne cork sounded in Jeremiah's office.

I laughed as I watched him fumble with the bottle, helpless against the foaming fountain.

As he poured into scotch glasses—which I'd have preferred to be filled with actual scotch—he said, "Never did I think I'd see the day when the Pattons were run out of town."

"Well, not all of them," I said, taking the glass he offered me.

"To Frank," he said with his glass in the air.

"To Frank," I echoed, wishing he were here.

We took simultaneous sips and made identical faces.

He put his on his desk. "It seemed like the proper drink to celebrate, but I forgot just how much I hated it."

"Oh, I remembered how bad it was."

"Next time, say speak up." He took his seat, smiling. But something about the expression was sad. "I have one more thing for you to sign today."

"What's that?" I asked as he picked up a folder I hadn't noticed on his desk.

"Have a look for yourself."

When he handed it over, curiosity prickled up and down my spine. I opened it. Saw Olivia's name. Stopped breathing.

The document went through some legalese I scanned, getting to the contract points.

The first of which granted me her fifty percent share.

I skimmed the rest, picking out a few other terms. But I couldn't think past the first one.

The entire farm.

Mine.

I looked up at Jeremiah, who had that same sad smile on his face.

"She asked me to give you this too."

I took the letter with shaking hands. Tore it open. Read it once fast, then again, slower. And with every word, a little piece of me fell apart.

Jake,

Please don't say no.

I know you're going to resist, but I've already relinquished my shares, and that's the case whether you sign the contract or not. So I hope you'll take the farm. It's yours.

It was always yours.

I came here with all the best intentions, and I'm leaving having failed at so many of them. But in this one final act, I'm going to make that right and do what I should have done from the start. Give the farm to you.

How can I say I'm sorry when words aren't enough? How can I explain how it feels to know that I broke the trust you give so sparingly? You were right—I came home like a bulldozer and changed everything. But I hope you know that I would never betray you. That everything I ever did was with the farm first, you second in my mind. Only I had it backward—it should have been you first, always.

Thank you for teaching me so much more than how to drive a tractor. You showed me what was important in my life and gave me what I was missing. You let me love you for a season, and that's a gift that will carry me through the rest of my days.

I will miss this place more than you know.

I will miss you most of all.

I hope someday, you'll forgive me. But in the meantime, please take care of the farm. Take care of Kit and Mack and Alice.

Take care of yourself.

All my love forever,
Olivia

I ran my thumb over the loops of her name with my heart nothing but glittering shards in my chest.

I should have been happy—it was what I thought I'd wanted, after all. But all I felt was deep, aching loss, coupled with an immediate rejection of her contract.

Because it wasn't what I'd wanted after all. Not without her.

If she'd handed this paper to me a few months ago, I'd have signed without question. But not now. Because somehow, over the course of one summer, I'd come to rely on her. I'd shared every moment with her as we navigated our new, solitary lives without Frank. Every struggle, every success. She'd become the only person I could share the farm with, just like Frank had intended.

She couldn't leave. I never wanted to leave.

Long ago, I'd let her leave here without a fight, and then I blamed her for it. I'd pushed her away and locked the door behind her. And here we were again, history repeating itself. Except this time, it was me who'd caused the mess.

It was *me* who didn't trust *her*. Not the other way around.

It wasn't her leaving me—I'd all but sent her away, fulfilling my prophecy, sabotaging myself, my happiness.

Everything *had* changed because of her, but not one single thing—not even the goats—was a detriment. I couldn't go back to the way things were. And I couldn't do this without her.

I'd fallen in love with her.

I couldn't help but wonder if Frank had intended that too.

What have I done?

It wasn't a dawning of realization, a slow rise of understanding. It was the crack of thunder.

She would never have put the farm in danger. She never would have sold. She couldn't have betrayed me even if she'd wanted to. Because she wasn't the one to sell out.

The papers in my hand were proof—she would sacrifice everything to do what she thought was right. Even considering the Pattons' money was all in the interest of the farm, just like she'd said. I'd just been too blind to see it. Too hurt to believe her.

I looked up at Jeremiah, who was watching me.

"I can't sign this." The words scratched their way up my dry throat.

"Well, why not?"

But I was already standing, folder under my arm. "Because without her, none of it matters."

"Well, son—if you've got something to say to her, you'd better hurry. She's leaving soon for the airport."

"Leaving?" I breathed.

He nodded. "Back to New York. Asked me not to tell you."

"She can't leave. She can't... I've got to—"

With a laugh, Jeremiah nudged me toward the door. "Go on, boy—get outta here quick."

And I left him smiling behind me as I ran for my truck.

I loved her.

And I had to make sure she knew.

FRENCH EXIT

Olivia

MY PINK SUITCASES WERE LINED UP LIKE CHEERFUL little soldiers on the porch.

I couldn't stop crying.

Jolene lay so still in my arms, I wondered if she knew what was happening.

"Kit's going to take such good care of you," I promised, rocking her in a porch chair, scratching her neck and looking into her sweet face. "You're going to be the most spoiled ever, you know that? She's going to f-feed you hamburgers and steak and chicken with gravy. And you'll have Bowie too. You'll never be a-alone."

The words dissolved, my eyes squeezed shut, and I gathered her up so I could bury my face in her scruff. She licked the tears from my cheek. I cried harder.

Alone again.

"Oh, honey," Kit said from behind me, her voice cracking. "Come here."

I stood, still holding Jolene in my arms as Kit wrapped me up in her arms, and for a moment, I leaned into her, tried to get it all out. But the tears were bottomless. By now, I knew that for fact.

When I broke away, I swiped at my cheeks.

"There has to be some way for you to stay," Kit said through tears of her own. "There has to be."

I shook my head. "It's okay, Kit. I-I'll be okay."

"Just talk to Jake. I know he'll come around."

"It's just better for everyone if I go. You all can get back to normal."

"Nothing will ever be normal again, not like it was before Frank died. And here I thought we'd found a new normal, one Frank would be so proud of."

"Me too."

When my chin wobbled, she snatched me up again.

I'd gotten word from Jeremiah that Patton had signed the contract. The farm had all the money it could ever want for. James Patton, gone. Chase taking over. Everyone had gotten what they wanted.

Except for me.

Kit let me go and tried to dry her tears. "I don't know how I'm ever going to get you to the airport in this state. Oh! I made you a meal. Let me go get it, and we'll … well, we'll go." She paused. "Are you sure there's nobody else you want to say goodbye to?"

I shook my head with a weak smile on my face. "I saw Presley last night, and Chase and I said goodbye this morning when he was making himself scarce."

"Anybody else?" she nudged.

Another shake of my head. "I can't. We said goodbye already. I can't do it again."

She pursed her lips when her face bent up and answered with a nod. With a whoosh, she headed inside.

I put Jolene on the ground and walked down the steps and a little bit away so I could see the farmhouse. It was where I'd truly grown up, the home I remembered best and knew so well. This farm was a sanctuary, one that had saved me as a little girl. All of my most meaningful experiences, all of my greatest joys, they'd been here, in this place. I thought I'd gotten it back. But then I'd lost it again.

It's for the best, I told myself.

I wondered if I'd ever convince myself it was true.

I looked down at Jolene. "All right, girl. It's time."

Those pink suitcases waited for me on the white porch, but for the first time, they brought me no relief. No flash of optimism. That first pink suitcase brought me to a farm. To animals and fun and a doting grandfather and adventure.

That pink suitcase had taken me away to a happier place. But this time, it was taking me away *from* one.

I decided then I should trade in my luggage for a black set.

I was halfway up the steps when I heard the distant hum of an engine and stopped. It wasn't an unusual sound on a farm, but not a sound we heard so close to the house. The closer it came, the louder it got, and I backed down the stairs, taking a few curious steps in the direction of the noise. I shielded my eyes from the blazing sun, staring at the peak of a slope that led down to the pastures.

A flash of sunlight against glass blinded me. I flinched before looking again as the top of a tractor came into view.

The top of a *pink* tractor.

Jake was behind the wheel.

My bruised heart climbed up my throat, jamming it. I couldn't understand what he was doing here, now. His was the last face I'd expected to see, the one I'd been trying and failing to let go. I couldn't believe he came here just to fight or to talk, not about anything good. But I couldn't let myself imagine that this was what I wanted most of all. Forgiveness. Acceptance. Faith.

Not until he stood, leaning out of the open side with one hand on the wheel and the other in the air. And on his face was the smile I loved so much. I could hear the laughter that went with it in my mind.

I laughed and ran toward him, shouting, "What are you doing?" as if he could hear me.

The second he figured he was close enough, he killed the engine and jumped out in almost the same motion.

"Thank God I caught you," he breathed as he approached.

"What are you—"

Without tracking the motion, I was in his arms. Surrounded by the heady scent of him. Caged by his body, flush with mine, his arms a velvety vise.

Taken completely by way of his lips against mine.

It was like I'd taken my first breath in a hundred years.

I breathed him in greedily, leaned into the kiss, into him, without questioning what or why or how. I didn't care if it was a dream. Because for at least this moment, he was mine again.

He broke the kiss, his hand cupping my jaw, his forehead pressed to mine. Then his lips to my hair when he pulled me into his chest and held me there.

And I held him, too afraid to speak. It might all disappear if I did.

"You're still here," he said softly.

I nodded into the divot of his chest.

He took a shaky breath, let it out gently. "I don't know how to ask you for forgiveness."

I pulled back to look up at him. "You?"

"I know it's hard to believe," he said with the uptick of one side of his mouth. But it faded. He smoothed my hair, peered into my face. "You gave me the farm."

"It was never really mine to start."

"I don't want it."

My brows quirked.

"Not if you're not here to share it with me."

I shook my head, baffled. "I don't understand. What happened? Why are you—"

"You happened, just like you always do. Everything you do is for the good of the people you love. Never for yourself. I was just too proud to see it, too ... too scared. I was so afraid of losing you, I made you leave." I must have looked confused, because he said, "You didn't expect me to show up, did you?"

"No."

"You gave me the farm—just gave it to me, fully intending to get in that truck and get on an airplane and leave everything you love here. And for no other reason than your conviction that it was the best thing for everyone. Everyone but you. I didn't trust you because I was a fool. I fought you because I was afraid. But you kept trying because you believe in me. And I called you faithless when it was me who had no faith. I didn't deserve your grace, Olivia."

"Jake, I ..."

"But you gave it to me anyway. Because you loved me despite it all. And I was so afraid you'd leave me, I ran you off myself. I love you. Do you ... do you have any idea how much I love you?"

He searched my eyes, swallowed hard.

And my heart stopped.

He loves me.

"And I almost let you go without telling you." He stroked my cheek. "Stay. I don't know who I am here without you, not anymore. And I don't want to know. You've changed everything for the better, me most of all. Without you, this farm has no heart or soul. And neither do I."

I wasn't sure when I'd started crying—probably somewhere near the *love* part—but my tears drew streaks of cold down my face. He thumbed the trail of one.

After a second, he said, "I don't think you've ever been quiet this long."

A laugh bubbled out of me, and I wrapped my arms around his neck to pull him to my upturned face, our lips connecting with the sweet familiarity of home. When we were breathless, I leaned back, my arms still around his neck.

"Well, if you love me, how could I leave? Like you said, everything I love is here."

"*If* I love you?" he said on a chuckle. "If I loved you any more, I might have a heart attack. I don't know how much more it can take."

"Then I'm not going anywhere."

"Good," he said against my lips.

And then he took them for his own.

I'd never been kissed before that moment. I'd never known surrender until he gave himself to me.

I'd never known the truth of love until I loved him.

We went up like a flame in a twist of bodies in perfect accord, and I'd have happily burned forever there in his arms.

I might have, if it wasn't for Kit.

We broke apart at her squeal of surprise, laughing as she dove between us.

"You two," she said through a sob. "You nearly put me in an early grave. Tell me it means you're staying, Livi."

"I'm staying," I promised, my eyes on Jake's.

"Forever, if I have anything to do with it," he answered.

To which Kit broke out into fresh happy tears. "That's it," she blubbered. "We're having a party tonight, and I'm gonna have Mack put meat on the smoker this minute. If I'm gonna have dessert ready, I'd better quit my sniveling and get busy."

"Cook when you're happy, cook when you're sad?" Jake teased.

"Cooking happens to be the right answer for any occasion, I've found. Now get your ass in the house with Livi's bags, Jake. Unpack them once and for all."

"Gladly," he said, pulling me back into his chest once Kit was free.

She simpered at the sight of us, hands over her lips before she waved us off and hoofed it into the house. A second later, I heard her out the back door calling for Mack and shouting that I was staying like the town crier.

I couldn't help but laugh.

"Think she's happy?" Jake asked.

"I think if she were any happier, she might explode in a cloud glitter and confetti."

"Then that makes two of us."

I turned in his arms to smile up at him. "Make it three."

"Goddamn, I'm glad I caught you before you left."

"When did you do *that*?" I asked, nodding to the tractor.

He glanced back at it like he'd forgotten it was there. "We've been working on it since last week. I was gonna surprise you with it but then ..."

"It's pink. You gave me a pink tractor." I beamed up at him. "You hate pink."

"Not as much as I love you. So much in fact, I was prepared to get on a plane, if that's what it took."

"Painted me a pink tractor *and* you would have gotten on a plane for the first time for me?"

"*And* gone to New York. It'd be a host of firsts. But there was no way I was letting you leave here forever, not without making sure you knew that I'm an idiot and that I love you."

"Say it again," I cooed.

With that tilted smile of his, he slipped his hand into my hair. "I'm an idiot. World's biggest asshole."

"No, the other part."

His smile widened. "Oh, the part where I love you?"

"Mhmm," I hummed.

"I'm sorry, Livi. For everything. I don't know how to make it right, what I did, what I said. You were going to leave, just like I was afraid you would. Except instead of you turning your back on us, I drove you away. Never again. If you ever *do* leave, it won't be on account of me. In fact, I might just hold you hostage."

Laughter bubbled out of me. "Gonna lock me in the barn with the goats you didn't want?"

"I was thinking more in the way of a ring on your finger and a new last name."

I blinked, unsure I'd heard him right. "Do you mean—"

"I mean that I want you here with me forever. Starting right now." He thumbed my cheek, smiling again. "If I didn't think you'd need a year to plan some big to-do, I'd throw you over my shoulder and drive you to the courthouse this minute."

"Don't act like you know me," I said on a laugh, though there were tears in my eyes.

"Oh, I know you, Olivia Brent, and you're the best thing to ever happen to me. Even next to Frank. Because he might have taught me what home meant, but you showed me how to love. How to trust. So someday, I'm gonna bring you a ring and get down on one knee and ask you that question. You're not even gonna see it coming."

I groaned. "Oh my God, you're going to drive me crazy waiting, aren't you?"

"A hundred percent. I'll even make sure Kit catches it on film for your social media."

A fake gasp. "You're on board with my social media? What are the odds I can get you to do the calendar too?"

"Don't press your luck."

I sighed. "I swear, one day I'm going to convince you."

"You have a better chance of convincing me to paint my truck pink."

One of my brows rose in challenge.

"Jesus," he said, laughing. "I don't stand a chance, do I?"

"Nope."

"Good thing I'd do anything for you. *Except* the calendar," he added when he saw my face. "I'm putting my foot down at the prospect of half the town having my naked chest on their refrigerators."

"You're no fun," I pouted.

"Well, I hope you don't love me for my sense of humor."

"I love you for many, many reasons. So many reasons that when you *do* get down on one knee and ask me *that* queston, I'll say yes."

Fire sparked behind his eyes. "Good. Then let's get these suitcases inside, empty them out, and put them away indefinitely."

"And then let's humor Kit and get through her party as quick as we can. Because all I really want is to lock us in my room for the next three days to make up for every second we were apart."

With that smile, he picked me up so we were nose to nose, chest to chest, my legs around his waist and our lips close enough to breathe each other.

"How about we start with an afternoon?"

"I'll take it. I'll take all of it. All of you."

"Good thing. Because I'm yours, Livi."

Our lips met with an exchange of hearts.

And I never wanted mine back, not if it meant that I could keep his forever.

EPILOGUE

Jake

IT'D BEEN THE HAPPIEST YEAR OF MY LIFE, THANKS TO HER.

I stood on the edge of the dancefloor at sunset with a whiskey in my hand, a smile on my face, and my eyes on my wife.

Olivia danced with the abandon she approached everything with. Her wedding dress was hitched by her fists so she didn't trip, exposing her pink rainboots. When she'd shown up here a year ago, they'd been spotless and unused. Now they were scuffed and banged up, the shine gone and the rubber worn. I'd tried to get her to buy new ones for the wedding, but she said it wouldn't be the same. It had to be these.

Half the town was here at the farm to celebrate. It'd taken her this long to plan it, as suspected, and she'd put every bit of her into it, just like everything she did. Just a few short hours ago, I'd stood under the last two elms at the end of the drive, sunlight dappling the seats lined up between the trees. Every one was full—Kit in the front row with her nose in a hanky and Olivia's aunt crying at her side. Maybe just a little in mourning that Olivia wouldn't be leaving the farm to go back to New York. She didn't yet know of Olivia's plans to convince her to move *here* and matchmake her. I didn't know with whom. The only unmarried man of her age was Buffalo Joe, and I had a feeling he had way too much body hair for her.

I stood under an archway of flowers with my heart beating in my throat, waiting for the moment my life would change.

And then I saw her at the end of that aisle on Mack's arm.

I have never in my life been so overcome as I was in that moment. As she made her way to stand by my side where she'd forever stay, I was stripped of everything but my love for her, leaving me with bone-deep appreciation that this woman would have chosen me when she could have had the world.

I held her hand, repeated the words. Listened to her vows with my throat in a vise, spoke mine with a rough voice and my heart too full to master myself. I promised her forever. She promised the same.

And a kiss sealed the vow.

It was the perfect way to mark the end of one life and the beginning of another.

I smiled at her as she bounced on the parquet with Presley and Priscilla, oblivious to me, though I was always aware of her. We could be miles apart, and I'd feel her as if she were next to me. Though the instance was rare—it was almost unheard of for us to be in separate places.

For two months, she waited on a proposal, and I led her on like a bastard, enjoying her squirm too much to give her the ring. Once, I got down on one knee right in front of her to tie my shoe. Once I took her to our picnic spot and watched her dig around in her dessert looking for hardware. The worst was when I gathered everybody up, stood them up on the porch expectantly, gave her a big speech … and handed her her birthday present—a fancy schmancy camera she'd been hinting at forever. I wasn't sure she'd ever forgive me for that one.

When it finally happened, I'd taken her out on the pink tractor, which had become an icon for the farm. It was sunset on one of the last days of summer, and she sat in my lap, leaning back into me lazily as we puttered up one of the higher pasture hills. From up there, you could see the ocean in the distance stretching to the horizon, the mountains on either side of us cradling our valley. I'd gotten down first, and when she'd stepped to the edge to jump down, I was on my knee with an open velvet box in my hand.

As predicted, she hadn't seen it coming.

The farm thrived under our watch and with the help of the Patton money. Our debts had been paid, our finances free and clear for the first time in a decade. Home deliveries had become our biggest earner, followed closely by tours and the shop, of course. James Patton had kept his promise to stay in Washington, and Chase had become an unexpected ally.

He stood on the other side of the dance floor mirroring me. When he raised his glass in my direction, I did the same, and we took a drink of comraderie.

I never thought I'd see the day when I shook hands with a Patton. And this was definitely the first Brent wedding a Patton had attended in a hundred and twenty-five years.

We'd even made the ice cream flavor together like he and Olivia had talked about—Peace Treaty. It was a creamy strawberry (Olivia) fudge (Chase) swirl mixed with salted caramel chunks (me), and we couldn't keep it in stock. With Chase in charge of the Patton farm, things around town had changed. For the first time in more than a century, we were equals, working in harmony, the feud finally put to bed by the generation with sense.

The only thing missing was Frank.

His absence had been felt more in the last few weeks than ever, especially today. Not long after we were engaged, I officially moved into the big house, and in the process, Olivia found Pop's letter on my dresser in the same spot it'd been in since I'd received it. To no one's surprise, she convinced me it was time, handing it to me before leaving me in my room alone.

I read it so many times, I knew it by heart.

BET THE FARM

Jake,

I'm sorry.

The last thing I ever wanted was to leave you with the farm in the state it's in, but if this letter is in your hands, I've failed. I know you must be surprised that I'd leave you half of all of this, but I hope you'll hear me when I say that this place is yours just as much as it is Olivia's.

Seven years of my life were spent without a son, raising my only kin—his only child—alone. Every day was a reminder of his absence. Every cricket Livi brought in to show me, every hug with her stringy arms, every little tear I wiped away left me wishing he was there. I thought I'd known loss when Janet died. But nothing can compare to outliving your child.

And then Livi was leaving, headed for a better life than I could give her, and I had to face the prospect of being alone again, more alone than ever. But then you knocked on my door, and I knew just how much we needed each other.

If I know Olivia, she's going to come in here like a bulldozer, and if I know you, you'll budge like a brick wall. But she needs you. And I know you don't want to admit it, but you need her too.

And I need you to take care of each other.

My greatest sadness is the thought of leaving you both alone, and the only comfort I have is knowing you'll be together. Take care of her, Jake. Take care of yourself and the farm.

If anyone can save it, it's the two of you.

Know that every time I called you son, it wasn't an endearment. It was a fact. I am the most fortunate man on earth to have found you, to have helped raise you, to be there for you just like you were so often for me, even when you didn't know how much you meant to me. I hope that you know how I love you, son. Now go out into the world and do good.

Forever your Pop,
Frank

Truth of it was, this world would never be the same without Frank Brent in it. But there wasn't a doubt in my mind that today would have made him almost as happy as it made me.

I'd never been so lucky as I'd been since she showed up with those stupid pink suitcases to steal my heart.

At the thought, I tossed back the end of my drink and made my way onto the dance floor as the song changed to a Patsy Cline song. Without a word, I scooped up my bride and spun her away, giving a polite *'Scuse me* to those around her.

Her chin tipped up as she laughed, and I beamed down at her as I took her on a turn.

"Hello, wife."

"Hello, husband."

I chuckled at the sound of the word on her lips, that fiery streak of possession and submission it somehow both contained hot in my chest.

"I'm glad you found me. I haven't seen you in three songs."

"I was there. You were just having too much fun. Didn't want to interrupt you."

"Marriage rule number one: always interrupt me to dance."

With a laugh, I turned us in a circle within a measure. "*That's* rule number one?"

"Yes, along with kiss me at least once a day and always let me have the good seat on the couch."

A pack of goat kids ran across the dancefloor in tuxedos and tutus with a wave of laughter in their wake.

"I can't believe you got Stanley to wear a bowtie," I said.

"It took a lot of convincing. Almost as much as it took *you* to do my calendar."

"That is not for commercial use, Olivia."

"Literally the best wedding present *ever*. Who needs silver servingware when you have your husband immortalized feeding baby cows without a shirt on?"

I rolled my eyes.

"I think my favorite is the one of you all sweaty in front of the hay bales with your jeans all low. You could be a part-time model."

"All I did was shuck hay."

"*That* is why you could be a model. You give good face when you don't even know you're giving good face. Your face is just a giver like that."

"What the hell does that even mean?" I asked on a laugh.

"It means I love you. It's almost time to go."

"Thank God. You know how long I've been waiting to get you out of this dress?"

"Well, I've only been in it for eight hours ..."

"Since I asked you to marry me."

Her cheeks flushed, the apples high with her smile. "You're such a closet romantic."

One of my brows rose. "Because I want to take your clothes off?"

"In this context, yes."

"God, I love you," I said, laughing again.

"Good thing. You're stuck with me now."

"Never wanted anything more."

I'd only just started kissing her before the music changed again, and Presley's voice came over the speakers, directing everyone to our designated exit. Olivia disappeared for a minute, coordinating her things with Presley, and I shook hands with those who offered, accepting kisses on the cheek and well wishes from the rest as they flowed toward the wide path they'd marked with lanterns in the grass. Presley appeared and began passing out sparklers. The sun hung low enough to kiss the treetops when Olivia slipped her arms around my waist and smiled up at me.

"You ready for this to be over?" she asked.

"Over? We're barely getting started."

She beamed. "See? Romantic."

"It's your fault. You made me love you like this."

"It was the boots, wasn't it?"

"A hundred percent the boots."

I leaned in to kiss her again, but Presley yelled, "Come on, lovebirds!"

"I swear to God if I get interrupted kissing my wife one more time …"

Olivia just laughed and grabbed my hand, and together we ran down the path toward the pink tractor where it sat waiting for us with cans dangling from the back. I climbed up first, then helped her into my lap. And when I turned it on, Olivia waved behind us, squealing through the lurch when I put it into gear.

And then there was nothing but me and her.

Off we bumbled, leaving the party behind us. I wondered for a minute what we looked like—her skirts took up almost the entire cab.

She smiled at me like she knew a secret.

"What?" I asked.

"We're married."

"Damn straight we are. You're all mine."

"Oh, I've been all yours forever."

"Yeah, but now there's a ring on your finger that tells everybody else. I want the whole world to know that you belong to me just like I belong to you." With one hand on the wheel, I tipped her so I could gaze upon the face I loved so desperately.

When I kissed her, I kissed her good and well. Kissed her like a man who owned the world. Kissed her like I was the luckiest man to ever walk the earth.

And this time, there were no interruptions.

THANK YOU

This book is one I've wanted to write for years, and on having the chance to do it, I was ecstatic. But early on, life intervened. The loss of our oldest dog to leukemia. An incredibly emotional political and news cycle. A child hospitalized after asking me for help—they no longer felt safe with themselves. A holiday season in and out of psychiatric facilities, beside myself with worry that I would lose my oldest child to the darkness of mental illnesses. Coming out on their behalf to our family as non-binary, doing my best to guide loved ones through their emotions and trying to find my way through my own. All that on top of a global pandemic and endless months spent isolated.

All along, I had this story, my little bright spot. Finding time to work was difficult. Finding joy in writing when our world was so dark was a big ask, but despite it all, this story was born.

I hope it means as much to you as it does to me.

The usual suspects get my forever thanks: My husband Jeff for being my support and inspiration. Kandi Steiner for being there with me always, talking me through every step of this process, dropping everything to pitch in as she does. Kerrigan Byrne for unending hours of discussion over plot and story, sometimes while shooting aliens together on the internet. Kyla Linde for being my work wife, helping me find the simplest solutions to big, scary story problems, and keeping me fresh in my metaphorical running shoes for sprints.

I wanted to thank a few more people—First my alpha and beta readers: Amy Vox Libris, Sarah Green, Sasha Erramouspe, Dani Sanchez, Kandi Steiner, Sara Sentz, Melissa Brooks, Danielle Lagasse, and Julia Huedorf. Thank you for your extreme patience and flexibility through my ever-changing schedule and delivery dates. Your feedback means everything to me. Everything. I couldn't have done it without your time, effort, support, and critical feedback. Thank you, thank you, thank you.

I'd also like to thank Jovana Shirley of Unforeseen Editing for her thorough work. Dani Sanchez for our weekly meetings set to hair pet, plan, hope, dream. Lauren Perry for the incredible photo shoot she did for teasers. Stacey Blake of Champagne Formatting for my gorgeous interiors. I'd like to thank Pinky at Morning Fresh Dairy (the home of Noosa yogurt) for sitting with me after my tour of the farm, answering the never-ending flow of questions, laughing with me over cow vaginas, and coming up with viable scenarios for Brent Farm.

To all the bloggers who read, review, post, squeal about books you love, thank you for making my dreams a reality. Thank you for your tireless work, for all the sleepless nights spent reading one more chapter. Forever grateful for you.

And to you, reader—thank you for spending these hours here in my heart. I hope it brought a little joy into your world.

OTHER BOOKS

CONTEMPORARY STANDALONES

Small Town Romance
Bet The Farm
Friends with Benedicts: Coming Spring 2021

Bright Young Things
Fool Me Once
Everyone wants to know who's throwing the lavish parties, even the police commissioner, and no one knows it's her ... not even the reporter who's been sneaking in to the parties and her heart.

The Bennet Brothers:
A spin on Pride & Prejudice
Coming Up Roses
Everyone hates something about their job, and she hates Luke Bennet. Because if she doesn't, she'll fall in love with him.

Gilded Lily
This pristine wedding planner meets her match in an opposites attract, enemies to lovers comedy.

Mum's the Word
A Bower's not allowed to fall in love with a Bennet, but these forbidden lovers might not have a choice.

The Austens
Wasted Words (Inspired by Emma)
She's just an adorkable, matchmaking book nerd who could never have a shot with her gorgeous best friend and roommate.

A Thousand Letters (Inspired by Persuasion)
Fate brings them together after seven years for a second chance they never thought they'd have in this lyrical story about love, loss, and moving on.

Love, Hannah (a spinoff of A Thousand Letters)
A story of finding love when all seems lost and finding home when you're far away from everything you've known.

Love Notes (Inspired by *Sense & Sensibility*)
Annie wants to live while she can, as fully as she can, not knowing how deeply her heart could break.

Pride and Papercuts (Inspired by *Pride and Prejudice*)
She can be civil and still hate Liam Darcy, but if she finds there's more to him than his exterior shows, she might stumble over that line between love and hate and fall right into his arms.

The Red Lipstick Coalition

Piece of Work
Her cocky boss is out to ruin her internship, and maybe her heart, too.

Player
He's just a player, so who better to teach her how to date? All she has to do is not fall in love with him.

Work in Progress
She never thought her first kiss would be on her wedding day. Rule number one: Don't fall in love with her fake husband.

Well Suited
She's convinced love is nothing more than brain chemicals, and her baby daddy's determined to prove her wrong.

Bad Habits

With a Twist (Bad Habits 1)
A ballerina living out her fantasies about her high school crush realizes real love is right in front of her in this slow-burn friends-to-lovers romantic comedy.

Chaser (Bad Habits 2)
He'd trade his entire fortune for a real chance with his best friend's little sister.

Last Call (Bad Habits 3)
All he's ever wanted was a second chance, but she'll resist him at every turn, no matter how much she misses him.

The Tonic Series

Tonic (Book 1)
The reality show she's filming in his tattoo parlor is the last thing he wants, but if he can have her, he'll be satisfied in this enemies-to-lovers-comedy.

Bad Penny (Book 2)
She knows she's boy crazy, which is why she follows strict rules, but this hot nerd will do his best to convince her to break every single one.

The Hardcore Serials

Read for FREE!
Hardcore: Complete Collection
A parkour thief gets herself into trouble when she falls for the man who forces her to choose between right and wrong.

HEARTS AND ARROWS
*Greek mythology meets Gossip Girl in a contemporary paranormal
series where love is the ultimate game and Aphrodite never loses.*

Paper Fools (Book 1)
Shift (Book 2)
From Darkness (Book 3)

ABOUT THE AUTHOR

Staci has been a lot of things up to this point in her life: a graphic designer, an entrepreneur, a seamstress, a clothing and handbag designer, a waitress. Can't forget that. She's also been a mom to three little girls who are sure to grow up to break a number of hearts. She's been a wife, even though she's certainly not the cleanest, or the best cook. She's also super, duper fun at a party, especially if she's been drinking whiskey, and her favorite word starts with f, ends with k.

From roots in Houston, to a seven year stint in Southern California, Staci and her family ended up settling somewhere in between and equally north in Denver. When she's not writing, she's reading, gaming, or designing graphics.

www.stacihartnovels.com
staci@stacihartnovels.com

Printed in the USA
CPSIA information can be obtained
at www.ICGtesting.com
LVHW051633041223
765671LV00045B/840